I0651213

John Ashton

English Caricature and Satire on Napoleon

Volume 1

John Ashton

English Caricature and Satire on Napoleon
Volume 1

ISBN/EAN: 9783337349806

Printed in Europe, USA, Canada, Australia, Japan

Cover: Foto ©Andreas Hilbeck / pixelio.de

More available books at **www.hansebooks.com**

THE EXILE.

A SKETCH FROM LIFE AT LONGWOOD.   APRIL 1820.

ENGLISH
CARICATURE AND SATIRE

ON

NAPOLEON I.

BY

JOHN ASHTON

AUTHOR OF 'SOCIAL LIFE IN THE REIGN OF QUEEN ANNE' ETC.

WITH 115 ILLUSTRATIONS BY THE AUTHOR

IN TWO VOLUMES—VOL. I.

London

CHATTO & WINDUS, PICCADILLY

1884

All rights reserved

PREFACE.

THIS book is not intended to be a History of Napoleon the First, but simply to reproduce the bulk of the Caricatures and Satires published in England on our great enemy, with as much of history as may help to elucidate them.

The majority of the caricatures are humorous ; others are silly, or spiteful—as will occasionally happen nowadays ; and some are too coarse for reproduction—so that a careful selection has had to be made. Gillray and Rowlandson generally signed their names to the work of their hands ; but, wherever a caricature occurs unsigned by the artist, I have attributed it, on the authority of the late Edward Hawkins, Esq., some time· Keeper of the Prints at the British Museum, to whatever artist he has assigned it. I have personally inspected every engraving herein described, and the description is entirely my own.

Should there, by chance, be an occasional discrepancy as to a date, it has been occasioned by the inconceivable contradictions which occur in different histories and newspapers. To cite an instance : in three different books are given three different dates of Napoleon leaving Elba, and it was only by the knowledge that it occurred on a Sunday, and by consulting an almanac for the year 1815, that I was able absolutely to determine it.

The frontispiece is taken from a very rare print, and gives a novel view of Napoleon to us, who are always accustomed to see him represented in military uniform.

That my readers may find some instruction, mingled with the amusement I have provided for them, is the earnest wish of

JOHN ASHTON.

CONTENTS

OF

THE FIRST VOLUME.

VOL. I. a

ENGLISH CARICATURE AND SATIRE

ON

NAPOLEON THE FIRST.

CHAPTER I.

BIRTH AND GENEALOGY—HIS OWN ACCOUNT—MAJORCAN OR GREEK
EXTRACTION—ENGLISH BIOGRAPHIES.

CURIOUSLY enough, it has never been practically settled whence the ancestors of Napoleon Bonaparte came. He, himself, cared little for the pride of birth, and when, during his Consulate, they manufactured for him a genealogy descending from a line of kings, he laughed at it, and said that his patent of nobility dated from the battle of Monte-notte.

But, still, one would think he ought to know, for family tradition is strong ; and if it can be trusted, this is his own account. 'One day Napoleon questioned Canova about Alfieri, and Canova found an opportunity to render an important service to Florence, &c. " Sire," said he, "authorise the President of the Academy of Florence to take care of the frescoes and pictures. I heartily wish it.

That will reflect great honour on your Majesty, who, I am assured, is of a noble Florentine family." At these words the Empress (Maria Louisa) turned towards her husband and said :—" What! are you not Corsican ? "   " Yes," replied Napoleon, " but of Florentine origin."   Canova then said :—" The President of the Academy of Florence, the Senator Allessandria, is of one of the most illustrious houses in the country, which has had one of its ladies married to a Bonaparte, thus you are Italian, and we boast of it." " I am, certainly," added Napoleon.'[1]

Prince Napoleon Louis Bonaparte (brother to the Emperor) published in 1830, at Florence, a French translation of an old book[2] about the sack of Rome, 1527, which gives an account of the family of the writer. But Majorca also puts in a claim to the older Bonapartes ; and in 1852, Don Antonio Furio, a learned man, Member of the Royal Academies of Belles Lettres of Barcelona and Majorca, &c., made a declaration as to ' the rank, dignity, and extinction of the noble family of Bonapart in the island of Majorca ;' and quotes from a book kept in the archives of Palma, in which are preserved the armorial escutcheons of the noble families of the Island, the arms of Bonapart—which were Dexter, on a field Azure, six stars, Or, placed two by two, Sinister, on a field gules, a lion rampant, Or ; and the Chief Or, bears a scared eagle, sable. He says the family came from Genoa to Majorca, in which island its members were considered noblemen, and they filled several distinguished offices. In a register of burials relating to knights and gentlemen, written in 1559, the antiquity and nobility of the Bonaparts are clearly authenticated ; and it would

---

[1] Chevalier Artand's *Italy*, p. 377 ; 'L'Univers pittoresque, Europe,' tome 2, Paris, 1857, ed. Didot.

[2] 'Ragguaglio Storico di tutto l' occorso, giorno per giorno, nel Sacco di Roma dell' anno 1527, scritto da Jacopo Bonaparte, gentiluomo Samminiatere ' (from San Miniato, near Florence) ' che vi se trovò presente.'

seem from Don Furio's account (for all of which he gives chapter and verse) that the learned jurisconsult Don Hugo Bonapart left Majorca and went to Corsica, where, in 1411, he was made Regent of the Chancery of that place ; and, as he settled there, his name was inscribed in the Golden Book of France.

This seems pretty circumstantial, until another theory appears—namely, his Greek extraction. Sir J. Emerson Tennent says:[1] 'There is a story relative to the family name of the Bonapartes, that somewhat excites curiosity as to the amount of truth which it may contain. In 1798, when Napoleon was secretly preparing for his descent upon Egypt, among other expedients for distracting and weakening the Porte, French emissaries were clandestinely employed in exciting the Greeks in Epirus, and the Morea, to revolt. In Maina especially (the ancient Sparta), these agents were received with marked enthusiasm, on the ground that Bonaparte was born in Corsica, where numbers of Greeks from that part of the Morea had found an asylum after the conquest of Candia, in 1669, but they were eventually expelled by the Genoese.

'One of the persons so employed by Napoleon to rouse the Greeks in 1798 was named Stephanopoli ; and one of the arguments which he used was, that Napoleon himself was a Greek in blood, and a Mainote by birth, being descended from one of the exiles who took refuge at Ajaccio in 1673. The name of this family, he said, was Calomeri, Καλόμερις,[2] which the Corsicans accommodated to their own dialect by translating it into *Buonaparte.*'

Another writer, signing himself *Rhodocanakis*, in the same periodical,[3] says: 'I am happy to be able to assert

---

[1] *Notes and Queries*, 3rd series, vol. xi. p. 307.
[2] From Καλὸς, good, and Μερὶς, part or share —Buona-parte.
[3] *Notes and Queries*, 3rd series, vol. xi. p. 507.

with confidence, and on the authority of General Kallergis, the intimate friend of the present Emperor, of Prince Pitzipios, and others, that the story devised by Nicholas Stepanapoulos, and mentioned by his niece, the Duchesse d'Abrantes, in her *Memoirs*, that Napoleon was a Greek in blood, and a Mainote by birth, being descended from the family of Calomeri, who took refuge at Ajaccio, Corsica, was never authoritatively denied. On the contrary, both the first and third Napoleon appeared pleased at the story, whenever it was alluded to in their presence ; probably because they thought it good policy not to deny what they might in future wish to turn to their advantage. As regards the name of Καλομέρης or Καλόμερος, there are still many families of that name in Greece.'

Now let us hear what Madame Junot, the aforesaid Duchesse d'Abrantes, the intimate friend of Napoleon, whose families were the closest of neighbours at Ajaccio, says on this subject.[1] 'When Constantine Comnenus landed at Corsica in 1676, at the head of a Greek colony, he had with him several sons, one of whom was named. Calomeros. This son he sent to Florence, on a mission to the Grand Duke of Tuscany. Constantine dying before the return of his son, the Grand Duke prevailed on the young Greek to renounce Corsica, and fix his abode in Tuscany. After some interval of time, an individual came from Italy—indeed from Tuscany—and fixed his abode in Corsica, where his descendants formed the family of Buonaparte ; for the name *Calomeros*, literally Italianised, signified *buona parte* or *bella parte*.[2]

'The only question is, whether the Calomeros who left

---

[1] *Memoirs of Madame Junot, Duchesse d'Abrantes*, Bentley, London, 1883. When quoting from her memoirs I always use this translation.

[2] Napoleon omitted the ' u ' in Buonaparte while general-in-chief in May 1796.

Corsica, and the Calomeros who came there, have a direct
filiation. Two facts, however, are certain—namely, the
departure of the one, and the arrival of the other. It is a
singular thing that the Comneni,[1] in speaking of the Bonaparte family, always designate them by the names *Calomeros*,
Calomeri, or *Calomeriani*, according as they allude to one
individual, or several collectively. Both families were united
by the most intimate friendship.

'When the Greeks were obliged to abandon Paomia
to escape the persecutions of the insurgent Corsicans,
they established themselves temporarily in towns which
remained faithful to the Republic of Genoa. When, at a
subsequent period, Cargesa was granted to the Greeks for
the purpose of forming a new establishment, a few Greek
families continued to reside at Ajaccio.'

I have been thus diffuse on his ancestry, because
English satirists could not tell the truth on the subject—
they were too swayed by the passion of the moment, and
had to pander to the cravings of the mob. Take an
example, from a broad sheet published in 1803, when our
island was in deadly fear of invasion, a ' History of Buonaparte.' 'Napoleon Buonaparte is the son of a poor lawyer
of Ajaccio, in Corsica, in which city he was born on the
15th of August, 1769. His grandfather, Joseph, originally
a butcher of the same place, was ennobled by Count
Nieuhoff, some time King of Corsica. He was the son of
Carlos Buona, who once kept a liquor shop, or tavern, but
who, being convicted of robbery and murder, was condemned to the Gallies, where he died in 1724. His wife,
La Birba, the mother of Joseph, died in the House of
Correction at Geneva (? Genoa). On the 3rd May, 1736,

---

[1] Madam Junot was very proud of her descent from Constantine Comnenus, the tenth Protogeras of Maina, who quitted Greece in 1675, landed at
Genoa Jan. 1, 1676, and arrived at Corsica March 14, 1676.

when Porto Vecchio was attacked, Joseph Buona brought to the assistance of King Theodore a band of vagabonds which, during the civil war, had chosen him for its leader. In return, Theodore, on the following day, created him a noble, and added to his name *Buona* the termination *Parté*. Joseph Buonaparte's wife *Histria*, was the daughter of a journeyman tanner of Bastia, also in Corsica.'

And yet one more, from another equally veracious 'life.' 'Buonaparte's great-grandfather kept a wine-house for factors (like our gin shops), and, being convicted of murder and robbery, he died a galley slave at Genoa, in 1724: his wife was likewise an accomplice, and she died in the House of Correction at Genoa in 1734. His grandfather was a butcher of Ajaccio, and his grandmother daughter of a journeyman tanner at Bastia. His father was a low petty-fogging lawyer, who served and betrayed his country by turns, during the Civil Wars. After France conquered Corsica, he was a spy to the French Government, and his mother their trull. What is bred in the bone will not come out of the flesh.'

CHAPTER II.

THE foregoing was the sort of stuff given to our grand-fathers for history ; nothing could be bad enough for Boney, *the Corsican Ogre*—nay, they even tortured his name to suit political purposes. It was hinted that the keeper of ' the Man with the Iron Mask,' who was said to be no other than the twin (and elder) brother of Louis XIV., was named *Bon part* ; that the said keeper had a daughter, with whom the Man in the Mask fell in love, and to whom he was privately married ; that their children received their mother's name, and were secretly conveyed to Cor-sica, where the name was converted into *Bonaparte*, or *Buonaparte* ; and that one of these children was the ancestor of Napoleon Bonaparte, who was thus entitled to be recognised, not only as of French origin, but as the direct descendant of the rightful heir to the throne of France.

They put his name into Greek, and tortured it thus :—
Napoleon, Apoleon, Poleon, Oleon, Leon, Eon, On,
Ναπολεων, Απολεων, Πολεων, Ολεων, Λεων, Εων, Ων,
which sentence will translate, ' Napoleon, being the lion of the nations, went about destroying cities.'

In the ' Journal des Débats,' 8 Avril, 1814, although not an English satire on his name, it is gravely stated that he was baptised by the name of Nicholas, and that he assumed the name of Napoleon as an uncommon one ; but this name, Nicholas, which was applied to him so freely in France, was but a cant term for a stupid blockhead. Whilst on this subject, however, I cannot refrain from quoting a passage from a French book : ' I do not know what fellow has held that *Napolione* was a demon, who in bygone times, amused himself by tormenting a poor imbe-cile. The fellow can not have read the life of the Saints : he would then have learned that St. Napolione, whose name is given at length in the legend, is as good a patron as any other ; that he performed seven miracles during his life, and twenty-two and a half after his death—for he had not time to finish the twenty-third : it was an unfortunate tiler who, in falling from a roof, broke both his legs. St. Napoleon had already set one, when an unlucky doctor prescribed some medicine to the sick man which carried him off to the other world.' [1]

There is an extremely forcible acrostic in Latin on his name, which deserves reproduction :—

	B ona
N ationibus [2]	U surpavit
A uctoritatem	O mnium
P rincipibus	N eutrórum
O bedientiam	A urum
L ibertatem	P opulorum
E cclesiæ	A nimas
O mni modo	R evera
N egans	T yrannus
	E xecrandus.

---

[1] *Buonaparte et la famille, ou Confidences d'un de leurs anciens amis*, Paris 1816.

[2] Denying by every means the authority of nations, obedience to princes, or liberty to the Church. He usurped the goods of all, the treasure of neutrals, the souls of nations : in very truth he was an execrable tyrant.

But not only was his name thus made a vehicle for political purposes, but the expounders of prophecy got hold of it, and found out, to their great delight, that at last they had got that theological bugbear, *the Apocalyptic beast.* Nothing could be clearer. It could be proved to demonstration, most simply and clearly. Every one had been in error about the Church of Rome ; at last there could be no doubt about it, it was NAPOLEON. Take the following handbill as a sample of one out of many :—

A PROPHECY

(*From the 13th Chapter of Revelations*)

ALLUDING TO

BUONAPARTE.

Verse 1st.

'And a Beast rose out of the Sea, having ten crowns on his head,' &c.

This Beast is supposed to mean Buonaparte, he being born in *Corsica,* which is an island, and having conquered ten kingdoms.

Verse 5th.

'And a mouth was given him speaking blasphemies ; and power given him upon the earth, forty and two months.'

Buonaparte was crowned in December, 1804 ; it is therefore supposed the *extent* of his assumed power upon earth will now be limited, this present month (*June*) 1808, being exactly the forty-second month of his reign.

Verse 16th.

'And he caused all to receive a mark in their hands, and no one could buy or sell, save those that had the mark of the Beast.'

To persons conversant in commercial affairs, these verses need no comment. There are, at present, some of *these marks* to be seen in this country ; they had the Crown of Italy, &c., at top, and are signed ' Buonaparte,' ' Talleyrand ' ; and all of them are numbered.

Verse 18th.

'Let him that hath understanding, count the number of the Beast, for it is the number of a man, and his number is SIX HUNDRED, SIXTY AND SIX.'

This verse is curious, and should be read attentively. The method of using letters for figures at the time the Revelations were written is proved by many monuments of Roman antiquity now extant.

The Ancient Alphabet of Figures		Buonaparte's name with the Figures			Ten Kingdoms conquered
A .	. . 1	N .	.	. 40	France
B .	. . 2	A .	.	. 1	Prussia
C .	. 3	P .	.	. 60	Austria
D .	. 4	O .	.	. 50	Sardinia
E .	. 5	L . .	.	. 20	Naples
F .	. 6	E .	.	. 5	Rome
G .	. 7	A .	.	. 1	Tuscany
H .	. 8	N .	.	. 40	Hungary
I .	. 9				Portugal
K .	. 10	B .	.	. 2	Spain
L .	. 20	U .	.	. 110	
M .	. 30	O .	.	. 50	
N .	. 40	N .	.	. 40	
O .	. 50	A .	.	. 1	
P .	. 60	P .	.	. 60	
Q .	. 70	A .	.	. 1	
R .	. 80	R .	.	. 80	
S .	. 90	T .	.	. 100	
T .	. 100	E .	.	. 5	
U .	. 110			———	
V .	. 120	The Number			
X .	. 130	of the Beast . 666			
Y .	. 140				
Z .	. 150				

Napole	an Buon	aparte
6	6	6

The above verses are not the only parts of the chapter which have reference to Buonaparte, but the *most prominent ones* ; the connection throughout has been clearly ascertained.

In a curious little book called *The Corsican's Down-fall*, by a Royal Arch Mason, published at Mansfield in 1814, at p. 6, it says, with reference to the numeration, 'The oldest treatise on the theory of arithmetic is comprised in the seventh, eighth, and ninth books of Euclid's *Elements*, about two hundred and eighty years before the Christian era. The first author of any consequence who used the modern way of computing by figures, instead of letters of the alphabet, was Jordanus of Namur, who flourished about 1200 ; and his arithmetic was afterwards published and demonstrated by Johannis Faber Stapulensis, in the fifteenth century. The name, then, and number of the Beast must be discovered (if at all) by the ancient method of computation in use at the time when the prophecies were written.'

But Bonaparte ungratefully refused to fulfil prophecy by being destroyed at the end of forty-two months, *i.e.* in June 1808, which must have put the expositors on their mettle. They were, however, fully equal to the occasion, and ingeniously solved the quotation this way.[1] 'Power was given unto him to continue forty-and-two months : now it is well known that he was self created, or crowned Emperor of France, on the 2nd day of December 1804, and that he reigned in full power and authority over the prostrate States upon the Continent until the 2nd day of May 1808, the very day on which the gallant Patriots of Spain made so noble and glorious a struggle to throw off the abominable yoke that he had imposed upon them,

[1] *The Corsican's Downfall*, p. 9.

which is exactly a period of three years and a half, or forty two months.'

An ingenious lunatic, named L. Mayer, found out another way of fathering the Mark of the Beast upon Napoleon. He took the number of sovereigns who had reigned in Europe until Napoleon's arrival—some he has left out to suit his convenience, but that is a trivial matter —the case had to be made out against the unfortunate Emperor.

Sovereigns included in the Number of the Beast.[1]

	Numbers
Roman Emperors	77
Popes	186
Kings of France	40
Kings of Spain	78
Kings of Portugal	26
Emperors of Germany .	57
Kings of Bohemia . .	31
Kings of Hungary	34
Kings of Poland . . .	35
Kings of Denmark . . .	35
Kings of Naples and Sicily	30
Kings of Sardinia	36
Bonaparte	1
	Total 666

The Society of Antiquaries have, among their hand-bills, one published in 1808, as follows:—

Mr. Urban,—The following singular coincidences may furnish matter for reflection to the curious. It has been generally admitted that the Roman Empire, after passing under *seven* different forms of government (or *seven* heads), was divided into *ten* kingdoms in Europe (the ten horns of Daniel and John) ; and that, notwith-

[1] *Buonaparte the Emperor of the French considered as the Lucifer and Gog of Isiah and Ezekiel, &c.*, by L. Mayer, Lond. 1806, p. 86.

standing the various changes Europe has undergone, the number
of kingdoms was generally about ten.

It is not a little surprising that the *Heads of the Family of
Napoleon*, who has effected such a change in the same Empire,
are exactly seven, viz.:—

      1. Napoleon.

      2. Joseph, King of Italy.

      3. Louis, King of Holland.

      4. Jerome.

      5. Murat, Duke of Berg and Cleves.

      6. Cardinal Fesch.

      7. Beauharnais, the adopted son of Napoleon.

And also that *the Members of the New Federation are just ten,*
viz.:—

1. Bavaria.	6. Ysembourg.
2. Wirtemberg.	7. Hohenzollern.
3. Baden.	8. Aremberg.
4. Darmstadt.	9. Salm.
5. Nassau.	10. Leyen.

It is also remarkable that in the *man's name*, NAPOLEON
BUONAPARTE, there are precisely three times six letters :—

Napole	on Buon	aparte	
6	6	6	=666

And in his name is contained the name given by John to the
King of the Locusts, who is called ' Apoleon,' or ' the Destroyer.'

Even the date of his birth was disputed, for some said
he was born on February 5, 1768—in his marriage registry
it is the same, and he used to tell De Bourrienne, his school-
fellow, that he was born on August 15, 1769, and it is so
noted in the registry of his entrance into the military school
at Brienne in 1779, and the Ecole Militaire in 1784, besides
being the date used in all documents necessary to his promotion. But probably his mother knew somewhat about

it, and Madame Junot says,[1] speaking of Madame Lætitia Bonaparte, ' I recollect she this day told us that, being at Mass on the day of the fête of Notre Dame of August, she was overtaken by the pains of childbirth, and she had hardly reached home when she was delivered of *Napoleon*, on a wretched rug. . . . I know not why,' said she, ' it has been reported that Paoli was Napoleon's godfather. It is not true ; Laurent Jiubéga [2] was his godfather. He held him over the baptismal font, along with another of our relations, Celtruda Buonaparte.' [3]

[1] *Memoirs*, p. 269.

[2] His nephew was afterwards prefect in Corsica. He was a relation of Napoleon.

[3] Daughter of Charles Bonaparte, the Emperor's uncle, and wife of Paraviccini, a cousin, also, of Napoleon.

CHAPTER III.

COUNT MARBŒUF, HIS PUTATIVE FATHER—POVERTY OF THE BONAPARTE
FAMILY—EARLY PERSONAL DESCRIPTION OF NAPOLEON—HIS OWN
ACCOUNT OF HIMSELF—SATIRISTS' NARRATION OF HIS SCHOOL-DAYS.

IN after life, when Napoleon was successful, and had made
a position, reports were spread that his real father was
Count Marbœuf, who had been in Corsica, and in after life,
or at all events at his entrance into it, acted as his bene-
factor and patron. Lætitia Ramolini, afterwards Madame
Lætitia Bonaparte, was very graceful and pretty, indeed
Madame Junot says of her,[1] 'Lætitia was indeed a lovely
woman. Those who knew her in advanced life thought
her countenance somewhat harsh ; but that expression
instead of being caused by any austerity of disposition,
seemed, on the contrary, to have been produced by
timidity.' Indeed, no one can look at any portrait
of Madame Mère, and not be struck with her lofty
beauty.

This scandal about Count Marbœuf, it must be remembered, is of French origin, and was well known, and
recognised, probably, at its value. To give one illustration,[2]
'La malignité a fait honneur de sa naissance au Comte de
Marbœuf, gouverneur de l'isle, qui rendait des soins assidus
à Madame Buonaparte, jeune femme, belle et interressante
alors.'

[1] *Memoirs*, p. 7.
[2] *Buonapartiana, ou Choix d'Anecdotes curieuses*, Paris, 1814.

All our English squibs repeat the tale, and the subjoined is certainly the cleverest of them.[1]

> About his parentage indeed,
> Biographers have disagreed ;
> Some say his father was a farmer,
> His mother, too, a *Cyprian* charmer :
> That his dad Carlo was quite poor,
> Letitia a French General's —— ;
> If, faithless to her marriage vows,
> She made a cuckold of her spouse,
> Then Nap (some characters are rotten)
> Has been a *merrily begotten.*
> But other writers, with civility,
> Insist he's sprung from *old Nobility*,
> And therefore to his father's name
> Attach the highest rank and fame :
> Nay, furthermore, they add as true,
> Nap was Paoli's godson too.
> But what to this said great Paoli ?
> ' I stood for one, but 'pon my soul, I
> At present do not rightly know
> Whether it was for Nap or Joe.'
> It was for Joe, if he'd have said it,
> But Joe has done him little credit.
> Now let the honest muse despise
> All adulation, barefaced lies,
> And own the truth—Then Boney's father
> Was member of the law, or rather,
> A pettifogger, which his friends,
> To serve their own politic ends,
> Would keep a secret, knowing well
> That pettifoggers go to Hell.
> When France occasioned some alarms,
> And Corsica was up in arms,

---

[1] *The Life of Napoleon, a Hudibrastic Poem in Fifteen Cantos, by Doctor Syntax* (William Combe). London, 1815.

This Carlo Bonaparte thought fit,
His parchments for the sword to quit.
He fought, they say, with some applause,
Tho' unsuccessful in the cause :
Meanwhile, with battle's din and fright,
His wife was in a dismal plight ;
From town to town Letitia fled,
To shun the French, *as it is said* ;
Tho' others whisper that the fair
Was under a French Gen'ral's care,
And that to keep secure her charms
She fondly trusted to his *arms.*
Be this however as it might,
After incessant fear and flight,
Letitia ('fore her time, mayhap)
Was brought to bed of Master Nap :
The Cause, we think, of his ambition,
And of his restless disposition.

The Bonaparte family was not rich, their sole means of living being from the father's professional exertions, and the family was very large, and many mouths to feed ; in fact, they were in somewhat straitened circumstances, but not in such squalid poverty as Gillray depicts them, in the accompanying illustration, where our hero may be seen, with his brothers and sisters, gnawing the *bony part* of a shin of beef.

Madame Junot [1] says, ' Saveria told me that Napoleon was never a pretty boy, as Joseph had been ; his head always appeared too large for his body, a defect common to the Bonaparte family. When Napoleon grew up, the peculiar charm of his countenance lay in his eye, especially in the mild expression it assumed in his moments of kindness. His anger, to be sure, was frightful, and though I

---

[1] *Memoirs,* vol. i. p. 10.

am no coward, I never could look at him in his fits of rage without shuddering. Though his smile was captivating, yet the expression of his mouth when disdainful, or angry, could scarcely be seen without terror. But that forehead which seemed formed to bear the crowns of a whole world; those hands, of which the most coquettish woman might have been vain, and whose white skin covered muscles of iron; in short, of all that personal beauty which distinguished Napoleon as a young man, no traces were discernible in the boy.'

DEMOCRATIC INNOCENCE.

The young Bonaparte and his wretched Relatives in their native Poverty,
while Free Booters in the island of Corsica.

Napoleon said of himself: ' I was an obstinate and in-quisitive child. I was extremely headstrong; nothing overawed me, nothing disconcerted me. I made myself formidable to the whole family. My brother Joseph was the one with whom I was oftenest embroiled; he was bitten, beaten, abused : I went to complain before he had time to recover his confusion.'

At ten years of age, through the medium of his patron, Count Marbœuf, he was sent to the military school at

Brienne, which he entered on April 23, 1779. Here he was shy and reserved, and not at all liked by his schoolfellows, who twitted him with his poverty, the country whence he came, his name, and made reflections on his mother ; the last particularly exasperating him. His veracious Hudibrastic historian says :—

When he two years at school had been,
He proved more violent and mean :
Unlike his sprightly fellow boys,
Amused with playthings and with toys ;
At shuttlecock he'd never stop,
Nor deign to whip the bounding top.
His garden was his sole delight,
Which ne'er improv'd his mental sight ;
But thus in childhood serv'd to show
He was to all mankind a foe.
His schoolfellows, in keen sedateness,
He robb'd to prove his urchin greatness :
Deluded by his wheedling art,
Some cheerfully resign'd a part
Of their possessions, and to these
He added what he chose to seize ;
Then, planting it with num'rous trees
And putting palisades all round,
He strutted monarch of the ground ;

  . . . . .

  . . . . .

'Twas on a welcome festive morn,
For some great saint divinely born.
No matter why, it was a jolly day,
Boys must be merry on a holiday ;
And now behold their bulging pockets,
Enrich'd with pistols, squibs, and rockets—
When some, but humbly begg'd his pardon
Threw fireworks into Boney's garden ;

'Twas chiefly manag'd by the breeze
Which sent them 'mong his plants and trees ;
Bursting, the cracks were oft repeated,
Nap's ears were with the thunder greeted ;
Th' explosions discomposed, I wot,
Th' arrangement of the lovely spot.
Nap saw it with corroding spite,
And now began his lips to bite ;
But strove his anger to restrain,
Until revenge he could obtain.

NAPOLEON BLOWING UP HIS COMRADES.

For weeks he plann'd what he should do,
And in about a month or two
Contrived his infamous design,
By having made a kind of mine
Beside the garden ; where, in haste,
Long trains of gunpowder he plac'd ;
Deliberately now, as stated,
He for the little fellows waited ;
And just as they were passing through it,
A lighted bit of stick put to it ;
The boys were suddenly alarm'd,
And some were miserably harm'd,

While all, with fright and consternation,
Were in a state of perturbation.
Th' *heroic* Boney, with a club,
Now came the sufferers to drub ;
But soon the master was in sight,
Which put the Conqueror to flight

CHAPTER IV.

NAPOLEON AT THE ECOLE MILITAIRE—PERSONAL DESCRIPTION—*PUSS IN BOOTS*—VISIT TO CORSICA—SOLICITS SERVICE IN ENGLAND—REPORTED VISIT TO LONDON—SIEGE OF TOULON.

ON October 14 or 17, 1784, he left Brienne for the Ecole Militaire at Paris.

Gillray, when he drew the picture (on next page) of the abject, ragged, servile-looking Napoleon, could hardly have realised the fact that Napoleon was then over fifteen years of age, and that, having been already five years at a military school, he must necessarily have carried himself in a more soldierly manner. He stayed at the Ecole Militaire till August 1875, when he obtained his brevet of second lieutenant of Artillery in the regiment of La Fère. Madame Junot[1] tells an amusing anecdote of him at this period, which I must be pardoned introducing here, as it helps us to imagine his personal appearance. ' I well recollect that on the day when he first put on his uniform, he was as vain as young men usually are on such an occasion. There was one part of his dress which had a very droll appearance— that was his boots. They were so high and wide, that his little thin legs seemed buried in their amplitude. Young people are always ready to observe anything ridiculous ; and, as soon as my sister and I saw Napoleon enter the drawing-room, we burst into a loud fit of laughter. At that early age, as well as in after life, Bonaparte could not relish a joke ; and when he found himself the object of merriment, he grew angry.

[1] *Memoirs*, vol. i. p. 33.

' My sister, who was some years older than I, told him that since he wore a sword he ought to be gallant to ladies; and, instead of being angry, should be happy that they joked with him. " You are nothing but a child—a little *pensionnaire*," said Napoleon, in a tone of contempt. Cecile, who was twelve or thirteen years of age, was highly indignant at being called a child, and she hastily resented the affront by replying to Bonaparte, " And you are nothing but a *puss in boots.*" This excited a general laugh among

DEMOCRATIC HUMILITY.

Bonaparte when a boy received thro' the King's bounty into the
Ecole Militaire at Paris.

all present, except Napoleon, whose rage I will not attempt to describe. Though not much accustomed to society, he had too much tact not to perceive that he ought to be silent when personalities were introduced, and his adversary was a woman.

' Though deeply mortified at the unfortunate nickname which my sister had given him, yet he affected to forget it; and to prove that he cherished no malice on the subject, he got a little toy made, and gave it to me. This toy consisted of a cat in boots, in the character of a footman running before the carriage of the Marquis de Carabas. It was very well made, and must have been rather expensive to him considering his straitened finances. He brought along with it a pretty little edition of the popular tale of *Puss in Boots*, which he presented to my sister, begging her to keep it as a *token of his remembrance.'*

Napoleon afterwards frequently called Junot, *Marquis de Carabas*, and, on one occasion, Madame Junot, in badinage, reminded Napoleon of his present to her, at which he got very angry.

During his sub-lieutenancy he was very poor, yet he managed to go to Corsica for six months, whilst Paoli, who had been living in England, was there. There is a curious idea that, about this time (mentioned in more places than one [1]), he applied for service under the British Government.

> At this time Bonaparte scarce knew
> What for his maintenance to do—
> So he sat down, and quickly wrote
> A very condescending note,
> (Altho' a wretched scrawl when written),
> Which to a Chieftain of Great Britain,
> He, soon as possible, dispatch'd,
> In which he swore he was attach'd
> Unto the British Constitution,
> And therefore form'd the resolution
> Of fighting in that country's cause,
> For George the Third, and for his laws,
> If that his services were needed,
> And to his wishes they acceded.
> It seems that Bonaparte could trade well,
> He'd fight for any one that paid well ;
> But he a disappointment got,
> Because his services were not

---

[1] For instance, see *Notes and Queries*, 3rd series, vol. vii. p. 364.

By Britain's chief Commander tried ;
The rank he sought for was denied.
This was the cause of great displeasure,
It mortified him above measure,
And he gave England now as many a
Curse, as before he e'er gave Genoa.

Nay, more extraordinary than all, it was even pretended
that he lived some time in England. The *Birmingham
Journal* of April 21, 1855, affirms, on the authority of ' Mr.
J. Coleman of the Strand, who is now 104 years of age,
and whose portrait and biographical sketch appeared in
the *Illustrated London News*, Feb. 1850, and who knew perfectly well M. Bonaparte, who, while he lived in London,
which was for five weeks, in 1791 or 1792, lodged in a house
in George Street, Strand, and whose chief occupation appeared to be taking pedestrian exercise in the streets of
London. Hence his marvellous knowledge of the great
metropolis, which used to astonish any Englishmen of
distinction, who were not aware of the visit. I have also
heard Mr. Matthews, the grandfather of the celebrated
comedian, Mr. Thomas Goldsmith of the Strand, Mr.
Graves, Mr. Drury, and my father, all of whom were tradesmen in the Strand, in the immediate vicinity of George
Street, speak of this visit. He occasionally took his cup
of chocolate at the Northumberland, occupying himself in
reading, and preserving a provoking taciturnity to the
gentlemen in the room ; though his manner was stern, his
deportment was that of a gentleman.'

Timbs [1] endorses this statement, in identically the same
words of a portion of the above, which he fathers on old
Mr. Matthews, the bookseller in the Strand, but we must
recollect that Mr. Timbs was writing the '*Romance* of
London.'

[1] *Romance of London*, vol. iii. p. 172, ed. 1865.

A personal description of Napoleon in 1793 may be interesting, especially as it comes from a trustworthy pen.[1] 'At that period of his life Bonaparte was decidedly ugly ; he afterwards underwent a total change. I do not speak of the illusive charm which his glory spread around him, but I mean to say that a gradual physical change took place in him in the space of seven years. His emaciated thinness was converted into a fulness of face, and his complexion, which had been yellow, and apparently unhealthy, became clear and comparatively fresh ; his features, which were angular and sharp, became round and filled out. As to his smile, it was always agreeable. The mode of dressing his hair, which has such a droll appearance as we see it in the prints of the bridge of Arcola, was then comparatively simple, for young men of fashion (the *Muscadins*), whom he used to rail at so loudly at that time, wore their hair very long. But he was very careless of his personal appearance ; and his hair, which was ill-combed and ill-powdered, gave him the look of a sloven. His little hands, too, underwent a great metamorphosis : when I first saw him, they were thin, long, and dark ; but he was subsequently vain of the beauty of them, and with good reason.

'In short, when I recollect Napoleon entering the courtyard of the Hotel de la Tranquillité in 1793, with a shabby round hat drawn over his forehead, and his ill-powdered hair hanging over the collar of his great-coat, which afterwards became as celebrated as the white plume of Henry IV., without gloves, because he used to say they were an useless luxury, with boots ill-made and ill-blackened, with his thinness and his sallow complexion ; in fine, when I recollect him at that time, and think what he was afterwards, I do not see the same man in the two pictures.'

[1] *Memoirs of Madame Junot*, vol. i. p. 73.

He was fortunate in obtaining a higher rank in the army, being promoted to be commandant of artillery, and he joined the army besieging Toulon on September 12, 1793. He found his chief, General Cartaux, incompetent, and, from representations made to Paris, Cartaux was superseded. There was very hard fighting at Toulon before it was taken, Admiral Hood, and General O'Hara, commanding the British forces. The latter being taken prisoner, much disheartened the English, but, at the final assault,

NAPOLEON WORKING THE GUNS AT TOULON.

when the town was retaken by the French, the English and Spanish gunners died fighting at their posts.

Our metrical History of Napoleon says,—

> The first shell 'gainst Toulon, 'tis said,
> The hand of Bonaparte had sped.

The vengeance of the French, on entering the town, was terrible ; but many thousands had taken shelter on board the British ships, leaving only a few hundreds to be executed 'according to law.' Our poem somewhat exaggerates.

One of the Jacobins, whom Hood
Had sent to prison for no good—
A noted character indeed—
By the republicans was freed.
As vengeance he on all design'd
Who to the English had been kind,
Or in their dreadful situation
Promoted the Capitulation,
This miscreant selected then
One thousand and four hundred men,
Whom they determin'd to assassinate—
A testimony of surpassing hate ;
And Boney was, with general voice,
For executioner their choice.
Indeed the choice was very good,
For Boney was a man for blood.
In sets, it was these wretches' lot,
To be brought forward to be shot :
Nap gave the order with composure,
The loaded guns were pointed so sure
A dreadful carnage soon ensued—
A carnage—horrible when view'd.
Yet, *gallant* Boney, with delight,
Remain'd spectator of the sight.
Nay, more, himself vers'd in hypocrisy,
He thought he might perhaps some mock'ry see :
So ' Pardon ! pardon ! ' loud he said,
To know if they were really dead ;
Some, who had counterfeited death,
Rose up, and were deprived of breath !
Poor souls ! they knew not when he said it
His word was not deserving credit.
However two there were more wise,   ⎫
Who, having put on death's disguise,   ⎬
Could not be tempted thus to rise,   ⎭
But tarried till the wolves were gone,
And then—a father found his son !

CHAPTER V.

NAPOLEON'S PROMOTION—HIS POVERTY—JUNOT'S KINDNESS—REVOLT OF THE SECTIONS—NAPOLEON'S SHARE THEREIN—MADE GENERAL OF THE INTERIOR—INTRODUCTION TO JOSEPHINE—SKETCH OF HER LIFE.

FOR the capture of Toulon, Bonaparte was speedily promoted; indeed, his superior officer, Dugommier, in his report, said, 'Reward and advance this young man, otherwise he will find means to advance himself.'

He afterwards joined the army at Nice, and was sent on a secret diplomatic mission to Genoa; on his return from which he was arrested and thrown into prison, where he remained a fortnight before he obtained his release. He was without any employment during the remainder of 1794, and till the autumn of 1795. He was then in very poor circumstances financially, and Madame Junot gives a graphic picture of his distress at this time.[1] 'Bonaparte's servant informed Mariette that the general was often in want of money;' but, he added, 'he has an aide-de-camp who shares with him all he gets. When he is lucky at play, the largest share of his winnings is always for his general. The aide-de-camp's family sometimes sends him money, and then almost all is given to the general. The general, adds the man, loves this aide-de-camp as dearly as if he were his own brother.' The aide-de-camp was Junot, who got a commission after Toulon.

[1] *Memoirs*, vol. i. p. 80

The wretched Boney, we are told,
Reduced, and shivering with the cold,
To public houses used to rove,
And warm his hands before a stove;
Nay, in Corrozza, it is said,
A large score still remains unpaid.
He in an humble garret slept,
Which never very clean was kept,
Hence got he a disorder, which
The vulgar people call the ' itch.'
    Long might have been poor Nap's dejection
But for a pending insurrection ;
For now was entertained th' intention
Of overturning the Convention.
The party by Barras were led,
He of the rebels was the head ;
But, neither brave nor skilful reckon'd,
He wish'd to have an able second.
This task, by many, as we find,
Was conscientiously declin'd ;
For every one of them well knew,
A dreadful slaughter must ensue.
Barras said in a thinking mood,
' I know a rascal fond of blood—
A little Corsican blackguard,
But now to find him may be hard.'
Then, having mentioned Boney's name,
They all agreed upon the same ;
And Tallien gladly undertook
For the said Corsican to look.
Soon Boney on their honórs waited,
Though all in rags as it is stated ;
And, matters being quick concluded,
No ' saucy doubts or fears ' intruded ;
Nap with a horse was soon provided,
And regimentals he beside had.

This scheme began they to contrive
In seventeen hundred, ninety five.
And of October, we may say,
The fourth was now a fatal day !
For, lo ! the insurgents sallied out,
And desolation spread about ;
All honest opposition fail'd
And blood-stain'd tyranny prevail'd.
Men, women, children, at a bitter rate
The cries of ' Treason,' did reiterate,
But nothing could their fury quell,
For women, men, and children fell !
　　Now, owing to this revolution,
. Was formed another Constitution ;
Nap this assembly went to meet,
And laid his *trophies* at their feet :
These trophies were *eight thousand carcases*,
Among the wounds, too, many a mark was his.
A *second* victory like this,
Was to Barras extatic bliss.
And Nap, for bravery extoll'd,
No longer a blackguard was called ;
But as a hero now regarded,
Was amply by Barras rewarded.
　　In this life there is many a change,
As unexpected and as strange :
Then let us hope that this day's sorrow
May be tranquillity to-morrow :
For, mark you how our hero rose,
Who wanted money, shoes, and clothes ;
All those he had—and, what is more,
His garret chang'd for a first floor ;
And such, too, was his happy lot,
That he a place for Lucien got ;
Who, after this notorious slaughter,
Had married an innkeeper's daughter.

This is the satirist's account of the revolt of the Sections, and Bonaparte's part therein. When applied to,
he accepted the command, but declared that he must act
untrammelled, and not like Menon, who failed through
having three representatives of the people to counsel him.
This was agreed to, and Barras was chosen chief, with
Napoleon under him. The insurgents numbered some
40,000, the troops but 7,000 ; and such was the moderation of the latter, that when the insurrection was quelled,
there were but seventy or eighty of the people killed, and
between three and four hundred wounded.

He was then made General of the Interior, and consequently Governor of Paris, and this position led him more
into society.

It is now that we come to a great epoch in his life, his
meeting with Josephine, which came about in a somewhat
singular manner. At one of his levées, a boy of twelve
years, or so, called upon him. The lad was Eugène de
Beauharnais, son of a general of the Republic, who was
executed a few days before the death of Robespierre, and
his errand was to petition Napoleon that his father's sword
might be given to him. To quote Napoleon's own words,
'I was so touched by this affectionate request, that I
ordered it to be given to him. On seeing the sword he
burst into tears : I felt so affected by his conduct, that I
noticed and praised him much. A few days afterwards,
his mother came to return me a visit of thanks ; I was
struck with her appearance, and still more with her *esprit*.'
He was always meeting her in society, especially at
Barras's house ; and this intimacy, ripening into affection,
brought about their marriage. The following series of
eight plates, illustrating her life, were drawn by Woodward.

Josephine (Marie Josephine Rose de la Pagerie) was
born at Martinique, according to De Bourrienne, on June 23,

1763, but others say it was the same day of the month, only four years later. She was the daughter of a planter in that island, and was a Creole, *i.e.* one born in a French West Indian settlement. She was fourteen years old when she was brought to France by her father, and being very graceful and pretty, it was not long before she was married, which was to the Vicomte de Beauharnais, on December 13, 1779. The union was not at first a happy one. She went to Martinique, to see her mother, and stayed there about fifteen months. Her husband was a general

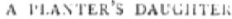

A PLANTER'S DAUGHTER.   A FRENCH COUNTESS.

in the army of the Rhine, but was singled out by Robespierre as a victim of his tyranny, was imprisoned and beheaded. Josephine was also imprisoned, and it was at La Force that she met with Madame Tallien—' Nôtre Dame de Thermidor,' as Arsène Houssaye calls her—who was also in prison. Here, uncertain as to their fate, the female prisoners played at mock trials and executions (for the trials always ended in condemnation), and day by day their numbers grew less, as they were taken away to the real tragedy which they had rehearsed. Scandal (French

before it became English) says that Barras, smitten by her
charms, had her released on condition that she became his

A WIDOW.   A PRISONER.

mistress.   Here is one French account : [1] ' A cette époque,
la jeune veuve du malheureux vicomte de Beauharnais,

A LOOSE FISH.   BARRAS' MISTRESS.

mort sur l'échafaud, languissait aux Magdelonettes, où,
depuis longtems, elle était détenue comme suspecte.   In-

[1] *Amours et Aventures du Vicomte de Barras*, Paris, 1817.

timement liée avec Hoche, elle le pria de parler pour elle à
Barras, alors tout-puissant. Celui-ci ne connaissait la vi-
comtesse que de réputation ; il voulut la voir, et lui rendit
visite dans sa prison. . . . Barras, séduit par la conversation et les charmes personnels de la jeune veuve, devint, à
la première visite, et son protecteur, et son ami. Deux
jours après, elle fut rendue à la liberté.'

That Josephine gave rise to this scandal, is probably
owing to her intimacy with Madame Tallien and Barras.
Barras, she was bound to be grateful to, for by his means,
a part of her husband's property was restored to her ; but
it was Tallien who, at his wife's entreaty, obtained the
liberty, both of Josephine and Duchesse d'Aiguillon.
Madame Tallien's receptions were the most brilliant in
Paris, where the prettiest and wittiest women met the men
most distinguished in any way, and common gratitude,
at least, would have led Josephine to the assemblies of her
dear friend, who had shared her imprisonment, and obtained her release.

CHAPTER VI.

LET us for a moment, as an antidote to the caricaturist's
pictures, see what was Josephine's dress at this period.[1]
'Here is Madame de Beauharnais, that excellent Josephine,
whose heart is not made for coquetry, but who throws a
childish joy into her dress.   With an air less dramatic and
superb than her rivals,[2] the joyous and kindly creole is,
perhaps, the most French of the three, Madame Tallien is
the most Greek, and Madame Viconti the most Roman.
Josephine wears a wavy dress, rose and white from top
to bottom, with a train trimmed at the bottom with
black bugles, a bodice six fingers deep, and wearing no
fichu; short sleeves of black gauze, long gloves covering
the elbow of *noisette* colour, which suits this beautiful
violet so well ; shoes of yellow morocco ; white stockings with green clocks.   If her hair is dressed after the
Etruscan manner, ornamented with cherry-coloured rib-
bons, I am sure it is impossible to approach nearer to
the antique.   To tempt the fashion is the sole ambition
of the pretty Josephine, but it happens that the celebrated
Madame de Beauharnais sets it.'

It is impossible to quit this subject without some

---

[1] *Notre Dame de Thermidor*, p. 429.
[2] Madame Tallien and Madame Viconti.

contemporary quotations, as they help us to realise the truth, or falsehood, of the caricaturist.[1] 'Madame Tallien was kind and obliging, but such is the effect on the multitude of a name that bears a stain, that her cause was never separated from that of her husband. The following is a proof of this. Junot was the bearer of the second flags, which were sent from the army of Italy to the Directory. He was received with all the pomp which attended the reception of Marmont, who was the bearer of the first colours. Madame Bonaparte, who had not yet set out to join Napoleon, wished to witness the ceremony; and, on the day appointed for the reception of Junot she repaired to the Directory, accompanied by Madame Tallien. They lived at that time in great intimacy; the latter was a fraction of the Directorial royalty with which Josephine, when Madame Beauharnais, and, indeed, after she became Madame Bonaparte, was in some degree invested. Madame Bonaparte was still a fine woman; her teeth, it is true, were already frightfully decayed, but when her mouth was closed she looked, especially at a little distance, both young and pretty. As to Madame Tallien, she was then in the full bloom of her beauty. Both were dressed in the antique style, which was then the prevailing fashion, and with as much of richness and ornament as were suitable to morning costume. When the reception was ended, and they were about to leave the Directory, it may be presumed that Junot was not a little proud to offer to escort these two charming women. Junot was then a handsome young man of five and twenty, and he had the military look and style for which, indeed, he was always remarkable. A splendid uniform of a colonel of huzzars set off his fine figure to the utmost advantage. When the ceremony was ended, he offered one arm to

---

[1] *Madame Junot's Memoirs*, vol. i. p 249.

Madame Bonaparte, who as his general's wife was entitled
to the first honour, especially on that solemn day ; and offering his other arm to Madame Tallien, he conducted them
down the staircase of the Luxembourg.   The crowd stepped
forward to see them as they passed along.   "That is the
general's wife," said one.   "That is his aide de camp," said
another.   "He is very young."   "She is very pretty.— *Vive
le General Bonaparte !— Vive la Citoyenne Bonaparte !*   She
is a good friend to the poor."   "Ah !" exclaimed a great
fat market woman, "She is *Notre Dame des Victoires !*"
"You are right," said another, "and see who is on the other
side of the officer ; that is *Notre Dame de Septembre !*"
This was severe and it was also unjust.'

We must not trust to the caricaturist's portrait of Josephine.   She was good looking and graceful then, but, afterwards, she did become very stout.   We must never forget
in looking over the folios of caricatures of this period, that
the idea of caricaturing then was to exaggerate everything,
and make it grotesque ; it is only of modern years that the
refinement of a Leech, Tenniel, or Proctor, gives us caricature without vulgarity.

After seeing Josephine as she really was, it will be worth
while to compare the satirist's idea of her, and her marriage
with Napoleon.

> Nap changed on entering Society,
> Obscurity for notoriety ;
> He to Barras only inferior,
> Commands the army of th' interior.
> As pride in office is essential,
> His manners now were consequential ;
> Conducting all affairs of weight,
> The little man was very great ;
> And by this sudden rise to dignity,
> He gave full weight to his malignity.

Barras, now moved by his persuasions,
Consulted him on all occasions ;
A greater compliment, too, paid he,
He got for him, a *cast off* lady :
A widow rich, as they relate,
But how so rich, 'tis hard to state,
Her spouse, for politics reputed,
By Robespierre was executed,
And she was by Barras *protected*,
Till he at length the fair neglected.
However, she procured with great art,
A man of colour for a sweetheart ;
By which no fortune's manifested,
For men of colour are detested ;
They married would have been, moreover,
But that—in stepped another lover ;

    .   .   .   .   .
    .   .   .   .   .

There are some writers who pretend,
The lady's virtue to defend ;
For, in the character they draw,
She's guilty of but one *faux pas* ;
But others, probably censorious,
Declare her lapses were notorious,
And that, devoid of sense and shame,
She even gloried in the same ;
So reckoning all things, the amount is,
She was a *condescending* countess.
The lady was, as it appears,
Older than Nap by twenty years ;
But, for a man, who scorned to prove
The votary or slave of love—
Whispering soft nonsense, and such stuff—
She certainly was good enough.
Short, like himself, and rather bulky,
But not so insolent and sulky.

As by Barras, too, recommended
(No matter from what stock descended),
It certainly must be allow'd
Of such a wife he should be proud.
So, locked together, soon were seen,
Brave Boney and fair Josephine.

The pictorial caricaturist, Gillray, gives us February 20, 1805, 'Ci-devant occupations, or Madame Tallien, and the

Empress Josephine Dancing Naked before Barras, in the Winter of 1797—a fact.'[1]

At the foot of this etching, which depicts the sensual *bon viveur*, Barras, looking on at the lascivious dancing of his two mistresses, Madame Tallien and Josephine, it says : 'Barras (then in power), being tired of Josephine, promised Bonaparte a promotion, on condition that he would take

[1] Gillray, evidently, was not particular as to dates, for Napoleon married Josephine in 1796.

her off his hands. Barras had, as usual, drank freely, and placed Bonaparte behind a screen, while he amused himself with these two ladies, who were then his humble dependents. Madame Tallien is a beautiful woman, tall and elegant. Josephine is smaller, and thin, with bad teeth something like cloves. It is needless to add that Bonaparte accepted the promotion, and the lady, now Empress of France !'

Barre, who notoriously wrote against Napoleon, says : [1] 'And not satisfied by procuring him a splendid appointment, he made him marry his mistress, the Countess de

Beauharnais, a rich widow, with several children ; and who, although about twenty years older than Bonaparte, was a very valuable acquisition to a young man without any fortune. The reputation of the Countess de Beauharnais was well established, even before the Revolution : but Buonaparte had not the least right to find fault with a woman presented to him by Barras.'

At all events they were married, and here is G. Cruikshank's idea of the ceremony, and here, also, he depicts the bridesmaids and groomsmen.

Their honeymoon was of the shortest, for De Bourrienne

[1] *History of the French Consulate under Napoleon Buonaparte, &c.,* by W. Barre, London, 1804.

says : ' He remained in Paris only ten days after his marriage, which took place on the 9th of March, 1796.
Madame Bonaparte possessed personal graces and many
good qualities. I am convinced that all who were acquainted
with her must have felt bound to speak well of her ; to few,
indeed, did she ever give cause for complaint. Benevolence
was natural to her, but she was not always prudent in its
exercise. Hence her protection was often extended to persons who did not deserve it. Her taste for splendour and
expense was excessive. This proneness to luxury became
a habit which seemed constantly indulged without any
motive. What scenes have I not witnessed when the
moment for paying the tradesmen's bills arrived ! She
always kept back one half of their claims, and the discovery
of this exposed her to new reproaches. How many tears
did she shed, which might easily have been spared !'

We here see the caricaturist's idea of Josephine as a
French general's wife.

A GENERAL'S LADY.

CHAPTER VII.

NAPOLEON MADE COMMANDER-IN-CHIEF OF THE ARMY OF ITALY—HIS SHORT HONEYMOON—HIS FIRST VICTORY—STATE OF THE FRENCH ARMY—THE ITALIAN CAMPAIGN—FRENCH DESCENT ON IRELAND— ITS RESULT—STATE OF ENGLAND.

NAPOLEON now waxed great. Through Barras' influence he was made Commander in Chief of the army of Italy, and bade adieu to his wife after the very brief period of conjugal life, as aforesaid, and, on the way to join the army, he visited his mother and family, at Marseilles, writing frequent and affectionate letters to his newly married bride.

Montenotte was his first victory, the precursor of so many ; and on April 11, 1796, he there defeated the Austrian general, Beaulieu, who was compelled to retreat, leaving behind him his colours, and cannon, about two thousand prisoners, and about a thousand killed.

The French army then was in a bad state, according to a serious historian.[1] 'The extreme poverty of the treasury may be understood from the fact that the sum of two thousand louis was all that could be collected to furnish him (Napoleon) with means for so important a command. By an organised system of pillage, says Lanfrey, the Republican coffers were soon replenished to the amount of several millions!' Another historian[2] says : 'Scherer, who was at that time commander-in-chief of the army of Italy, had recently urged for money to pay his troops, and for horses to replace those of his cavalry which had

---

[1] R. H. Horne.   [2] G. M. Bussey.

perished for want of food ; and declared that, if any delay took place in furnishing the requisite supplies, he should be obliged to evacuate the Genoese territory, and repass the Var. The Directory found it easier to remove the General than to comply with his request.' Our poetic history relates :—

> Such was the army's sad condition,
> They had no clothes nor ammunition,
> Besides, a scarcity of food,
> And even that little, was not good.
> They had no money—may be said—
> And why? The men were never paid.
> But his intentions wisely Nap hid,
> Whose methods were as strange as rapid.
> He promis'd, when he was appointed,
> To get them everything they wanted ;
> And, what is more, too, their protector be,
> Without expense to the Directory.
>
> .   .   .   .   .
>   .   .   .
>
> In his deceptions he succeeded,
> And now procur'd all that he needed.
> His troops which were with hunger nigh dead,
> Were with good victuals soon provided ;
> They for new clothes exchang'd their rags,
> And then with Rhino fill'd their bags ;
> While Nap, as you may well believe,
> These people laughed at in his sleeve.

It is not within the province of this work to follow Napoleon in his victorious career in Italy, except the English caricaturist should notice him, and he had not yet attained to that questionable honour ; but a very brief synopsis of his battles in 1796 may be acceptable. Monte-notte, April 11 ; Millesino, April 14 ; Dégan, April 15 ; Mondovi, April 21 : Lodi, May 10 ; Lonado, August 3 ;

Castiglione, August 5 ; Roveredo, September 4 ; Bassano, September 8 : San Giargo, September 13 ; Arcola, November 15.

Barre says : 'The campaign in Italy was extremely brilliant, and withal revolutionary. Buonaparte attributed all the glory almost exclusively to himself. His secretary, who wrote his despatches, did it so as to flatter the generals and the army, but still as if all the merit belonged to the commander-in-chief. It seems that General Berthier made a bargain with Buonaparte, to whom he sold his talents for the sake of becoming rich without any responsibility. When Buonaparte was raised by the mixed faction, he made Berthier Minister of War ; and in that capacity he has shown himself more rapacious than any of his predecessors. Every contractor is obliged to give him *one hundred thousand livres* as a present (*pot de vin*) with out which there is no contract.' He tells a story which bears somewhat on the above. 'It happened once, that whilst he was playing at cards, having General Massena for his partner, that general made a mistake ; when Buonaparte started, all of a sudden, in a violent passion, and exclaimed, *Sacré Dieu ! General, you make me lose.* But General Massena instantly retorted with a happy sarcasm : *Be easy, General, remember that I often make you win.* Buonaparte could never forget nor forgive that *bon mot.*' This story also figures in poetry :—

> In numbers being three to one,
> A Battle at Monte Notte he won ;
> The Austrian General he defeated,
> And therefore with huzzas was greeted.
> But, tho' of this affair Conductor,
> Massena had been his instructor.
> Yet, when (would you believe it, Bards ?)
> Nap's partner at a game of Cards,

He scrupled not his friend t' abuse—
'Zounds ! general, how you make me lose ! '
The general, patient all the while,
Thus answer'd with a gracious smile,
' For such a loss don't care a pin,
Remember, Nap, I've made you *win*.'
Tho' nothing but the truth he spoke,
Nap never could forgive the joke.

It is impossible to pass over in silence an event which happened in 1796, in which, although Napoleon was not personally interested, all England was. This was no less than an attempted invasion of Ireland by the French ; relying on being supported by the Irish, who were disaffected then, as now. The expedition failed, although it was numerous and well-found, having General Hoche and 25,000 men with it. By defective seamanship, many of the ships were damaged, and a 74 gun ship, the *Seduisant*, was totally lost. Only one division, commanded by Admiral Bouvet, reached Ireland, but anchored in Bantry Bay, where they did nothing, but speedily weighed anchor, and returned to France. The following is an official letter on the subject :—

Dublin Castle, December 29, 1796.

My Lord [1]—The last accounts from General Dalrymple are by his aide-de-camp, Captain Gordon, who left Bantry at ten o'clock A.M. on Tuesday, and arrived here this morning. Seventeen sail of French ships were at that time at anchor on the lower part of Bear island, but at such a distance that their force could not be ascertained. A lieutenant of a French frigate was driven on shore in his boat, in attempting to quit his vessel, which was dismasted, to the admiral. He confirms the account of the fleet being French, with hostile views to this country, but does not appear to know whether the whole fleet, which consisted of about 17 sail of the line, 15 frigates, and including transports and luggers, amounted

---

[1] The Lord Mayor of London, Thomas Blackhall.

to fifty sail, were all to re-assemble off Bantry. General Hoche was on board, commanding a considerable force. I have the honour to be, my lord,

Your lordship's most obedient servant,

T. PELHAM.

Just let us glance for one moment at the social position of England at that time. For the first three months of the year the quartern loaf was 1*s.* 3*d.* ; in April it fell to 10*d.* : in June it rose to 11*d.* ; in September it fell to 8¼*d.* ; at which it remained all the year. There was a surplus of revenue over expenditure of over twenty-three millions, which must have gratified the Chancellor of the Exchequer ; the exports exceeded those in 1795 by 1,781,297*l.*, and the London Brewers brewed 142,700 more barrels of porter than the previous year ; 3 per cent. Consols varied from 71 in January (the highest price) to 56¾ in December (nearly their lowest).

CHAPTER VIII.

NAPOLEON DESPOILS ITALY OF HER WORKS OF ART—THE SIEGE OF
MANTUA—WÜRMSER'S SURRENDER—EARLIEST ENGLISH CARICATURE
OF NAPOLEON—INVASION OF ENGLAND—LANDING IN PEMBROKESHIRE
—NELSON'S RECEIPT TO MAKE AN OLLA PODRIDA—'THE ARMY OF
ENGLAND.'

SUCH a subject as the spoliation of Italian works of art
was not likely to go a-begging among caricaturists, so
George Cruikshank illustrated the poet Combe.

SEIZING THE ITALIAN WORKS OF ART.

As Nap (for his extortions fam'd),
Of livres twenty millions claim'd ;
Which sum, we also understand,
Pope Pius paid upon demand ;
And sixteen million more, they say,
Was bound in two months' time to pay
With these exactions not content,
To further lengths our hero went ;

A hundred paintings, and the best,
Were, we are told, his next request.
At his desire, the precious heaps came,
(It was indeed a very deep scheme),
Loretta's statues so pleased Boney,
They instantly packed up *Madona* :
These relics then, without delay,
To Paris Boney sent away ;
And there they formed an exhibition
As proof of Papal superstition.

At the siege of Mantua, Würmser sent his aide-de-camp
Klenau to Napoleon to treat for terms of peace. G. Cruik-

NAPOLEON AND HIS GUARD.

shank depicts the scene. Klenau is brought in blindfolded,
and Bonaparte, surrounded by his guard, strikes a melodramatic attitude, worthy of a pirate captain at a trans-
pontine theatre.

The real facts are thus described by Horn. 'Mantua
was now without hope of relief. The hospitals were
crowded, the provisions exhausted ; but Würmser still
held out. Napoleon informed him of the rout and disper-
sion of the Austrian army, and summoned him to surrender.
The old soldier proudly replied that "he had provisions for

a year ; " but a few days afterwards he sent his aide-de-
camp, Klenau, to the head-quarters of Serrurier to treat for
a surrender.

'At the conference, a French officer sat apart from the
two others, wrapped in his cloak, but within hearing of
what passed.   After the discussion was finished, this officer
came forward and wrote marginal answers to the conditions
proposed by Würmser ; granting terms far more favourable than those which might have been exacted in the
extremity to which the veteran was reduced. " These,"
said the unknown officer, giving back the paper, " are
the terms that I grant, if he opens his gates to-morrow ;
and if he delays a fortnight, a month, or two months, he
shall have the same terms.   He may hold out to his last
morsel of bread ; to-morrow I pass the Po and march upon
Rome."   Klenau, recognising Napoleon, and struck with
the generosity of the conditions he had granted, owned
that only three days' provisions remained in Mantua.'

The earliest English caricature of Napoleon that I have
met with, was published on April 14, 1797, all those hitherto given, being of later date.   It is not worth reproducing,
as the artist had evidently no knowledge of what manner
of man Napoleon was.   It is called the ' French Bugabo[1]
frightening the Royal Commanders.'   Bonaparte (a perfectly fanciful, and horrible sketch) is seated on the back of
some impossible Saurian—meant, probably, for the devil—
who is vomiting armies and cannon.   He calls out, ' Egad,
they run well.   Courez donc Messieurs les Princes ! ! !'
Of the two royal commanders running away, Frederick
Duke of York is calling out to his companion, ' I wish I
was at York. Come on, Charles, follow me.'   Fox, who
acts the part of ' the sweet little cherub that sits up aloft,'
says, ' Run, Frederick, run Charles, Mack, Wurmsell, Kell ;

[1] A bogey, a bugbear.

well done D'Alvinzi, now Davidovich.' The poor Pope is being trodden under the beast, and cries out, 'Oh Lord ! this rebel son of mine pays me no homage whatever.'

Of all the attempts of the French to invade England, perhaps the most ludicrous was that which took place in February 1797. On the 22nd of that month, a French corvette, and a lugger, made for the coast of Pembrokeshire, and there landed some 1,200 men. Two days after, they surrendered to Lord Cawdor, and were sent to Haverford-west : but, before the arrival of the military, the peasants attacked them with rough weapons, such as pikes and scythes. The ships, which brought this invading army over, were captured on their return to Brest. The following is an official letter to the Lord Mayor, respecting the event :—

My Lord,—I have the honour to acquaint your lordship that intelligence has been received that two French Frigates, a Corvette, and a lugger, appeared off the East of Pembrokeshire, on the 22nd instant, and, on the evening of that day, disembarked some troops (reported by deserters to be about 1,200 men, but without any field pieces). Every exertion had been made by the Lord Lieutenant, and gentlemen of that county, and its neighbourhood, for taking the proper steps on this occasion ; and the greatest zeal and loyalty has been shewn by all ranks of people. Immediately, on an account having been received at Plymouth, of this force having appeared in the Bristol Channel, frigates were despatched from Plymouth in quest of them.

> I have the honour to be, &c.
>
> PORTLAND.

In the 'Times' of March 13, 1797, is the following :—

Commodore NELSON'S *Receipt to make an Olla-Podrida.*

Take a Spanish first-rate, and an 80 gun ship and after well *battering* and *basting* them for an hour, keep throwing in your *force balls*, and be sure to let them be *well seasoned.* Your *fire* must never *slacken* for a single moment, but must be kept up as *brisk* as possible during the whole time. So soon as you perceive your Spaniards to be well *stewed* and *blended* together you must then throw your own ship on board of the two-decker. Lash your sprit-sail-yard to her mizen-mast : then jump into her quarter gallery, sword in hand, and let the rest of your boarders follow as they can. The moment you appear on the 80 gun ship's quarter deck, the Spaniards will all throw down their arms and fly : you will then have only to take a hop, step and a jump, from your *stepping stone*, and you will find yourself in the middle of the first-rate's quarter-deck with all the Spaniards at your feet. Your Olla Podrida may now be considered as completely *dished* and fit to be set before his MAJESTY.—*Nelson's New Art of Cookery.*

Negotiations for peace with France had been going on during the year, and Lord Malmesbury went over to Lisle to conduct them on the part of the English, but they came to nothing. The French, however, in order to keep us in anxiety, massed large quantities of troops on their coast, which the Directory ordered should be called the 'Army of England,' and they gave Bonaparte the command of it. It was destined to come to nothing. Napoleon had made peace with the Austrians, and was then given the above command.

> Among themselves [1] they had indeed,
> On Nap's departure all agreed ;
> For, one of his prodigious sway,
> 'Twas policy to send away.
> So Barras, who had such a wise head,
> Albion's immediate fall advised.
> And to send Boney, he thought best,
> To head the army in the West,
> Which had a pompous appellation,
> As 'twas to rouse the English nation ;

---

[1] The Directory.

The ' Army of England ' it was named,
Though never for an action famed ;
They had, indeed, for the occasion,
(We mean of the resolv'd invasion),
Rafts and Balloons, and ships for diving,
And other matters were contriving.
The business settled, Barras wrote
To his *dear* Bonaparte a note.
' Your loving friend now reinstates you,
Another victory awaits you—
To Albion's shores conduct your army,
There's nothing there that can alarm ye ;
I will each necessary thing lend,
That you may sack the Bank of England ;
On London's Tower let them see
The Standard of French Liberty.'
Some of the Ministers it seems
Thought this the maddest of all schemes ;
Tho' Barras with fine words embellish'd it—
Not even Mr. Boney relish'd it ;
And very soon, it must be own'd
The project wisely was postpon'd.

Thus stood things at the end of 1797, a year which left
the public pulse—the Three per Cent. Consols— at 49 (they
had, in September, dropped to $47\frac{7}{8}$), and the quartern loaf
about eightpence all the year through.

CHAPTER IX.

IN 1798 the caricatures with regard to the relations between
France and England became more numerous, and in this
year the personal entity of Napoleon is confessed, and his
likeness, a somewhat rough one, but still recognisable, is
established.   An early one in this year is, the ' Storm
Rising, or the Republican Flotilla in danger,' Feb. 1798, by
Gillray.   Fox, Sheridan, the Duke of Bedford, and Mr.
Tierney are represented as working a windlass, which is
used to pull over the Flotilla.   This is represented by a huge
raft bristling with cannon ; a large fort is in the centre, and
minor ones all around which bear flags inscribed ' Liberty,
Atheism, Blasphemy, Invasion, Requisitions, Plunder,
Beggary, Murder, Destruction, Anarchy, and Slavery.   It
is represented as coming from Brest, where the devil is seen
dancing on a guillotine, fiddling, and singing, " Over de
Vater ! over de Vater to Charley ! " '   Fox's coat lies on the
ground, together with a paper, a ' List of the New Republican Ministry.   Citizen Volpone (Fox) Premier.'   Their
designs, however, are being defeated by Pitt, who as Eolus,
is raising a storm, and blowing against the Flotilla, the
Admirals Duncan, Curtis, Howe, Gardiner, Trollope,
Colpoys, St. Vincent, Seymour, Parker, and Onslow.   A

somewhat similar idea was worked out in a caricature by
Isaac [1] Cruikshank, January 28, 1789.

In March Sir John Dalrymple drew, and Gillray etched,
a series of four caricatures. The first was called the 'Consequences of a successful French Invasion,' and it shows
the French clearing out the House of Commons, and the
members in fetters. The second engraving is, 'We explain

de Rights of Man to de Noblesse.' Paine's doctrines are
being carried out in far more than their entirety. A
guillotine takes the place of the throne, and the French
commander orders, à la Cromwell, one of his men, 'Here,
take away this bauble! but if there be any gold on it take
it to my lodging.'

The next one is a slap in the face for Ireland, and is

---

[1] He was the father of our great caricaturist, George; but there is little
doubt from the internal evidence of the pictures, that George either wholly
produced, or materially helped in the execution of many caricatures signed
with his father's name.

called, ' We fly on the wings of the wind to save the Irish Catholics from persecution,' and French sympathy is shown by a priest being stabbed, and the holy vessels trampled on.

The fourth is 'Me teach de English Republicans to work,' and the French are represented as cruel taskmasters. Men and women are put to work in the fields, and Republicans, with fearful whips, keep them up to the mark of efficiency. Others are harnessed to a plough, and are kept well to their work by a most cruel lash.

Napoleon gave up all idea of invading England, and in May the expedition to Egypt was formed.

Fox's French proclivities are shown in a caricature (the Shrine of St. Anne's Hill,[1] May 26, 1798, Gillray) where he is seen on his knees before an altar, on which are a cap of liberty, and two busts of Robespierre and Buonaparte. The reredos is composed of a guillotine, and the tables of the ten commandments are labelled ' Droit de l'homme. 1. Right to worship whom we please. 2. Right to create and bow down to anything we chuse to set up. 3. Right to use in vain any name we like. 4. Right to work 9 days in the Week and do what we please on the tenth. 5. Right to honor both Father and Mother when we find it necessary. 6. Right to Kill. 7. Right to commit Adultery. 8. Right to Plunder. 9. Right to bear what Witness we please. 10. Right to covet our Neighbour's house and all that is his.' Nichols, Tierney, Lauderdale, Bedford, Lansdowne, and Norfolk, appear in the upper background as Cherubin.

When the invasion panic was abroad, patriotism was rampant, and everybody was very brave—on paper. This was the sort of stuff the people were fed on, of which I will give but two or three verses out of the eight.[2]

---

[1] Fox's residence.
[2] *The True Briton*, May 11, 1798.

While deeds of Hell deface the World,
And GALLIA's throne in ruin lies,
While round the Earth revolt is hurl'd,
And Discord's baneful Banner flies—
Loud shall the loyal BRITON sing
To arms ! to arms ! your bucklers bring,
To shield our Country, guard our King,
And GEORGE and ENGLAND save.

Ne'er shall the desolating Woe
That shades with horror Europe o'er,
To us her hideous image shew,
Or steep in blood this happy shore ;
Firm as our rock-bound Isle we'll stand,
With watchful eye and iron hand,
To wield the might of BRITAIN's land,
And GEORGE and ENGLAND save.

Oh, happy Isle ! wise order'd State !
Well temper'd work of Freedom's hand !
No Shock of Realms can touch thy fate,
If Union bind thy sea-girt Land !
Vainly the storms shall round thee ring,
While BRITAIN's sons in concord sing,
We'll shield our Country, guard our King
And GEORGE and ENGLAND save.

To give some idea of the commotion caused by the
threat of invasion, and yet not to be wearisome on the subject, I will only give the warlike items in the number of
the *True Briton*, from which the above verses are taken,
and which may be accepted as a fair sample. ‘We understand that the Duke of Bedford has received an answer
from his Royal Highness the Commander in Chief to his
offer of service, that it would be highly acceptable to the
Government if he would exert his influence in Devonshire
for the defence of the Coast.’ ‘His Grace the Duke of

Grafton has not only offered to furnish his waggons and
horses to Government, in case of emergency, but has also
expressed his desire to encourage all his neighbours and
tenants to assist with their persons and teams as far as
may be in their power.' 'Last week there was a respect-
able Meeting of the Inhabitants of Stowmarket, at which
it was unanimously agreed to form a Volunteer Corps of
Infantry for the defence of that Town and Hundred.' 'In
the county of Bedford, Lord Ongley, Mr. Trevor, and Mr.
Whitbread, raise, each of them, a troop of Yeomanry. The
town of Bedford raises a troop of Volunteer Cavalry.' 'A
Meeting was held at Newmarket on Sunday last, after
Divine Service, for aiding Government in case of Invasion,
pursuant to the Regulations of Mr. Dundas's Defence Bill ;
when the Inhabitants all came forward in a very laudable
manner for that purpose, and most of the labourers offered
their services as pioneers, or in any other capacity that
may be deemed necessary.' 'The farmers of the Parish of
Tarvin, in Cheshire, have set a noble example to their
brethren throughout the Kingdom, in having entered into
an agreement that they will, at a moment's notice, in case
of actual invasion, or imminent danger thereof, furnish
their respective teams, with able horses and drivers, for the
service of Government, free from any payment or gratuity
whatever ; and the number of each which they bind themselves to furnish, are 39 waggons, 68 carts, 347 horses, and
an adequate number of drivers.'

This is the voluntary, patriotic side of the question ;
take next day's paper, and we see, 'There was a sharp
press from the ships in Yarmouth Roads on Tuesday evening, by which means some good Seamen were procured.'

There is a vast amount of humour in 'Anticipation,
Ways and Means, or Buonaparte really taken' (I. Cruikshank, August 13, 1798). This represents a booth at a

country fair, where a Pierrot in tricolour costume (Fox), is showing to a lot of yokels a highly imaginative show canvas of Napoleon, with huge mouth and teeth, goggle eyes, two daggers, and immense boots and spurs. ' To be seen here alive, the noted Bony Parte, from Egypt. ☞ An undoubted likeness.' With tears streaming down his cheeks, he assures his audience that ' he is certainly taken. I never was so pleased at any event in the whole course of my life.'

Pitt, who, suffering from gout, sits down and acts as trumpeter to the show, addresses the people thus: 'Believe me, I do not mean to deceive you this time : he is really *taken*, and in this Booth at this present moment. Out with your pence good people—don't be so shy—Tumble up Mr. Bull—the only booth in the fair! don't be alarm'd —he is perfectly tame I assure you.'

The expedition to Egypt may be said to be the starting-point from which came the numerous caricatures of Napoleon. Before this, he had been known only by his victorious career in Italy, and had never come into active hostility with England ; but now that we were to measure our strength with the Chief of the 'Army of England,' he became an important person, and, consequently, the carica-turists, ever feeling the public pulse, took him up, and found it to their benefit.

The occupation of Egypt by the French, if successful, would have led to their attacking our empire in India, and this was Napoleon's design. Why the flotilla was ever allowed to go on its way unmolested, is hard to conceive ; but it was so, and on May, 19, 1798, sailed out of Toulon 13 sail of the line, 7 frigates, 62 gunboats, and 400 transport vessels, having 20,000 troops and large quan-tities of military stores on board. There were also 121 men learned in different branches of science, who accompanied the expedition, and the whole was under the supreme command of Napoleon.

On June 11 they reached Malta, which surrendered without resistance, and then went on their way. Nelson followed them, and got to Malta, where he arrived on the 22nd, only to find that the French had left some days before, on which he sailed for Alexandria, getting there on June 28, but found no news of the French fleet; so, instead of waiting for them, he steered northward for Caramania, and then went to Sicily; whence, after refitting, he sailed again for Alexandria.

In the meantime the French, of course, took advantage of his (to them) lucky absence; and, on July 2, they disembarked the army, and took possession of Alexandria, but not without some loss on the side of the French; and the bodies of the soldiers thus slain were by Napoleon's orders buried at the foot of Pompey's Pillar, and their names were to be engraved on the Column.

And now, as it will be a frequent article of impeachment against Napoleon in this book, let us examine into the truth of his turning Mahometan, and see, first, what foundation it had in fact from the mouths of his own countrymen. De Bourrienne gives a proclamation made by Napoleon to his soldiers before their arrival in Egypt, from which I extract only those sentences bearing on this subject :—

Head Quarters, on board the ' Orient.'
The 4th Messidor, Year VI. (June 22, 1798.)

Soldiers,—The people amongst whom you are going to live, are Mahometans. The first article of their faith is this : 'There is no God but God, and Mahomet is his Prophet.' Do not contradict this. Behave to them as you have behaved to the Jews—to the Italians. Pay respect to their muftis, and their imams, as you did to the rabbis and the bishops. Extend to the ceremonies prescribed by the Alcoran, and to the Mosques, the same toleration which you showed to the synagogues, to the religion of Moses, and of Jesus Christ. The Roman legions protected all religions.

And again, the same author says : 'On arriving at Alexandria, the General in Chief issued a proclamation to the people of Egypt, which, besides adverting to the insults and extortions experienced by French merchants from the Beys, contained the following passages :—

' " People of Egypt,—You will be told that I am come to destroy your religion—do not believe it. Be assured that I come to restore your rights, to punish the usurpers, and that I respect more than the Mamelukes, God, his prophet, and the Alcoran. Tell them that all men are equal in the eye of God ; wisdom, talents, and virtue make the only difference.

' " Cadis, Sheiks, Imans, Scorbajis, tell the people that we are the friends of the true Mussulmans. Have we not destroyed the Pope, who says that war ought to be made upon Mussulmans ? Have we not destroyed the Knights of Malta, because those bigots believed that God required them to raise their swords against the Mussulmans ? " '

And again (still quoting from the same authority), in a proclamation to the people of Cairo, dated from Ghizeh, 4th Thermidor, year VI. (July 22, 1798) : 'Fear nothing for your families, your houses, or your property ; and least of all, for the religion of the prophet, which I respect (*j'aime*).'

In another proclamation to the inhabitants of Cairo, according to 'Buonapartiana,' he is made to say : 'Make known to the people that since the world has been a world, it was written, that having destroyed the *enemies of Islamism*, *the Cross* should be thrown down ; I have come from the extreme confines of the West, to fulfil the task which has been imposed upon me. Shew your people that in the book of the Koran, in more than twenty passages, that what has happened has been predicted, and that what will happen is equally explained.'

In a French History[1] he is described as conversing with the Muftis and Imams in the Pyramid of Cheops. At p. 171 he says, ' Honour to Allah !' at p. 172, ' Glory to Allah ! There is no other God but God, Mahomet is his prophet, and I am one of his friends ;' and at p. 173, ' Mufti, I thank you, the divine Koran is the joy of my soul,

DEMOCRATIC RELIGION.

Bonaparte turning Turk at Cairo for Interest, after swearing on the Sacrement to support yᵉ Catholic Faith.

and the occupation of my eyes. I love the prophet ; and I am reckoning, before long, to see and honour his tomb in the Holy City.'

It is not worth while to multiply instances. His policy led him to conciliate the people, and, probably, his utter- ances were rather more in accordance with their religious ideas than would have been conformable in the mouth of a zealous Christian. But to the English caricaturist and satirist they were *bonnes bouches*, and they twisted and

[1] *Histoire de Bonaparte, Premier Consul, Depuis sa Naissance, jusqu'à la Paix de Lunéville*, Paris, chez Barba, 1801.

distorted them to suit their purposes. It became almost an article of belief with the average Englishman, that Napoleon had embraced the Mahometan religion. Were there not his own proclamations to prove it? Gillray even depicted him as undergoing a ceremony of reception into the Mahometan religion, surrounded as he is by Muftis, one of whom puts a turban on his head, another sonorously reads from the Koran, whilst a third brandishes a fearful knife for circumcision.

CHAPTER X.

CONDUCT OF FRENCH SOLDIERY—NAPOLEON'S HATRED OF ENGLAND—THE
EGYPTIAN CAMPAIGN—DESTRUCTION OF THE MAMELUKES—BATTLE
OF THE NILE—TARDY NEWS THEREOF.

AFTER the entry into Alexandria, Napoleon, by several
proclamations, imposed the strictest discipline upon his
soldiers ; and, although it is possible some irregularities
may have occurred on the part of the troops, such scenes
as were depicted by Cruikshank and Combe, one with his
pencil, the other with his pen, were simply impossible.

> He took the City by surprise,
> For he was always very wise,
> And with extreme amaze and dread,
> To mosques the people gladly fled.
> Regenerators yet annoy'd them,
> For they o'ertook and soon destroy'd them ;
> And horrible indeed to tell,
> Both men and women quickly fell ;
> Nay, even the infants at the breast !
> How sad the cries of the distrest !
> As *trophies* of this *glorious* fight,
> The spears held up the babes to sight ;
> While this unparalleled ferocity
> Was call'd *amazing generosity.*

The *avowed* object of Napoleon's expedition was to
punish the Beys, of whom there were twenty-four, who kept
up a force of some eight thousand Mamelukes, splendid

cavalry, recruited from slaves bought in Georgia, the Caucasus, and even in Europe. The pretence against them was injustice and oppression against French merchants ; but the *real* reason for it is in the proclamation dated on board the 'Orient,' of 4th Messidor, year VI. : 'Soldiers, you are about to undertake a conquest, the effects of which on civilisation and commerce are incalculable. *The blow you are about to give to England, will be the best aimed, and the most sensibly felt, she can receive, until the time when you can give her her death blow.*[1] . . . The Destinies are with us.

MASSACRE IN EGYPT.

The Mameluke Beys who favour exclusively English commerce, whose extortions oppress our merchants, and who tyrannise over the unfortunate inhabitants of the Nile, a few days after our arrival will no longer exist.'

With what intensity Bonaparte hated England! For example, take this little extract from Madame Junot,[2] to whose brother Napoleon was speaking : '"England !" he then rejoined. "So you think in Paris that we are going to attack it at last ? The Parisians are not mistaken ; it is indeed to humble that saucy nation that we are arming.

[1] The italics are mine.—J. A.   [2] *Memoirs*, vol. i. p. 209

England! If my voice has any influence, never shall England have an hour's truce. Yes, yes, war with England for ever, until its utter destruction." '

Alexandria was taken and garrisoned; but this was only the commencement of the campaign. Cairo must be reached speedily, and at all hazards. Then came that terrible march across the desert, from the 7th to the 10th of July —with generals all but mutinous, with Lannes and Murat dashing their cocked hats on the sands and trampling upon them in sight of the soldiers; the burning sun, the scarcity of water, harassed by enemies, human and insect—what joy could exceed theirs when they reached the Nile at Rahmanié! That wild rush into the water, without even thinking of the depth, and then the welcome shade and the juicy melons in such abundance; it must have been a glimpse of heaven to those poor half-maddened, half-starved soldiers.

After a brief rest they pushed on towards Cairo. On July 19 they sighted the pyramids; on the 21st they had to encounter Mourad Bey, who had a force of 8,000 Mamelukes, forty pieces of cannon, and 20,000 infantry. Then was it that, pointing to those grand historical monuments, Napoleon addressed his soldiers with the ever-memorable and oft-quoted speech: 'Soldiers! From the summit of those pyramids forty centuries look down upon you.'

We know the issue of that battle—how, out of 8,000 Mamelukes that proudly sat their steeds that morning, 6,000 bit the dust ere night. The French that day drank deep of blood, for 10,000 of the Egyptian troops lay dead on the field; they took 1,000 prisoners, and all their artillery and baggage. They could make no further stand, and the way to Cairo was open. A small force under Dupuy took possession of the city, which they found almost deserted, and on July 24, the *Sultan Kebir*, or *King of Fire*, as the natives had christened Napoleon, made his formal entry into Cairo. A brief rest to tranquillise the place and restore confidence to its returning inhabitants, and then, leaving Desaix in charge of the city, Napoleon went in pursuit of Ibrahim Bey, and drove him into Syria.

But what news was to welcome the conqueror back to Cairo? Sad indeed was the tale he heard—nought less than the destruction and capture of his whole fleet, save two ships, which effected their escape. Nelson had made up for lost time, and on August 1 he fought the ' Battle of the Nile,' when 'L'Orient' was blown up, and young Casabianca, the son of the captain of the ship, with it. We all know the poem by Mrs. Hemans commencing, 'The boy stood on the burning deck.'

De Bourrienne does not disguise the effect this disaster had upon Napoleon. He says : ' The catastrophe of Aboukir came like a thunderbolt upon the General-in-Chief. In spite of all his energy and fortitude, he was deeply distressed by the disasters which now assailed him. To the painful feelings excited by the complaints and dejection of his companion-in-arms, was now added the irreparable misfortune of the burning our fleet. He measured the fatal consequences of this event at a single glance. We were now cut off from all communication with France, and all hope of returning thither, except by a degrading capitulation with an implacable and hated enemy. Bonaparte had lost all chance of preserving his conquest, and to him this was indeed a bitter reflection.'

But with what different feelings was the news received in England ! There was no steam, no electricity, then ; men did not receive their news red-hot as we do now, but had to wait for it, more or less calmly, according to their temperament. Let us take this battle of the Nile as an

example. It was fought on August 1. On September 1
the ' True Briton ' (from which the following extracts are
taken) gives its readers an ' Extract from a letter from
Strasbourg, of the 20th August,' in which a circumstantial
account of the total destruction and capture of the French
fleet by that of England is given, together with a veracious
statement that ' the latter lost their Admiral Nelson, who,
nevertheless, two hours before he died of his wounds,
received General Buonaparte on board his ship (the ' Cul-
loden ') *Prisoner, with all his General Staff.*' This corre-
spondent's veracity is only equalled by his impartiality.

On September 17 we hear of the sailing of the English
fleet from Syracuse in quest of her enemy. On September
21 we have a quotation from the ' Redacteur ' of September
14: ' The same Letters inform us, that the Squadron of
Admiral Brueys had anchored on the coast of *Bignieres*,
and was preparing to return to France, when it was
attacked by the English Squadron, which was superior to
ours, both in the number and the size of the vessels; that
on both sides the action was maintained with a degree of
obstinacy, of which History affords no example; that
during the action the Vessel of the French Admiral was
burnt; that two or three French Ships sunk; and that some
others, both French and English, ran aground after having
lost all their Masts; and that, finally, some other French
ships, quite disabled, remained on the spot where the Battle
was fought.'

CHAPTER XI.

RECEPTION OF THE NEWS OF THE BATTLE OF THE NILE—NELSON SENDS FRENCH ADMIRAL'S SWORD TO THE CITY OF LONDON—VARIOUS CARICATURES ON THE BATTLE—TYPICAL JOHN BULL.

IT was not till October 2 that a glimmer of the truth, through rather a roundabout channel, appeared in the papers ; and later on that day appeared a 'London Gazette extraordinary,' with Nelson's despatches, which were very brief. Who can wonder at the excessive national rejoicing? People were drunk with joy. Take a few paragraphs from the 'Times' of October 3 :—

'DRURY LANE.—After the play, the news of Admiral Nelson's glorious victory produced a burst of patriotic exultation that has been rarely witnessed in a theatre. " Rule Britannia " was unanimously called for from every part of the house, and Messrs. Kelly, Dignum, Sedgewick, Miss Leak, and Mrs. Bland, came forward and sung it, accompanied by numbers of the audience. It was called for, and sung, a second time. The acclamations were the loudest and most fervent we have ever witnessed.

'The following lines, written for the occasion, were introduced by Mr. Dignum and Mr. Sedgewick—

> Again the tributary Strain
> Of grateful Britons let us raise,
> And to the Heroes on the Main,
> Triumphant add a Nelson's praise.

> Though the *Great Nation* proudly boasts
> Herself invincible to be ;
> Yet our brave NELSON still can prove
> BRITANNIA, Mistress of the Sea.

The audience were not satisfied with this repeated mark of exultation, but in the effusion of enthusiastic loyalty, called for " God save the King," which was received with reiterated plaudits.'

'Immediately that the news of the gallant victory obtained by Admiral NELSON was known at Lloyd's, a subscription was opened for the relief of the widows and orphans of the brave men who perished in fighting for their country.' [1]

'Every man in this country may address Admiral NELSON with SHAKESPEARE,

> Horatio, thou art e'en as *brave* a man
> As e'er my understanding cop'd withal.

The Capture of the French Fleet by NELSON, has reduced BUONAPARTE to the situation of *Macbeth*,

> There is no going hence, nor tarrying here.'

' A person last night, in the gallery of Drury Lane house, calling frequently for the tune of BRITONS STRIKE HOME,[2] was immediately silenced by the appropriate observation of another at some distance from him, " Why, damn it, they have—have not they ? " '

' An affray happened last night opposite to the Admiralty, where the crowd was very great.   The mob, as usual,

---

[1] Eleven hundred guineas were collected at once on the first day, besides which, the *Times*, October 4, says, ' The Royal Exchange and London Assurance Companies have subscribed 100 guineas each, and the East India Company have voted 1,000*l.* towards this benevolent and patriotic fund.'

[2] From *Bonduca*, by Henry Purcell, A.D. 1710.

insisted on every person of genteel appearance pulling off their hats ; six Officers passing along, were ordered to pay the same compliment to the mobility, and, refusing to do so, the populace attempted to force their hats off. The Officers drew their swords, and it was said that some persons were wounded.'

The next day's 'Times' (October 4) says : ' To shew the zeal for Illumination in honour of our late splendid Victory, a chaise last night passed through the town, in which were three Ladies, with large cockades in their head dresses. The inside of the chaise was lighted up ; a postillion was on each horse with flambeaux in their hands, besides two out-riders, also carrying flambeaux.'

' It was remarked by a loyal Hibernian, on the official news of Admiral Nelson's victory, that nothing on *earth* could resist us by *sea.*'

The mob after a day or two became so uproarious that the magistrates were compelled to order the cessation of the illuminations.

On October 3 the Court of Common Council met, two hundred strong, when the Lord Mayor read the subjoined letter from Nelson—

> Vanguard, Mouth of the Nile :
> August 8th, 1798.

My Lord,—Having the honour of being a freeman of the City of London, I take the liberty of sending to your Lordship the sword of the commanding French admiral, Monsieur Blanquet, who survived after the battle of the 1st, off the Nile, and request that the City of London will honour me with the acceptance of it, as a remembrance that Britannia still rules the waves ; which that she may for ever do, is the fervent prayer of

> Your lordship's
> Most obedient Servant
> HORATIO NELSON.

Right hon. the Lord Mayor of London.

Naturally, this gratifying memorial of this splendid victory was welcomed with enthusiasm, and orders were given to provide a suitable case, with inscription, for it ; and the Council voted Nelson a sword, value 200 guineas ; also the freedom of the City in a gold box, value 100 guineas, to Captain Berry, who was captain of the admiral's flagship, the 'Vanguard ;' and the thanks of the court to every one concerned.

The caricaturists soon pounced upon the subject, and the way in which the news of the victory was taken by different statesmen is very amusingly shown. (Gillray, October 3, 1798.) Burdett, who is always represented with his crop of hair combed over his eyes, is reading the 'Extraordinary Gazette,' and, in astonishment, exclaims, 'Sure I cannot see clear ?' Jekyll is telling Lord Lansdowne how nine French ships of war were captured and two burnt ; but his lordship claps his hands to his ears, and calls out, ' I can't hear, I can't hear.' The Duke of Bedford will not believe it, and is tearing up the notification of 'the complete destruction of Buonaparte's Fleet,' exclaiming, 'It's all a damn'd Lye ;' whilst poor Erskine, with Republican briefs before him, drops the paper which tells him of the capture of Bonaparte's despatches, and, with a smelling-bottle to his nose, plaintively calls out, 'I shall faint, I, I, I.' The poor Duke of Norfolk, whose many empty bottles of port testify to his inebriate condition, is very ill, and gives his opinion that ' Nelson and the British Fleet' is 'a sickening toast.' Tierney is in despair, and with the 'End of the Irish Rebellion ' in his pocket, and on his knees a paper, End of the French Navy. Britannia rules the Waves,' calls out, with upturned eyes, ' Ah ! our hopes are all lost.'

Moodily, with his head resting on his hands, sits Sheridan, with a ' List of the Republican Ships taken and destroyed ' before him, and his thoughts are of prudence,

' I must lock up my Jaw.' Black-visaged Fox, wearing a Cap of Liberty, has kicked over the stool that hitherto has supported him, and mournfully bidding ' Farewell to the Whig Club,' says, ' and I—— end with Éclat.'

This victory of the Nile is very graphically depicted (Gillray, October 6, 1798) in the ' Extirpation of the Plagues of Egypt ;—Destruction of Revolutionary Crocodiles ;—or —The British Hero cleansing y^e Mouth of y^e Nile.' Here

Nelson has half-a-dozen crocodiles (typical of captured French ships) hooked and in his power, whilst, with a stout cudgel of ' British Oak,' he is spreading deadly blows and consternation into a quantity of tricoloured crocodiles. The blowing up of the ' Orient ' is shown by one crocodile which is thus being destroyed.

Another caricature (October 7, 1798) of the victory of the Nile is ' The Gallant Nellson bringing home two uncommon fierce French Crocodiles from the Nile as a present to the King.' The one-armed hero is leading by a chain Fox and Sheridan, who have their jaws muzzled by rings, and Fox's mouth is also secured by a padlock, 'a mouthpiece for hypocrites.' They are both weeping copiously, after the fabled manner of crocodiles. Nelson is saying, ' Come along you Hypocritical dogs, I dare say your Dam'd sorry now for what you've done. No, no, I shall bring you to my MASTER ;' whilst.John Bull, habited as a countryman, exclaims, 'Aye, aye, what ! Horatio has got 'em at *last.* Why, these be the Old Cock Deviles. I thought as how he would not go so far for nothing.' This goes well with that of October 3.

A very curious caricature is (Ansell, October 24, 1798) Bonaparte in Egypt, ' A terrible Turk preparing a Mummy for a *present* to the Grand Nation.' A Turk, terrible indeed, has Napoleon by the throat, and, with sword in hand, is going to despatch him, saying, 'As for you, you Dog of no Religion, I'll sacrifice you at the tomb of the Prophet, whose name you have prophaned for the purposes of Murder, Rapine, and Plunder.'

Napoleon, whose defenceless state is typified by his swordless scabbard being broken, is endeavouring to mol-lIfy the wrath of the Turk. 'Now, mild and gentle Sir, don't be so rough : do you think I would cut your throat, ravish your wives, or plunder your house ? No, by Mahomet I would not. Sacrè Dieu, I would not. Ah, Diable, you'll choak me.'

Fox, Erskine, Sheridan, and the Duke of Norfolk are kneeling down, begging for Napoleon's life, whilst a Turk, who exclaims, 'You agree together so well, I think I'll fix you together for life,' has a bowstring ready to strangle all four. Pleads Fox, ' Pray don't hurt our dear friend, he wou'd not hurt Man, Woman, or Child. He can't bear the sight of blood ; as for plunder or deception, he is the determined enemy to both, by —— he is, and we are ready to swear it.' Sheridan and Erskine say—the one, 'd—n me if he ayn't, and we are ready to swear it ;' the other, 'I'll swear it, I, I, I, swear it.'

'John Bull taking a luncheon' (Gillray, October 24, 1798) is an extremely graphic caricature, and introduces us to the popular idea of John Bull, who, certainly, is never represented in this period with any of the refinement that Leech, Doyle, Tenniel, or any of our modern caricaturists depict him ; tastes and habits were coarser then than now, and John Bull was always shown in the rough. The

second portion of the title of the picture helps us to realise the popular fancy, 'or—British Cooks cramming old *Grumble Gizzard* with Bonne Chére.' All his admirals and captains are bringing him food. Nelson presents him with a *Fricasee à la Nelson*, a huge dish of French ships ; others are bearing dishes, such as *Desert à la Warren, Fricando à la Howe, à la Gardner, à la Bridport, à la Vincent, Dutch Cheese à la Duncan.*

John Bull is seated, devouring these viands, which are to be washed down with mighty draughts of *True British Stout*, exclaiming, 'What! more Frigasees ? why you sons o' b——s, you, where do you think I shall find room to stow all you bring in ?' Fox and Sheridan are seen through an open window, running away, calling out, ' Oh curse his Guts, he'll take a chop at us next.'

There is another one with similar *motif* by Ansell, November 1, 1798.

The 'destruction of the French Collossus' (Gillray,

November 1, 1798) is a painful picture.   The huge creation strides from Egypt to France ; its head being a skull, with vipers crawling in and out—its hands and feet being imbrued in blood ; it clutches the guillotine, and tramples the Bible, Crucifix, and scales of Justice under foot.   Round its neck is the bleeding head of Louis XVI. Britannia (typified by a shield of the national flag) hurls a thunderbolt, and shatters the huge statue into pieces.

CHAPTER XII.

REVOLT AND MASSACRE AT CAIRO—CARICATURES OF THE CAPTURE OF
FRENCH SHIPS—FIGHTING FOR THE DUNGHILL, ETC.—PRICE OF
BREAD AND CONSOLS IN 1798.

I HAVE omitted an episode which, to be chronologically correct, should have been introduced earlier; and here, as usual, we find a French authority for what might seem an English slander: Émile de la Bédolière, in his 'Tableau Chronologique de l'Histoire de Napoléon,' gives the story of the revolt at Cairo very tersely :—

October 21.—' During two months the Mussulmans patiently supported the yoke of the conquerors; but the establishment of a registration of landed property became the cause of a violent insurrection.

'On the 30th Vendemaire, year VII. (October 21, 1798), a multitude ran through the streets, and massacred all the French they met. Bonaparte repaired to the scene, and took measures to cut the communications between the different quarters of the city, which were in the hands of the insurgents. Fifteen thousand of them took refuge in the great mosque, and refused to surrender. A hail of bombs, shells, and bullets, threatened to engulph them under the débris of their last asylum   Soon they uttered lamentable cries, implored the mercy of the general-in-chief, and surrendered at discretion.'

Combe thus versifies this event :—

Mock liberty caus'd disaffection,
And soon commenc'd an insurrection.
According to our hero's plan
Of course a massacre began :
The streets were clear'd, and all the men
Ran to the mosques for refuge then.
The troops, tho', having forc'd the doors,
Strew'd with combustibles the floors,
And such indeed the conflagration,
It was a grand illumination ;
With screams and groans the air was fill'd,
For some were burn'd and some were kill'd—
All indiscriminately slain,
Who had for quarter begg'd in vain.
　　　At length our hero was inclin'd
Tho' somewhat slowly, to be kind ;
He granted quarter, and he trusted
All would be quietly adjusted.
He knew, which certainly was verified,
They had sufficiently been terrified.

Cruikshank, of course, grossly exaggerates the fact, and represents the French soldiery savagely attacking, even with pickaxes, the Egyptians who are endeavouring to escape from the mosque.

In November (12th) of this year, Rowlandson produced a plate called 'High fun for John Bull, or the Republicans put to their last shift.' This represents him as being in great glee at having captured so many ships, whilst the French are hard at work making fresh ones, which they are baking by batches in a *Dutch Oven* (an allusion to their being built in Holland). A Frenchman, with a large trayful of ships, calls out, 'Sacre dieu, Citoyens, make a Haste wit one autre Fleet, den we will shew you how to make one grande Invasion.' Another, a Spaniard, with a tray of cannon on his head, says, 'How ! That Nelson, wit one Arm and Eye can take our Ships by Dozens, then vat shall we do against the autres, wid two Arms and Eyes, dey will have two dozen at a time." A stolid Dutchman is baking a batch, grumbling the while, ' Donder and Blaxam to dis Fraternization ; instead of smoaking mine Pipes and sacking De Gold, dis French Broders make me build ships dat Mynheer Jan Bull may have de Fun to take dem.' Another Frenchman adds, 'Well you may talk, make haste, when dat English Nelson take our ships by the Douzaine.'

John Bull, who holds a whip in his hand, says, ' What ! you could not find that out before, you stupid Dupes ; but since you began the fun, you shall keep on. So work away, Damn ye, else Jack Tar will soon be idle.' A sailor carrying a trayful of ships on his head, calls out, ' Push on, keep moving, I'll soon come for another cargo. Old England for ever. Huzza ! '

'Fighting for the Dunghill—or—Jack Tar settling Buonaparte,' is by Gillray, November 20, 1798. Napoleon is terribly punished, his body being a mass of bruises and wounds, the worst being a large one in the breast, and labelled *Nelson*. Blood is streaming from his nose, and Jack is driving him out of the world altogether, having his

foot upon Malta, whilst Napoleon is insecure in Turkey
This engraving is an extremely typical one of the burly,
beef-fed Englishman, and the 'skinny Frenchman,' the
'Johnny Crapaud' of the time, any number of whom an
Englishman was supposed to be a match for—

> One skinny Frenchman, two Portugee,
> One jolly Englishman beat 'em all three.

Napoleon is depicted by Gillray (December 8, 1798)
as being in a fearful rage—and an extremely diverting
sketch it is. It is called ' Buonaparte hearing of Nelson's
Victory, swears by his sword to extirpate the English from
off the Earth. See Buonaparte's Speech to the French
Army at Cairo, published by authority of the Directory in
Volney's Letters.' His melodramatic pose, and costume,
are superb. A huge cocked hat and feathers, the hat
adorned with a crescent (to show his supposed Mahometan
proclivities), as well as a tricoloured cockade, surmounts his
head, which bears a most ferocious expression, somewhat
heightened by the formidable pigtail which he wears. A
huge green necktie is round his neck, and he wears a tricoloured scarf, in which are stuck a pistol and dagger ; boots,
with huge spurs, add to the dignity of the costume. He
is waving his bloody sword, and stamps upon a paper,
' Nelson's Victory over the Fleet of the Republic,' while he
shouts out : ' What ? our Fleet captured and destroyed by
the slaves of Britain ? by my sword and by holy Mahomet
I swear eternal Vengeance ! yes, when I have subjected
Egypt, subdued the Arabs, the Druses, and the Maronites ;
become master of Syria ; turn'd the great river Euphrates,
and sailed upon it through the sandy deserts ; compelled
to my assistance the Bedouins, Turcomans, Kurds, Arme-
nians, and Persians ; formed a million of cavalry, and
pass'd them upon rafts, six or seven hundred miles over the

Bosphorus, I shall enter Constantinople. Now I enter the Theatre of Europe, I establish the republic of Greece, I raise Poland from its ruins, I make Prussia bend ye knee to France, I chain up ye Russian bear, I cut the head from ye Imperial Eagle, I drive the ferocious English from the Archipelago, I hunt them from the Mediterranean, and blot them out from the catalogue of Nations. Then shall the conquer'd Earth sue for Peace, and an Obelisk be erected at Constantinople, inscribed " To Buonaparte, conqueror of the World, and extirpator of the ENGLISH NATION." '

This brings the year 1798 to a close of the prosperity, or otherwise, of which we may judge by the price of the quartern loaf, which averaged 8½d. for the year, and by the three per cent. Consols., which were 49⅝ in January, and 52⅝ in December ; but in this, as in other stocks, there was much fluctuation : for instance, in September Consols. were 49⅛ ; then came the news of the victory of the Nile, and up they went to 56½, only, however, to fall to 50½. But they rose again in November to 57⅞, fell again to 52⅛, and rose in December to 56.

CHAPTER XIII.

THE new year opens with a somewhat curious print by
I. Cruikshank, January 1, 1799, of the 'Ghost of Buonaparte appearing to the Directory.' The latter are in fearful dismay at the apparition, which, attired in the airiest of
costume, shakes his notched sword at them, saying, ' Regi-
cides, Parricides, Matricides, and Patricides, this is the
effect of your insatiable thirst for Conquest ; this is your
reward for my glorious Achievements in Italy, Germany,
&c.—to die by the hand of an Assassin, a d--d Mussulman :
and all my Brave Legions Destroyed by Water melons and
the Arabs. Go, Murderers in cold blood, may your conscious
guilt ever prey upon your vitals, and may the name of
Nelson ever haunt you, sleeping and waking '! What is
meant by his dying ' by the hand of an Assassin,' I do not
know ; but probably some rumour was afloat to that effect, as
Barre observes : 'Whilst Buonaparte and his army were thus
cut off from Europe, the most absurd reports were spread
(no doubt by the partisans of the artful Corsican) representing him as a victim of the Directory, who had thought
proper to remove so great, famous, and fortunate a general.

'They pretended that the Directory, unable to repay
the signal services of Buonaparte, and, fearing, at the same
time, his popularity, had contrived, with Talleyrand, to flat-

ter the ambitious vanity of that young conqueror with an expedition, which would raise his fame above the glory acquired by Alexander, or Cæsar. They added, that, as Buonaparte was sure of being director at the next election, the Directory had resolved to put him out of the way, by sacrificing him and his army; having even directed that the fleet should be exposed to certain destruction, in order that no possibility could exist of his return.'

The 'Times' of January 2, 1799, has the subjoined :—

The following Epigram has been handed about in Paris. The French points are all that can be remembered by the Gentleman who has put it in an English dress.

> ' France, to get rid of Turbulence,
> Sends her best Soldiers far from hence,
>   With promises, and wishes, hearty ;
> Pleas'd and content that what so e'er
> May happen either here or there,
>   To hazard all *in Bonâ-parte.*

> ' And still, though rous'd by home alarms,
> Nay, threatened by the world in arms,
>   France holds her head up bold and hearty—
> Since now each Directorial Elf,
> By losing *Bonaparte's* self
>   Enjoys the loss *in Bonâ-parte.'*

Meanwhile Napoleon was taking things pretty easily in Egypt, enjoying himself after his manner. It is a marvel that none of the English caricaturists ever depicted this portion of his life. True, Gillray, as we have seen, drew him in Turkish costume; but he never wore it but once, and then but for a very short time. But why did they spare him in his *amour* with Madame Fourès (Pauline, or *Queen of the East*, as the army christened her)? De Bourrienne makes no secret of it. He says : 'About the middle of September in this year (1798), Buonaparte ordered to be brought to the house of Elfy Bey, half a dozen Asiatic women, whose beauty he had heard highly extolled. However, their ungraceful obesity displeased him, and they were immediately dismissed. A few days after, he fell violently in love with Madame Fourés,[1] the wife of a lieutenant of Infantry. She was very pretty, and her charms were enhanced by the rarity of seeing a woman, in Egypt, who was calculated to please the eye of a European. Bonaparte engaged, for her, a house adjoining the palace of Elfy Bey, which he occupied. He frequently ordered dinner to be prepared there, and I used to go there with him at seven o'clock, and leave him at nine.

'This connection soon became the general subject of gossip at head-quarters. Through a feeling of delicacy to M. Fourés, the General in Chief gave him a mission to the Directory. He embarked at Alexandria, and the ship was captured by the English, who, being informed of the Cause of his mission, were malicious enough to send him back to Egypt, instead of keeping him prisoner.'

But he was not one to waste much time in dalliance. Turkey was not at all satisfied with the occupation of Egypt, and two armies were assembled, one in Syria, and one at Rhodes; the former of which had already pushed forward into Egyptian territory as far as El-Arisch, and also a train of artillery had been placed at Jaffa (the ancient Joppa). The commander of this *corps d'armée* (Achmet Pacha) had earned the unenviable title of *Djezzar*, or *the Butcher*. Napoleon, very early in the year 1799, marched against him, his busy brain having schemed the plan of crushing these Turkish troops, a demonstration against Constantinople itself, a forced peace with the Porte, and

---

[1] There is a long account of this lady in *Amours secrètes de Napoléon, des Princes et Princesses de sa famille, &c.*, by M. de B. . . . 2 vols., Paris, 1844, 12mo.

then hey! for India. To pave the way for this latter he actually wrote to Tippoo Sahib, saying he was coming to deliver him from the English yoke, and requesting his answer, which he might possibly have received, had not Tippoo been killed on May 4 of that year.

Napoleon, by way of conciliating the Egyptians, assisted at the celebration of 'Ramadan,' with great pomp, which, naturally, would afford his detractors another opportunity for outcry at his Mahometan proclivities. As soon as it was over, he set out against Achmet Pacha, and, on February 17, El-Arisch capitulated, and the army marched to Gaza. How the vanguard lost their way, and their terrible sufferings in the desert, it boots not to tell. Gaza was taken, its stores were confiscated, and then Jaffa was their bourne, which was reached, and invested, on March 4.

Before reading the sad page of history which Jaffa gives us, let us glance at one or two caricatures which appeared in England about this time. Napoleon had taken with him, in his expedition to Egypt, Denon and divers other learned men to investigate the archæology of the country, &c., and most valuable were the services of 'the Institute,' as this body of *savants* was called. They furnished some fun to the army, and the cry, when any danger threatened, of 'the Asses and the *Savants* to the centre,' was naturally productive of mirth; the army also christening the asses '*Demi-savants.*'

Gillray makes great fun of the expedition to Egypt, and satirises the French soldiers unmercifully; nor do the poor *savants* who accompanied the army fare any better. A good example is the 'Siege de la Colonne de Pompée, or Science in the Pillory,' published March 6, 1799. At the foot of the picture is: 'It appears by an intercepted letter from General Kleber, dated Alexandria, 5 brumaire, 7th year of the Republic, that when the garrison was obliged to

retire into the New Town, at the approach of the Turkish
Army, under the Pacha of Rhodes, a party of the *sçavans*,
who had ascended Pompey's Pillar for scientific purposes,
was cut off by a Band of Bedouin Arabs, who, having made
a large Pile of Straw, and dry Reeds, at the foot of the
Pillar, set fire to it, and rendered unavailing the gallant
defence of the learned Garrison, of whose Catastrophe the
above design is intended to convey an idea.

> 'To study Alexandria's store
>   Of Science, Amru deem'd a bore
>   And briefly set it burning.
>   The Man was ignorant, 'tis true,
>   So sought one comprehensive view
>   Of the light shed by learning.
>   Your modern Arabs grown more wise,
>   French vagrant Science duly prize ;
>   They've fairly bit the biters.
>   They've learnt the style of Hebert's Jokes,
>   Amru to books confined his Hoax ;
>   These Bedouins roast the writers.'

The *savants* are, indeed, in a parlous state, on the broad
summit of the pillar, exposed to fire from below, and the
guns and pistols of the Arabs ; they defend themselves
as well as possible by hurling their globes, and scientific
instruments, at their assailants, who are exceedingly astonished at them.   A balloon, La Diligence d'Abyssinie,
is fired at, and struck, the aeronauts, one of whom has a
parachute, being precipitated to the ground.

'The Institute,' which was modelled on that of Paris, also
gave scope to Gillray's facile pencil, and he published a series
of half a dozen plates, in the first one of which it was most
amusingly caricatured.   It was published on March 12,
1799, and called, 'L'Insurrection de l'Institut Amphibie—
The pursuit of Knowledge.'   A *savant* is depicted as study-

ing a work ' Sur l'Education du Crocodile,' some plates from which have dropped out. They show how useful the crocodile may become, by training, to tow vessels, and to ride and drive on land. He evidently is intending to put his theories into practice, for he has brought with him, to the river's side, a saddle, a fearfully cruel bridle, and a huge whip, when he is seized by an enormous saurian, and devoured. Another learned man, who has been reading ' Les Droits du Crocodile,' drops it, when he finds one of these creatures asserting its rights by seizing his coat-tails.

CHAPTER XIV.

TAKING OF JAFFA, AND MASSACRE OF SOLDIERS—DE BOURRIENNE'S
ACCOUNT—NAPOLEON'S OWN VERSION.

IT is sad to turn from this rollicking fun to the episode of
Jaffa ; but it cannot be dismissed, as it has afforded so much
employment to the detractors of Napoleon, and to the
English satirists of the time.   First of all, let us give the
version of an eye-witness (De Bourrienne), friend of, and
secretary to, Napoleon.   It is rather long, but no word of it
can be omitted, as it gives every argument that can be
brought forward to palliate the sickening massacre.

'On the 4th of March we commenced the siege of Jaffa.
That paltry place, which, to round a sentence, was pom-
pously styled the ancient Joppa, held out only to the 6th of
March, when it was taken by storm, and given up to pillage.
The massacre was horrible.   General Bonaparte sent his
aides de camp, Beauharnais and Croisier, to appease the
fury of the soldiers as much as possible, to observe what
was passing, and to report to him.   They learnt that a
considerable part of the garrison had retired into some vast
buildings, a sort of caravanserais, which formed a large
enclosed court.   Beauharnais and Croisier, who were distinguished by wearing the aide de camp scarf on the arm,
proceeded to that place.

'The Arnauts and Albanians, of whom these refugees
were almost entirely composed, cried, from the windows,

that they were willing to surrender, upon an assurance
that they would be exempted from the massacre to which
the town was doomed ; if not, they threatened to fire on
the aides de camp, and to defend themselves to the last
extremity. The two officers thought that they ought to
accede to the proposition, notwithstanding the decree of
death which had been pronounced against the whole garrison, in consequence of the town being taken by storm.
They brought them to our camp in two divisions, one consisting of about two thousand five hundred men, the other
of about fifteen hundred.

'I was walking with General Bonaparte, in front of his
tent, when he saw this multitude of men approaching, and,
before he even saw his aides de camp, he said to me in a
tone of profound sorrow, "What do they wish me to do with
these men ? Have I food for them ? ships to convey them
to Egypt or France ? Why, in the Devil's name, have
they served me thus ?" After their arrival, and the
explanations which the General in Chief demanded, and
listened to with anger, Eugene and Croisier received the
most severe reprimand for their conduct.

'But the deed was done. Four thousand men were
there. It was necessary to decide upon their fate. The
two aides de camp observed, that they had found themselves
alone in the midst of numerous enemies, and that he had
directed them to restrain the carnage. "Yes, doubtless,"
replied the General in Chief, with great warmth, "as to
women, children, and old men—all the peaceable inhabitants ; but not with respect to armed soldiers. It was your
duty to die, rather than bring these unfortunate creatures
to me. What do you want me to do with them ?" These
words were pronounced in the most angry tone.

'The prisoners were then ordered to sit down, and were
placed, without any order, in front of the tents, their hands

tied behind their backs. A sombre fury was depicted in their countenances. We gave them a little biscuit and bread, squeezed out of the already scanty supply for the army.

'On the first day of their arrival, a council of war was held in the tent of the General in Chief, to determine what course should be pursued with respect to them. The Council deliberated a long time without coming to any decision.

'On the evening of the following day, the daily reports of the generals of division came in. They spoke of nothing but the insufficiency of the rations, the complaints of the soldiers—of their murmurs and discontent at seeing their bread given to enemies, who had been withdrawn from their vengeance, inasmuch as a decree of death, in conformity with the laws of war, had been passed on Jaffa. All these reports were alarming, and especially that of General Bon, in which no reserve was made. He spoke of nothing less than the fear of revolt, which would be justified by the serious nature of the case.

'The Council assembled again. All the generals of division were summoned to attend, and, for several hours together, they discussed, under separate questions, what measures might be adopted, with the most sincere desire to discover and execute one which would save the lives of these unfortunate prisoners.

'Should they be sent to Egypt? could it be done?

'To do so, it would be necessary to send with them a numerous escort, which would too much weaken our little army in the enemy's country. How, besides, could they and the escort be supported till they reached Cairo, having no provisions to give them on setting out, and, their route being through a hostile territory, which we had exhausted, which presented no fresh resources, and through which we, perhaps, might have to return?

'Should they be embarked?

'Where were the ships? where could they be found? All our optical instruments, directed over the sea, could not descry a single friendly sail. Bonaparte, I affirm, would have regarded such an event as a real favour of fortune. It was, and I am glad to have to say it, this sole idea, this sole hope, which made him brave, for three days, the murmurs of his army. But in vain was help looked for, seawards—It did not come.

'Should the prisoners be set at liberty?

'They would then proceed to St. Jean d'Acre to reinforce the Pacha, or else, throwing themselves into the mountains of Naplouse, would greatly annoy our rear and right flank, and deal out death to us, as a recompense for the life we had given them. There could be no doubt of this. What is a Christian dog to a Turk? It would even have been a religious and meritorious act in the eyes of the Prophet.

'Could they be incorporated, disarmed, with our soldiers in the ranks?

'Here again the question of food presented itself in all its force. Next came to be considered the danger of having such comrades, while marching through an enemy's country. What might happen in the event of a battle before St. Jean d'Acre? Could we even tell what might occur during the march? and—finally—what must be done with them when under the ramparts of that town, if we should be able to take them there? The same embarrassments with respect to the questions of provisions, and security, would then recur with increased force.

'The third day arrived without its being possible, anxiously as it was desired, to come to any conclusion favourable to the preservation of these unfortunate men. The murmurs in the camp grew louder—the evil went on increasing—remedy appeared impossible—danger was real and imminent.

'The order for shooting the prisoners was given and executed on the 10th of March. We did not, as has been stated, separate the Egyptians from the other prisoners. There were no Egyptians.

'Many of the unfortunate creatures composing the smaller division, which was fired on close to the sea-coast, at some distance from the other column, succeeded in swimming to some reefs of rocks out of the reach of musket shot. The soldiers rested their muskets on the sand, and, to induce the prisoners to return, employed the Egyptian signs of reconciliation, in use in that country. They came back ; but, as they advanced, they were killed, and disappeared among the waves.'

Thus far De Bourrienne. Now let us hear what Napoleon himself says of the matter.[1] 'He spoke about the measures which he had caused to be taken at Jaffa. "After the assault," said he, "it was impossible to restore any kind of discipline until night. The infuriated soldiers rushed into the streets in search of women. You know what kind of people the Turks are. A few of them kept up a fire in the streets. The soldiers, who desired nothing more, whenever a shot was discharged, cried out that they were fired upon from certain houses, which they immediately broke open, and violated all the women they found."

'I replied[2] that Miot . . . positively asserted that he (Napoleon) had caused between three and four thousand Turks to be shot, some days after the capture of Jaffa. Napoleon answered : "It is not true that there were so

[1] Napoleon in Exile, or a Voice from St. Helena, &c., by Barry E. O'Meara. 2 vols., London, 1822. Vol. ii. p. 127.
[2] Ibid., vol. i. p. 329.

many. I ordered about a thousand or twelve hundred to be shot, which was done. The reason was, that amongst the garrison of Jaffa, a number of Turkish troops were discovered, whom I had taken a short time before at El-Arish, and sent to Bagdat upon their parole not to serve again, or to be found in arms against me for a year. I had caused them to be escorted twelve leagues on their way to Bagdat, by a division of my army. But those Turks, instead of proceeding to Bagdat, threw themselves into Jaffa, defended it to the last, and cost me a number of brave men to take it, whose lives would have been spared, if the others had not reinforced the garrison of Jaffa. Moreover, before I attacked the town, I sent them a flag of truce. Immediately afterwards we saw the head of the bearer elevated on a pole over the wall. Now, if I had spared them again, and sent them away upon their parole, they would directly have gone to St. Jean d'Acre, where they would have played over again the same scene that they had done at Jaffa. In justice to the lives of my soldiers, as every general ought to consider himself as their father, and them as his children, I could not allow this.

' " To leave as a guard a portion of my army, already small and reduced in number, in consequence of the breach of faith of those wretches, was impossible. Indeed, to have acted otherwise than I did, would probably have caused the destruction of my whole army. I, therefore, availing myself of the rights of war, which authorise the putting to death prisoners taken under such circumstances, independent of the right given to me by having taken the city by assault, and that of retaliation on the Turks, ordered that the prisoners taken at El-Arish, who, in defiance of their capitulation, had been found bearing arms against me, should be selected out and shot. The rest, amounting to a

considerable number, were spared.   I would," continued he,
" do the same thing again to-morrow, and so would Welling-
ton, or any general commanding an army under similar
circumstances!"'

Between these two partial accounts there are grave dis-
crepancies—both parties trying, as far as possible, to excuse
the deed ; but, if De Bourrienne can be relied on, his
account of the cold-blooded massacre must be the true one,
for he says, ' I confine myself to those details of this act of
dreadful necessity of which I was an eye-witness.'

CHAPTER XV.

THE MASSACRE AT JAFFA (*continued*)—ENGLISH EVIDENCE THEREON—SIEGE OF ST. JEAN D'ACRE—CAPTURE OF NAPOLEON'S BATTERING TRAIN—FAILURE OF THE SIEGE, AND RETREAT TO JAFFA.

IT is a singular thing, that, even in the very meagre accounts, of transactions in Egypt no mention of this should have got into the English newspapers ; but I have searched, and can find none.   But when, in 1803, this country was in fear of invasion, it was brought up, and used with great effect, in stimulating patriotism.   Take, as an instance, one [1] out of the thousands of broadsides which then flooded the country, and we shall find that the fact, although broadly stated, has not been exaggerated.

' On the 7th that town was taken by assault. This affair is on all hands allowed to have been bloody in the extreme ; but a tale has been brought to light, and attested by persons of undoubted credit, so bloody, so diabolical, as to outstrip everything which such an expression is calculated to describe.

' It is asserted that three days after the capture of the town, three thousand eight hundred prisoners were marched to a rising ground, and there massacred by means of musquetry, grape shot, and the bayonet. This fact was first made known in Europe by Sir Sidney Smith, and Mr. Morier, Secretary to Lord Elgin, now a prisoner in Paris ; its history has been minutely given by Colonel Sir Robert

---

[1] *History of Buonaparte*, price 6*d*.   Printed by Cox, Son, & Baylis, 75 Great Queen Street.

Wilson, of Hompesch's hussars, and its truth has been attested by Dr. Wittman who accompanied the army of the Grand Vizir.'

This Dr. Wittman was the physician to the British Military Mission, which went with that army through Turkey, Syria, and Egypt, and who wrote a narrative of his travels, in which, at p. 128, he says the unfortunates were dragged 'to the sand hills, about a league distant, in the way to Gaza, and there most inhumanly put to death. I have seen *the Skeletons of those unfortunate victims*, which lie scattered over the hills ; a modern Golgotha, which remains a lasting disgrace to a Nation calling itself civilised.'

Sir Robert Wilson says : 'Vollies of musquetry and grape instantly played against them ; and Buonaparte, who had been regarding the scene through a telescope, when he saw the smoke ascending, could not restrain his joy, but broke out into exclamations of approval ; indeed, he had just reason to dread the refusal of his troops thus to dishonour themselves. Kleber had remonstrated in the most strenuous manner, and the officer of the Etat-Major, who commanded (for the general to whom the division belonged, was absent) even refused to execute the order without a written instruction ; but Buonaparte was too cautious, and sent Berthier to enforce obedience. . . . The bones still lie in heaps, and are-shown to every traveller who arrives ; nor can they be confounded with those who perished in the assault, since this field of butchery lies a mile from the town.'

Combe, of course, does not forget this incident.

> Another bloody work ensued
> Which the brave Nap with rapture view'd—
> He near four thousand prisoners had,
> The number almost drove him mad ;
> Because so many men to feed,
> Required a deal of food indeed.

He chid his troops for being so good,
And said such mercy was of no good.
Resolv'd to get rid of his burthen,
(Tho' Kleber ventur'd to demur then,)
He bade his troops the men surround,
And march them to a rising ground ;
The soldiers did as he directed,
And they by Boney were inspected ;
It seems our hero was inclin'd
If *'twas his interest*, to be kind ;
Now Nap, among these Captives rude,
An aged Janizary view'd ;
And, with a contumacious sneer,
Said he 'Old man, what brought you here ?'
The Janizary, no way frighten'd,
Although unconscious how it might end,
Replied 'That question soon I can, Sir,
By asking you a like one, answer,
To serve your Sultan, you'll rejoin—
And the same answer now is mine.'
This frankness all around delighted,
And admiration, too, excited.
Behold—our very hero smiled,
As if he had been reconciled.
That smile, some whispered, is a gracious one.
This guess was not, tho', a sagacious one ;
The Janizary was not spared,
His fellow-prisoners' fate he shared ;
But previously brave Nap withdrew,
And at a distance had a view ;
The signal given—none dared to stop—
The musquetry went pop—pop—pop.
Nap thro' his spy glass marked the fun,
And cried out 'bravo' when 'twas done—
His soldiers, who the dead surrounded,
Humanely stabbed and killed the wounded.

Napoleon now turned his attention to the siege of St.
Jean d'Acre, where the garrison had the advantage of
European aid, besides which, Sir Sydney Smith cruised
about the fort, and Napoleon's battering-train, which had
been captured, was duly pointed at the besiegers.   He was,
besides, called off to help Kleber, who was in an awkward
situation at Mount Thabor, and had been fighting Achmet
Pasha, who had a considerably superior force, from six in
the morning till one in the afternoon.   Not one moment
too soon did Napoleon make his appearance ; but he turned
the tide of battle, and the Turks were defeated with the
loss of 5,000 or 6,000 men, and all their stores, &c.

Back they went to St. Jean d'Acre, and did their best
at the siege ; but it was not to be.   Reinforcements were
thrown into the town, Napoleon's army grew smaller, provisions got scarcer, the plague was in their midst ; so, sending his sick and wounded to Jaffa, he raised the siege and
began to retreat on May 20.

O'Meara tells us Napoleon's version of the causes which
led to this.[1] '"The chief cause of the failure there was that
Sir Sydney Smith took all my battering-train, which was
on board of several small vessels.   Had it not been for
that, I would have taken Acre in spite of him.   He behaved
very bravely, and was well seconded by Phillipeaux, a
Frenchman of talent, who had studied with me as an
engineer. . . . The acquisition of five or six hundred seamen as cannoniers, was a great advantage to the Turks,
whose spirits they revived, and whom they showed how to
defend the fortress.

'"But he committed a great fault in making sorties,
which cost the lives of two or three hundred brave fellows,
without the possibility of success.   For it was impossible he
could succeed against the number of the French who were

[1] Vol. i. p. 209.

before Acre. I would lay a wager, he lost half of his crew in them. He dispersed proclamations among my troops which certainly shook some of them, and I, in consequence, published an order, stating that he was *mad*, and forbidding all communication with him. Some days after, he sent, by means of a flag of truce, a lieutenant, or a midshipman, with a letter containing a challenge to me, to meet him at some place he pointed out, in order to fight a duel. I laughed at this, and sent him back an intimation that when he brought Marlborough to fight me I would meet him. Notwithstanding this, I like the character of the man." '

The French reached Jaffa on May 24, and found the hospitals full of wounded and those sick of the plague. Compelled still to retreat, it was necessary to remove the sick ; and, to encourage his soldiers in the task, and to show them how little was the risk, Napoleon is said to have handled several of the infected.

CHAPTER XVI

RETREAT FROM JAFFA — POISONING OF FIVE HUNDRED SOLDIERS — DIF-
FERENT ENGLISH AUTHORITIES THEREON — NAPOLEON'S OWN STORY,
ALSO THOSE OF LAS CASES AND O'MEARA - RETREAT TO CAIRO.

BUT this retreat became the subject of a dreadful accusation against Napoleon, which must have hit him hard
at the time of his projected invasion in 1803—aye, quite as
hard as the massacre at Jaffa. It was nothing less than
that he poisoned, with opium, 500 of his sick soldiers, before
he left Jaffa. There was a solid foundation for this fearful
charge, as will be shown hereafter. Combe speaks of it
thus—

> Another great thing Boney now did,
> With sick the hospitals were crowded,
> He therefore planned, nor planned in vain,
> To put the wretches out of pain ;
> He an apothecary found—
> For a physician, since renown'd,
> The butchering task with scorn declined,
> Th' apothecary, tho', was *kind*.
> It seems that Romeo met with such a one,
> This is a mournful theme to touch upon,
> Opium was put in pleasant food,
> The wretched victims thought it good ;
> But, in a few hours, as they say,
> About six hundred, breathless lay.

The truth of this has never been accurately established,
but I fancy, at that time, there were very few Englishmen

who did not thoroughly believe it. Sir Robert Wilson wrote : 'Buonaparte finding that his hospitals at Jaffa were crowded with sick, sent for a physician, whose name should be inscribed in letters of gold, but which, from important reasons, cannot be here inserted ; on his arrival, he entered into a long conversation with him respecting the danger of contagion, concluding at last with the remark, that something must be done to remedy the evil, and that the destruction of the sick at present in the hospital, was the only measure which could be adopted. The physician, alarmed at the proposal, bold in the confidence of virtue,

POISONING THE SICK AT JAFFA.

and the cause of humanity, remonstrated vehemently, respecting the cruelty, as well as the atrocity, of such a murder ; but, finding that Buonaparte persevered and menaced, he indignantly left the tent, with this memorable observation ; "Neither my principles, nor the character of my profession, will allow me to become a murderer ; and, General, if such qualities as you insinuate are necessary to form a great man, I thank my God that I do not possess them."

'Buonaparte was not to be diverted from his object by moral considerations ; he persevered, and found an apothe-

cary, who (dreading the weight of power, but who since has
made an atonement to his mind, by unequivocally con-
fessing the fact) consented to become his agent, and to
administer poison to the sick.   Opium, at night, was
distributed in gratifying food, the wretched, unsuspecting,
victims banqueted, and, in a few hours, five hundred and
eighty soldiers, who had suffered so much for their country,
perished thus miserably by the order of its idol. . . .

'If a doubt should still exist as to the veracity of this
statement, let the Members of the Institute at Cairo be asked
what passed in their sitting after the return of Buonaparte
from Syria ; they will relate, that the same virtuous physician,
who refused to become the destroyer of those committed to
his protection, accused Buonaparte of high treason, in the
full assembly, against the honour of France, her children,
and humanity ; that he entered into the full details of the
poisoning of the sick, and the massacre of the garrison,
aggravating these crimes by charging Buonaparte with
strangling, previously, at Rosetta, a number of French and
Copts, who were ill of the plague ; thus proving that this
disposal of his sick was a premeditated plan, which he
wished to introduce into general practice.   In vain Buonaparte attempted to justify himself ; the members sat petri-
fied with terror, and almost doubted whether the scene
passing before their eyes was not an illusion.'

Dr. Wittman assures his readers that whilst he was in
Egypt with the army, a man was pointed out to them as
having been the executioner of Napoleon's commands to
poison the sick and wounded French soldiers in the hospitals of Jaffa.

Barre says : 'Although neither Sir Robert Wilson nor
Dr. Wittman mention the name of the worthy physician
who refused with horror, and of the infamous wretch, who
basely consented to become the executioner of the sick

soldiers, it is now well known that the former was the worthy physician Dr. Desgenettes, and the latter, one Rouyer, an infamous apothecary, who thus became the murderer of his own countrymen, in compliance with the wishes of a Corsican assassin.'

In a little periodical, called ' Ring the Alarum Bell ! ' (which only ran four numbers), published in 1803, is the following, written by a General Danican : ' In 1801, I met at a lazaretto in Sicily, with a number of French Soldiers just come from Alexandria. With one of them I contracted habits of intimacy during my stay, and who frequently related to me some curious particulars of the conduct of Buonaparté in Egypt. . . . Having been witness to the poisoning scene at Caiffa he related to me the following anecdote. A grenadier, who had lost two brothers, was amongst the unfortunate wretches slightly affected with the pestilential disease. From what he had previously observed in the hospital, he had become more suspicious than his companions in distress, and he had scarcely taken the *Corsican physic*, than he immediately discharged it, made his way out of the hospital, and escaping the guard, whom he contrived to knock down, he gained the column under the command of Kleber, at whose feet he threw himself, and, in the intercession, almost of despair, conjured him to let him mount one of the camels, describing what he had escaped from, and venting the most energetic maledictions on the *Poisoner in Chief.* The poor wretch, in the most piteous manner, assured General Kleber that he would keep at a distance from the army, so that no one should be in any danger of catching his disorder, except the camel. Kleber granted his request ; the grenadier was saved and recovered, and was alive when the English landed under the brave Abercrombie.'

Now let us hear the Emperor's side of the question,

beginning with De Bourrienne. 'Orders were given directly
to undermine the fortifications and blow them up ; and, on
the 27th May, upon the signal being given, the town was
in a moment laid bare. An hour afterwards, the General
in Chief left his tent and repaired to the town, accompanied by Berthier, some physicians and surgeons, and his
usual staff. I was also one of the party. A long and sad
deliberation took place on the question, which now arose,
relative to the men who were incurably ill of the plague,
or were at the point of death. After a discussion of the
most serious and conscientious kind, it was decided to
accelerate a few moments, by a potion, a death which was
inevitable, and which otherwise would be painful and
cruel. . . .

'I cannot say that I saw the potion administered. I
should state an untruth if I did. I cannot name any
person concerned in the matter, without hazarding a mis-
representation. But I well know that the decision was
come to after that deliberation, which was due to so important a measure ; that the order was given, and that the
infected are dead. What! shall that which formed the
subject of the whole conversation of the head quarters, on
the day after leaving Jaffa, and was spoken of without any
question of its reality ; which was regarded by us as a
dreadful, but unavoidable, misfortune ; which was never
mentioned in the army but as a fact, of which there was no
doubt, and only the details of which were inquired after—
I appeal to every honourable man who was present, for the
truth of what I state—shall that, I say, be now stigmatized
as a malignant calumny, fabricated to injure the reputation
of a hero, who, were this the only reproach that might be
addressed to him, would go down with little blemish on
his character, to posterity ?'

Las Cases is specially wroth with Sir Robert Wilson,

but, even he, cannot successfully whitewash his beloved emperor. His attempted vindication is too long to be re-produced *in extenso*, but it goes to prove how widely spread in the army was the belief that the sick were hurried to their rest at Jaffa. 'A circumstance, which will not a little sur-prise those who have yet to learn how little credit is due to public report, and which will serve to show the errors that may creep into history, is that Marshall Bertrand, who was himself with the army in Egypt, (though certainly in a rank which did not enable him to come into immediate contact with the General in Chief) firmly believed, up to the period of his residence at Saint Helena, the story of poison having been administered to sixty invalids. The report was circulated, and believed, even in our army ; therefore, what answer could be given to those who tri-umphantly asserted, " It is a fact, I assure you, I have it from officers who served in the French army at the time." Nevertheless, the whole story is false. I have collected the following facts from the highest source, from the mouth of Napoleon himself.

' 1st. That the invalids in question who were infected with the plague, amounted, according to the report made to the General in Chief, only to *seven* in number.

' 2nd. That it was not the General in Chief, but a pro-fessional man, who, at the moment of the crisis, proposed the administering of opium.

' 3rd. That opium was not administered to a single individual.

' 4th. That the retreat having been effected slowly, a rear-guard was left behind in Jaffa for three days.

' 5th. That on the departure of the rear guard, the invalids were all dead, except one or two, who must have fallen into the hands of the English.'

But Las Cases, in his zeal, tries to prove too much ; for,

in a later passage, he says, that since his return to Paris he has had opportunities of conversing with those whose situation and profession naturally rendered them the first actors on the scene, and he finds 'that no order was given for the administering of opium to the sick,' and ' That there was not at the period in question, in the medicine chest of the army, a single grain of opium for the use of the sick.' So he admits that the emperor had the proposition made to him, by a man who must have known he had not the means to carry it out.

Is Barry O'Meara to be trusted ?   Let us hear what his testimony is (also professedly from the emperor's own lips).   '" Previously to leaving Jaffa," continued Napoleon, " and after the greatest number of the sick and wounded had been embarked, it was reported to me that there were some men in the hospital so dangerously ill, as not to be able to be moved.   I ordered, immediately, the chiefs of the medical staff to consult together upon what was best to be done, and to give me their opinion on the subject. Accordingly they met, and found there were seven or eight men so dangerously ill, that they conceived it impossible to recover, and also that they could not exist twenty-four or thirty-six hours longer ; that, moreover, being afflicted with the plague, they would spread that complaint amongst all who approached them.   Some of them, who were sensible, perceiving they were about to be abandoned, demanded with earnest entreaties, to be put to death.   Larrey was of opinion that recovery was impossible, and that those poor fellows could not exist many hours ; but as they might live long enough to be alive when the Turks entered, and experience the dreadful torments which they were accustomed to inflict upon their prisoners, he thought it would be an act of charity to comply with their desires, and accelerate their end by a few hours. Desgenettes did not approve of this, and replied, that his profession was to cure the sick, and not to despatch them.

'"Larrey came to me immediately afterwards, informed me of the circumstances, and of what Desgenettes had said ; adding, that perhaps Desgenettes was right. 'But,' continued Larrey, 'those men cannot live more than a few hours, twenty-four, or thirty-six at most ; and, if you will leave a rear-guard of cavalry to stay and protect them from advanced parties, it will be sufficient.' Accordingly I ordered four or five hundred cavalry to remain behind, and not to quit the place until all were dead. They did remain, and informed me that all had expired before they had left the town ; but I have heard since, that Sydney Smith found one or two alive when he entered it. This is the truth of the business. . . .

'"You have been amongst the Turks, and know what they are ; I ask you now, to place yourself in the situation of one of those sick men, and that you were asked which you would prefer, to be left to suffer the tortures of those miscreants, or to have opium administered to you ?" I replied, "Most undoubtedly I would prefer the latter." "Certainly, so would any man," answered Napoleon ; "if my *own son* (and I believe I love my son as well as any father does his child) were in a similar situation with those men, I would advise it to be done ; and, if so situated myself, I would insist upon it, if I had sense enough, and strength enough to demand it. . . .

'"If I had thought such a measure, as that of giving opium, necessary, I would have called a council of war, have stated the necessity of it, and have published it in the order of the day." He afterwards goes on to say that if he had done so, some of his soldiers would have been sure to have shot him.'

I have gone thus at length into these occurrences at Jaffa, to show how widely spread was the belief in them, and also to prove that these scandals were not of British origin. Whatever amount of truth there may be in them, readers must judge, as I have laid both sides fairly before them. That there was foundation for them, there can be no doubt—but we know that a tale does not lose in telling.

The return to Cairo, and the battle of Aboukir, are soon dismissed by the satirist, and not chronicled by the caricaturist.

CHAPTER XVII.

THE OLD RÉGIME AND THE REPUBLICANS—THE 'INCROYABLES'—
NAPOLEON LEAVES EGYPT—HIS REASONS FOR SO DOING—FEELING
OF THE ARMY—ACCUSED OF TAKING WITH HIM THE MILITARY
CHEST.

IT is refreshing, and like going among green pastures and
cool streams, to leave for a while political caricature, with
its ambitions, and its carnage, and find a really funny
social skit, aiming at the follies of the times, even if it be
only in ridiculing extravagance in dress.

Exceedingly droll is a social caricature by Gillray
(August 15, 1799), where a courtly old gentleman of the
Court of Louis XVI. bows low, saying, 'Je suis votre tres
humble serviteur,' whilst the ruffianly French 'gentleman of
the Court of Égalité' replies with a sentence unfit for reproduction. (See next page.)

Littré, in his magnificent dictionary, gives a very terse
definition of these 'Incroyables': 's. *m.* Nom donné aux
petit maîtres sous le Directoire, parce qu'on les entendait
s'ecrier a tout propos, c'est vraiment incroyable ; et, parce
que leur costume était tellement exagéré qu'il dépassait la
croyance commune.' They were Napoleon's detestation,
according to Madame Junot, and she describes them with
feminine minuteness. 'They wore grey greatcoats with
black collars and green cravats. Their hair, instead of
being *à la Titus*, which was the prevailing fashion of the
day, was powdered, plaited, and turned up with a comb,

while on each side of the face hung two long curls, called dog's ears (*oreilles de chien*).   As these young men were very frequently attacked, they carried about with them large sticks, which were not always weapons of defence ; for the frays which arose in Paris at that time were often provoked by them.'

Pardon must be begged for this digression, and the matter in hand strictly attended to.

Napoleon left Egypt on August 23, 1799, and reached

A FRENCH GENTLEMAN OF THE   A FRENCH GENTLEMAN OF THE
COURT OF LOUIS XVI.   COURT OF ÉGALITÉ.

France October 8 of that year.   The causes for this step will be detailed a little later on.   Meanwhile the caricaturist was watching events on the Continent, and, after his lights, depicting them.   With those not personally affecting Napoleon we have nothing to do ; and of him—Egypt being a far cry—we have but few, until after his return, when he was brought prominently before European notice.

Gillray thought he saw his power declining, and on September 1, 1799, he published 'Allied Powers, Unbooting Egalité.' In this picture Napoleon is being badly treated. One foot is on a Dutch cheese, which a Hollander is plucking away ; a British tar has him fast round the waist, and arms ; whilst a Turk, of most ferocious description, his dress being garnished with human cars, is pulling his nose, and slashing him with his scimitar, St. Jean d'Acre, which is reeking with blood. Prussia, backed up by Russia, is drawing off Italy, which serves as a boot for one leg, and, with it, a large quantity of gold coin.

The causes which induced Napoleon to leave Egypt cannot better be made known, and understood, than by quoting from De Bourrienne, who was an actor in this episode. He says : 'After the battle,[1] which took place on the 25th July, Bonaparte sent a flag of truce on board the English Admiral's ship. Our intercourse was full of politeness, such as might be expected in the communications of the people of two civilised nations. The English Admiral gave the flag of truce some presents, in exchange for some we sent, and, likewise, a copy of the French Gazette of Francfort, dated 10th June, 1799.[2] For ten months we had received no news from France. Bonaparte glanced over this journal with an eagerness which may easily be conceived.

' " Heavens ! " said he to me, " my presentiment is veri-

---

[1] Of Aboukir.

[2] Which probably gave details of the defeats of the French by Suwaroff, who is thus described in the *Vienna Gazette* (according to his portrait by Gillray, May 23, 1799) : ' This extraordinary man is now in the prime of life, six feet ten inches in height, never tastes either wine or spirits, takes but one meal a day, and every morning plunges into an ice bath ; his wardrobe consists of a plain shirt, a white waistcoat and breeches, short boots, and a Russian cloak ; he wears no covering on his head either by day or night ; when tired, he wraps himself up in a blanket, and sleeps in the open air ; he has fought twenty-nine pitched battles, and been in seventy-five engagements.'

fied : the fools have lost Italy. All the fruits of our
victories are gone ! I must leave Egypt ! "

'He sent for Berthier, to whom he communicated the
news, adding that things were going on very badly in France
—that he wished to return home—that he (Berthier) should
go along with him, and that, for the present, only he,
Gantheaume, and I, were in the secret. He recommended
him to be prudent, not to betray any symptoms of joy, nor
to purchase, or sell, anything.

'He concluded by assuring him that he depended on
him. " I can answer," said he, " for myself and Bourrienne."
Berthier promised to be secret, and he kept his word. He
had had enough of Egypt, and he so ardently longed to
return to France, that there was little reason to fear he
would disappoint himself by any indiscretion.

'Gantheaume arrived, and Bonaparte gave him orders
to fit out the two frigates, the *Muiron* and the *Carrère*,
and the two small vessels, the *Revanche* and the *Fortune*,
with a two months' supply of provisions for from four,
to five, hundred men. He enjoined his secrecy as to the
object of these preparations, and desired him to act with
such circumspection that the English cruisers might have
no knowledge of what was going on. He afterwards
arranged with Gantheaume the course he wished to take.
Nothing escaped his attention.'

Bonaparte concealed his operations with much care ;
but still some vague rumours crept abroad. General
Dugua, the commandant of Cairo, whom he had just left,
for the purpose of embarking, wrote to him on August 18
to the following effect :—

'I have this moment heard, that it is reported at the
Institute, you are about to return for France, taking with
you Monge, Berthollet, Berthier, Lannes, and Murat.
This news has spread like lightning through the city, and

I should not be at all surprised if it produced an unfavour-able effect, which, however, I hope you will obviate.'

Bonaparte embarked five days after the receipt of Dugua's letter ; and, as may be supposed, without replying to it.

On August 18, he wrote to the Divan of Cairo as follows : 'I set out to-morrow for Menouf, from whence I intend to make various excursions to the Delta, in order that I may, myself, witness the acts of oppression which are committed there, and to acquire some knowledge of the people.'

He told the army but half the truth : 'The news from Europe,' said he, 'has determined me to proceed to France. I leave the command of the army to General Kleber. The army shall hear from me forthwith. At present I can say no more. It costs me much pain to quit troops to whom I am so strongly attached. But my absence will be but temporary, and the general I leave in command has the confidence of the government, as well as mine.'

At night, in the dark, on August 23, he stole on board : and who can wonder if the army expressed some dissatis-faction at his leaving them in the lurch ? From the many works I have consulted, whilst writing this book, I can believe the words of General Danican (who has been before quoted) in 'Ring the Alarum Bell !'—'Immediately after Buonaparte's midnight flight from Egypt, with the Cash of the army, he was hung in effigy by the Soldiers ; who, in dancing round the spectacle, sang the coarsest couplets (a copy of which I have now in my possession) written for the occasion, to the tune of the *Carmagnole,* beginning : "So, Harlequin has at length deserted us !— never mind my boys, never mind ; he will at last be really hanged ; he promised to make us all rich ; but, instead, he

has robbed all the cash himself, and now's gone off : oh !
the scoundrel Harlequin, &c., &c." '

This charge against Napoleon, of running away with
the treasure-chests, is, like almost all the others, of French
origin. Hear what Madame Junot says, as it shows the
feeling of the French army on this point, that some one
had taken them (for Napoleon's benefit) : 'A report was
circulated in the army that Junot was carrying away the
treasures found in the pyramids by the General in Chief.
He could not carry them away himself' (such was the

FLIGHT FROM EGYPT.

language held to the soldiers), 'and so the man who
possesses all his confidence is now taking them to him.'
The matter was carried so far that several subalterns, and
soldiers, proceeded to the shore, and some of them went
on board the merchantman which was to sail with Junot
the same evening. They rummaged about, but found
nothing ; at length they came to a prodigious chest, which
ten men could not move, between decks, "Here is the
treasure!" cried the soldiers ; "here is our pay that has
been kept from us above a year; where is the key?" Junot's
valet, an honest German, shouted to them in vain, with all

his might, that the chest did not belong to his chenerâl. They would not listen to him.

'Unluckily, Junot, who was not to embark till evening, was not then on board. The mutineers seized a hatchet, and began to cut away at the chest, which they would soon have broken up, had not the ship's carpenter come running out of breath. "What the devil are you at?" cried he, "mad fellows that you are: stop! don't destroy my chest— here's the key." He opened it immediately, and lo!—the tools of the master carpenter.'

Barre, of course, alludes to this alleged robbery, and Combe writes of his desertion of his troops as follows :—

> Aboukir castle having won,
> Our hero thought it best to run.
> The bravest man will run away,
> When it is dangerous to stay ;
> But, as he to his troops declared,
> By him all dangers should be shared,
> And that on no account he'd leave them,
> 'Twas proper he should now deceive them.
> The cunning he display'd in fight,
> He manifested in his flight.
> On some pretence, it seems, he wrote
> To certain generals a note,
> Acquainting them with what he wanted,
> The time and place, too, he appointed.
> These generals, so well they fared,
> The *fame* of his desertion shared.
> When to th' appointed place they got,
> Nap was already on the spot ;
> And, what of all things made them glad,
> The military chest he had !
> He left his army,—but we find
> He left these words for them behind :
> ' This parting grieves me sore, altho' meant
> To be for only a short moment.'

I 2

This caricature is presumably by Gillray, although it is not signed by him ; and, as it was published on March 8, 1800, it is absolutely prophetic, for Napoleon is pointing to a future imperial crown and sceptre.   This is especially

BUONAPARTE LEAVING EGYPT.

For an Illustration of the above see the intercepted Letters from the Republican General Kleber to the French Directory respecting the Courage, Honor, and Patriotism of ——, the Deserter of the Army of Egypt.

curious, as it shows how, even then, the public opinion of England (of which, of course, the caricaturist was but a reflex) estimated him.

CHAPTER XVIII.

NAPOLEON'S ARRIVAL IN PARIS—HIS POPULARITY—DISSOLUTION OF THE
COUNCIL OF FIVE HUNDRED—GRAPHIC DESCRIPTION OF THE SCENE
—NAPOLEON, SIÈYES, AND DUCOS NAMED CONSULS.

NAPOLEON arrived in Paris at, for him, a happy moment, for the Directory was then as good as defunct. There was a feeling that a strong hand was needed to guide the affairs of the nation, and Generals Moreau and Jubert had already been offered the post of First Magistrate of the Republic, and each had declined the honour. When Napoleon landed, he was hailed as THE MAN, and his arrival was telegraphed to Paris, where it created an immense sensation.

On the day after his arrival, he had an interview with the Directors, to whom he explained the state of the army in Egypt, and told them, how, having heard of the disasters that had befallen their armies, he had returned home to help them ; but, although he was offered his choice of commands, he would have none of them, and lived quietly at Paris. The Council of Five Hundred even gave him a public dinner [1]—but he was steadily working out the ends he had in view.

What that was, was evident to the English people, for

---

[1] In the *Times* of November 15, 1799, we read of this dinner (November 7) that ' Buonaparte gave the toast, "To the union of all Frenchmen."' The same paper records that Bonaparte had presented Moreau with a robe enriched with diamonds, which he brought from Egypt, and was valued at 10,000 livres. This probably purchased his aid in the *coup d'état* of the 18th Brumaire.

his aim was shown very amusingly in a caricature by an unknown artist (November 1799). Napoleon, who, even then,
is represented as crowned, appears as a crocodile, in jack-
boots and sword, squeezing the life out of two frogs, whilst the
dismay of the others is most comically rendered : a body-
guard of crocodiles, in military uniform, back up their leader.

On November 9, he was made commandant of the
forces in Paris, which prepared him for the explosion of
the 18th Brumaire, year 8 (November 10, 1799). The
expulsion of the Council is most graphically told in the
'Times' of November 18, eight days after the event,
showing how slowly news travelled then. The scene must
have been painted by an eye-witness, for it gives the whole
previous debate—which at last turned on Napoleon's
appointment as commandant. It is so well told, I cannot
help giving it in its entirety.

'*Grandmaison.* "We are only offering crossing and
contradicting propositions, without coming to any decision :
I move that you begin by declaring the appointment of
Buonaparte to be unconstitutional."

'"Yes, yes," was resounded from several parts of the Hall.

'L. (*ucien*) Buonaparte quitted the Chair, which he gave
up to Chazal, and said, "I entreat the Council calmly to
reflect on the commotion that has manifested itself. It
may not be needless to represent"—(Here he was inter-
rupted by a loud voice, who said, "Do not attempt to
amuse us")—"I propose" (continued Lucien Buonaparte)
"that you summon the General who commands to appear
before you."

'"We do not acknowledge him," exclaimed several
Members.

'"When cool consideration" (observed Buonaparte)
"shall have stilled in your breasts the extraordinary emotion
which you have testified" (*murmurs*), "you will, perhaps, be

sensible of the injustice done General Buonaparte. Whatever may be the event, I now, in your presence, lay down
on the altar of the Country, the badge of Magistracy with
which the people had invested me."

'On saying these words, he laid down his badge of office
on the President's table : upon which the doors of the Hall
were opened, and twenty Grenadiers entered. They
advanced towards the Bureau, took L. Buonaparte into
custody, and, placing him in the midst of them, they conducted him out of the Hall.

'The Council was seized with extreme agitation. Cries,
vociferations, and tumultuous confusion, arose from the
Members suddenly quitting their places. Not a word
could be distinctly heard.

'Grandmaison, Blin, Delbrel, Bigonnet, Sherlock, Cro-
chon, and several other Members, pressed forward towards
the tribune.

'Sherlock made an effort to speak, but could scarcely
make himself heard among the tumult. " I move," said he,
" that you call back your President, whose resignation you
have not accepted."

' " He could have done nothing better," exclaimed several
Members, "than to have given it in."

' Meantime, at a distance was heard the sound of drums
that beat the *pas de charge.* . . . Soon after, for the third
time, the doors of the Hall were thrown open ; and a third
time the spectators endeavoured precipitately to escape by
leaping out of the windows.

'An officer came forwards, followed by a numerous
guard, exclaiming with a loud voice, " *General Buonaparte
orders the Hall to be cleared.*" Upon which, the troops
advanced into the Hall, the further part of which remained
occupied by the Deputies, who had not retired. The
soldiers suspended their march for a moment, in order to

afford time for the Hall to be cleared. About a Dozen of Members, among whom was Blin, remained near the Tribune, or at the Bureau ; one of them who was at the Tribune, exclaimed,

' " What are you, Soldiers ? are you anything else than guardians of the National Representation ; and do you dare to menace its safety, to incroach on its independence —is it thus that you tarnish the laurels which your courage has won ? "

' This harangue was coldly listened to by the soldiers, who advanced into the Hall with drums beating. The Members who stood near the Bureau and the Tribune, were at length obliged to yield their places to the soldiers, who took possession of them. As the latter advanced into the Hall, these members went out at the opposite door. In a few minutes the Hall was completely cleared. It was then five o'clock.

' Several members set out immediately for Paris, others remained at St. Cloud to observe the deliberations of the Council of Elders, and the extraordinary movement of the troops who filled the square of the palace. From time to time were heard the cries of *Vive Buonaparte* ! *Vive la République* !

' General Buonaparte, on hearing the Council of Five Hundred had withdrawn, advanced towards the soldiers and harangued them.

' He entreated them to remain calm, and to rest assured that the good cause should triumph. They all answered by shouts of *Vive Buonaparte* ! '

The scene depicted in the accompanying illustration is somewhat dramatically told by Napoleon himself in his proclamation of 19th Brumaire : ' I presented myself before the Council of Five Hundred, alone, unarmed, my head uncovered, just as the Ancients had received and applauded me. My object was to restore to the majority the expression of its will, and to secure to it its power.

'The stilettos which had menaced the Deputies, were instantly raised against their deliverer. Twenty assassins rushed upon me, and aimed at my breast. The grenadiers of the legislative body, whom I had left at the door of the hall, ran forward, and placed themselves between me and the assassins. One of these brave grenadiers (Thorne [1]) had his clothes pierced by a stiletto. They bore me off.'

DISSOLUTION OF THE COUNCIL OF FIVE HUNDRED.

Th' appointed meeting now took place,
Producing tumult and disgrace,
Some of the members, when desired,
Refused to take the oath required,
Insisting Nap should not be spared
But as an outlaw be declared.
As President Nap's brother sat,
So Lucien *hemm'd* and *haw'd* at that.
But so outrageous was the strife,
He found it hard to save his life ;
His eloquence he now display'd,
'Napoleon must be heard,' he said.
Then Boney came—in great dismay ;
Th' Assembly ordered him away—

[1] A gross exaggeration, for he only had his coat torn by a Deputy who had sufficient courage to collar him.

But such an order was mere *fudge*,
The brave Napoleon scorn'd to budge ;
And several began to push in,
To tear to pieces Nap and Lucien.
Nap gave the word—his troops attended,
By grenadiers he was defended ;
Tremendous now the hurly-burly,
Each phiz appear'd confounded surly ;
They drew their daggers in a rage,
And civil war began to wage.
Amidst these violent attacks,
Now some were thrown upon their backs,
And others fell upon their faces,
And others, on their —— proper places ;
While many, uttering sad groans,
Were found upon their marrow bones.

Gillray, of course (November 21, 1799), touched on it, but not very effectively, his picture ' Exit Libertè a la Francais !—or—Buonaparte closing the Farce of Egalité, at Saint Cloud, near Paris, November 10, 1799,' being the weakest caricature of any on this subject. Napoleon is directing his troops, who are charging the Council with fixed bayonets.

The Council met again at night, but simply to do as they were bid. Thorne, the grenadier with the torn coat, was decreed to have deserved well of his country, as were also Napoleon, Lefebvre, Murat, Berthier, and many others. Sixty-one members of the Council were expelled, and Article two of the Resolution, passed that night, says,—

' The Legislative Body creates provisionally an Executive Consular Committee, composed of Citizens Syeyes and Roger Ducos, Ex-Directors, and Buonaparte, General. They shall bear the name of Consuls of the French Republic.'

CHAPTER XIX.

NAPOLEON TAKES THE LEAD—SIÈYES AND DUCOS ARE DEPOSED—CAM-
BACÉRÈS AND LEBRUN NAMED SECOND AND THIRD CONSULS—
NAPOLEON'S LETTER TO GEORGE THE THIRD—REPLY TO SAME.

NAPOLEON had now got his foot fairly on the ladder, but it was he alone who was to mount it. At the first meeting of the Consuls, Sièyes asked, ' Which of us is to preside ? ' Ducos had grasped the position, and replied, ' Do you not see that the General presides ? '

There is a caricature by Cawse (November 30, 1799) of ' Satan's return from ~~Egypt~~ Earth. Discovered in Council with Belzebub and Belial—a Sketch after Fuseli [1] ! ! ! ' Here Napoleon forms the centre figure, one foot resting on a skull, the other on the Marseillaise hymn and the Council of Five Hundred. Behind him is a glory, with a trinity formed of three daggers—Sièyes, Ducos, and Buonaparte. Devils surround him, and, at his feet, is a howling French mob.

> Our hero, now, the people guided,
> And a new government provided.
> First Consul, *modestly* he claim'd,
> Two others were Sub-Consuls named ;
> But these were not in Boney's way,
> For the first Consul had full sway.
> And now these Consuls took an oath,
> For Nap to swear was never loth.

[1] This was one of Fuseli's celebrated 'Milton Gallery,' a series of 47 pictures, produced between the years 1790 and 1800.

> Thus elevated, Josephine
> Imagin'd she would be a queen ;
> But she by Nap was harshly told,
> That six and forty was too old ;
> His mother, who the lady hated,
> Advised him to be separated ;
> By her persuasions, Nap, of course
> Began to think of a divorce.
> He ponder'd ev'ry afternoon,
> And rubbing once his forehead, soon
> The lady's banishment decreed,
> Because—their tempers disagreed.
> In fact, her faults he recollected,
> And her caresses now rejected.
> But, as 'twill not improve our morals,
> We'll pass these matrimonial quarrels.
> As Nap a love of pow'r betray'd,
> He great munificence display'd ;
> For he rewarded with donations,
> His friends, especially relations.
> He to his mother acted handsome,
> As he bestowed on her a grand sum ;
> For Joe, and Lucien, he provided,
> Who, at this time, in France resided—
> How suddenly success awaits men !
> Both Joe, and Lucien, he made Statesmen.

It was not probable that Napoleon would rest contented with the provisional position he occupied. A fresh government had to be constituted, of which he must be the head : and so the Constitution of December 13 was manufactured, and afterwards passed into law. Article 23 provided, 'The sittings of the Senate are not to be public.' Article 24, 'The Citizens Sièyes, and Roger Ducos, the Consuls quitting their functions, are appointed members of the Conservative Senate. They shall assemble along with the second and third Consuls nominated by the present Constitution. These four Citizens shall appoint the Majority of the Senate, which shall then complete itself, and proceed to the elections entrusted to it.'

Article 39. 'The Government is entrusted to three Consuls appointed for ten years, and indefinitely re-eligible. Each of them is to be elected individually with the distinct quality of Chief, Second, or Third Consul. The first time the Third Consul shall only be named for five years. For the present time General Bonaparte is appointed Chief Consul, Citizen Cambaceres, now Minister of Justice, Second Consul, and Citizen Lebrun, Member of the Committee of Antients, Third Consul.' Article 41. 'The Chief Consul is to promulgate the laws : he is to name and revoke at pleasure the Members of the Council of State; the Ministers, Ambassadors, and other principal foreign agents, the officers of the army by land and sea, the members of local administration and the Commissioners of the Government at the Tribunals. He is to appoint all Judges, Criminal and Civil, as well as Justices of the Peace, and the Judges of Cassation, without the power of afterwards revoking them.' Article 43. 'The salary of the Chief Consul shall be 500,000 francs for the 8th year ' (ending September 22, 1800). 'The salary of the other two Consuls shall be equal to three-tenths of that of the first.' So that we see Napoleon fully knew how to take care of himself.

On January 1, 1800, Gillray published 'The French Triumvirate settling the New Constitution'—and mighty wise they look. (See next page.)

In the year 1799, Consols ranged from 55 in January to 62¼, the closing price in December. Bread, however, was dear, the average of the quartern loaf being 13*d.*

It was in the latter part of this year that Napoleon notified to George the Third his elevation to the dignity of First Consul, and appropriately chose Christmas Day on which to date his letter, which breathed (sincerely or not) ' Peace on earth, goodwill towards men.'

Bonaparte, First Consul of the Republic, to His Majesty the King of Great Britain and Ireland.

Paris 5 Nivôse year VIII. of the Republic.

Called by the wishes of the French Nation to occupy the first magistracy of the French Republic, I deem it desirable, in entering on its functions, to make a direct communication to your Majesty.

CAMBACÈRÈS.   LE-BRUN.   BUONAPARTE.

Must The War, which for four years, has ravaged every part of the world, be eternal? Are there no means of coming to an understanding?

How can the two most enlightened nations of Europe, more powerful and stronger than is necessary for their safety and independence, sacrifice to the idea of a vain grandeur, the benefits of commerce, of internal prosperity, and domestic happiness? How is it they do not feel that peace is as glorious as necessary?

These sentiments cannot be strangers to the heart of your Majesty, who rules over a free nation, with no other view than to render them happy.

Your Majesty will only see in this overture my sincere desire to effectually contribute to a general pacification, by a prompt step, free and untrammeled by those forms, which, necessary, perhaps, to disguise the apprehensions of feeble states, only prove in the case of strong ones, the mutual desire to deceive.

France and England, by abusing their strength, may for a long time yet, to the misery of all other nations, defer the moment of their absolute exhaustion ; but I will venture to say that the fate of all civilised nations, depends on the end of a war which envelopes the whole world.

signed BONAPARTE.

The British Government did not quite see it, but considered that the claws of the French eagle required yet more cutting. They had been partially operated on at the Nile, and at Acre. Italy was no longer under French rule. Suwarrow's victories had severely crippled the French, who were, besides, very weak financially. Add to this, that there were 140,000 Austrians gathering along the Rhine. But still it was judged they were yet too sharp for the peace of Europe.

The answer from the English Court,
Vex'd Nap, according to report :
'Twas to the Minister address'd,
It being candidly confess'd
That there appear'd not the least cause
To break through ceremonial laws ;
In this his Majesty agreed,
Peace was desirable indeed,
If that his Majesty were able
T' obtain one permanent and stable ;
But that at present there was poor hope
For England, and indeed for Europe,

> Till France her lawful princes own'd
> The Bourbons—whom she had dethron'd.

This, really, was the tenor of Lord Grenville's reply, dated January 4, 1800, which is far too long, and uninteresting, to reproduce.

Gillray caricatured this letter of Napoleon's (February 24, 1800) in ' *The Apples and the Horse dung, or Buonaparte among the Golden Pippins* ; from an old Fable. Explanation.—Some horse dung being washed by the current from a neighbouring dunghill, espied a number of fair apples swimming up the stream, when, wishing to be thought of consequence, the horse dung would every moment be bawling out, "Lack-a-day, how we apples swim!" *See* Buonaparte's " Letter to his Majesty," and Mr. Whitbread's " Remarks upon the Correspondence between Crowned Heads." ' Although Gillray did not choose a very savoury subject to illustrate his caricature, yet there is much humour in it.

CHAPTER XX.

BATTLE OF MARENGO—DEATH OF DESAIX—SAID TO HAVE BEEN ASSAS-
SINATED—NAPOLEON'S LOVE FOR HIM—SOUP KITCHENS AT PARIS—
LAVISH EXPENDITURE OF NAPOLEON'S GENERALS.

THERE was very little caricature of Napoleon in the year 1800, for the best of reasons, that we had very little to do with him, as he was occupied till May in settling his Government, and then he left for his Italian campaign. But in this year (May 12) Gillray issued a series of eight

DEMOCRATIC CONSOLATIONS.

Buonaparte on his Couch surrounded by the Ghosts of the Murder'd—
the dangers which threaten his Usurpation, and all the Horrors of Final
Retribution.

plates, 'Democracy, or a Sketch of the life of Buonaparte,' of which I have already given three—'Democratic Inno-cence,' 'Democratic Humility,' and 'Democratic Religion.' As four are not very interesting, I have not given them,

only the last of the series, which, evidently, was meant to
be extended.

Combe, even, had very little to say of this time, lightly
touching the passage of the Alps, the occupation of Milan
and Pavia, the defeat of the Austrians at Montebello, and
the battle of Marengo, where he makes an assertion I cannot find elsewhere, nor trace to any French source, except
De Bourrienne.

> Soon after this the gallant fellow
> The Austrians drove from Montebello,
> And then did he, with all his men go,
> To aid the battle of Marengo ;
> Here was indeed a bold resistance,
> Brave Boney saw it at a distance :
> And at this time, it is not doubted,
> Nap's army was completely routed ;
> Indeed, it grieves the muse to say,
> Our hero cried, and ran away ;
> But brave Desaix, who was not idle,
> His horse soon grappled by the bridle,
> And turning round the Consul's phiz,
> He said, while anger ruffled his,
> ' Citizen Consul, look before ye—
> That is the road to fame and glory.
> Nap bit his lip, and swore by heaven,
> Th' offence was not to be forgiven ;
> Indeed, as many understand,
> That hour the Gen'ral's fall he plann'd.
> By Victor and Desaix defeated,
> The Austrians in their turn retreated.
> This Victor, who destruction hurl'd
> Made always a great noise in the world,
> For he had been a drummer, so
> The way to *beat* he'd cause to know.
> But, while victorious, now we find
> Desaix received a shot behind,

His Aid-du-camp was bribed to do it,
And well, too, the First Consul knew it ;
Besides the shot, a base attack !
He got a stab, too, in the back ;
He fell, and instantly expir'd—
His death by Boney was desired :
Yet when they told him he was dead,
'Why can't I weep?' he faintly said.

This scandalous accusation is too contemptible to be
thought true for a moment; but I must reproduce it, to show
what was said of Napoleon in England. Yet, in a portion
of it, there is a small substratum of truth. Hear what De

Bourrienne says : 'The death of Desaix was not perceived
at the moment it took place. He fell without saying a
word, at a little distance from Lefebvre-Desnouettes. A
battalion-sergeant of the ninth brigade of light infantry,
commanded by Barrois, seeing him extended on the
ground, asked permission to pick up his cap. It was
found to be perforated behind ; and this circumstance
leaves it doubtful whether Desaix was killed by some
unlucky inadvertency while advancing at the head of his

troops, or by the enemy when turning towards his men to encourage them.'

Other accounts speak of his being shot in the breast.

How Napoleon loved Desaix, is best told by them who knew him well, and let them bear witness against this gross calumny. De Bourrienne says : 'After supper, the First Consul dictated to me the bulletin of the battle. When we were alone, I said to him, " General, here's a fine victory. You recollect what you said the other day, about the pleasure with which you would return to France after striking a grand blow in Italy : surely you must be satisfied now ? "—" Yes, Bourrienne, I am satisfied. But Desaix ! . . . Ah, what a triumph would this have been if I could have embraced him to-night on the field of battle ! " As he uttered these words, I saw that Bonaparte was on the point of shedding tears, so sincere and profound was his grief for the death of Desaix. He certainly never loved, esteemed or regretted, any man so much.'

O'Meara writes : ' Asked him if it were true that Desaix had, a little before his death, sent a message of the following purport to him : " Tell the First Consul that I regret dying before I have done sufficient to make my name known to posterity." Napoleon replied, " it was true," and accompanied it with some warm eulogiums on Desaix.'

As a matter of fact Napoleon could not sufficiently honour the memory of his comrade, so highly did he estimate him. He spoke, in his bulletins, of the irreparable loss his death caused him ; he took for his own aides-de-camp, Rapp, and Savary, who had acted in this capacity to Desaix. A medal was struck in his honour, his statue should have been erected on the Place des Victoires, solemn ceremonies were ordered, masses were said, and a monument was raised, by subscription, on the Place Dauphine, Paris.

It is amusing to read in the newspapers of the day
(with the exception of the ' Times') the spiteful things said
against Napoleon. But Cobbett, in the ' Porcupine,' outdoes
them all, and spits his venom on the most harmless deeds.
' The late establishment of Soup shops in Paris, naturally
excites some curious ideas. Madame Bonaparte, their
patroness, who is also a sprig of nobility, seems in no
small degree attached to the ancient regimen ; hence
probably her wish to revive soup meagre, frogs, &c. Nor
is it less remarkable that the French should wish to
establish soup shops, just at the time when they were
falling into disuse in this country.' [1] ' The *Morning Post*
tells us that "the Chief Consul has taken a thousand subscription tickets for the *soup establishments* at Paris." This
is at once a proof of that *plenty* which we have been told
exists in France, and of the Charity of the Chief Consul.
If ever there was a country more degraded than all others,
it is France. Should there be, amongst the people of that
country, one man left, who entertains antient notions,
what must be his mortification and shame to see his
countrymen not only ruled, but actually fed like paupers,
by a low bred upstart from the contemptible island of
Corsica ! And this, ye gods ! is the *Grand Nation* ! This
is the nation who is to change the public law of Europe !
This is the nation to whom Britons are requested to bow
down their heads ! To return to the " *soup establishments,*"
we should be glad to know how the Corsican came by the
money to purchase a thousand tickets. Was it part of the
dower which Barras gave him with his bride ? We rather
think he wrung it from the hands of the sovereign people.
What a base, what a despicable, race of slaves ! They
submit to assessments, forced loans, requisitions, and con-
fiscations ; they see their treasure seized on by millions

[1] No. 8, Nov. 7, 1800.

upon millions, and they applaud the " *charity* and *generosity*'
of the plunderer in chief, because he bestows on them the
fractions in soup maigre ! ' [1]

Cobbett did not write with ink, but with gall, and was
not at all particular as to the veracity of his statements.
Take the following examples : [2] ' *Lucien Buonaparte* is
holden in detestation in France.   His office, as Minister of
the Interior, gives him the command of very large sums,
which he wastes in every kind of dissipation, and in the
most scandalous manner, in order, forsooth ! to support his
rank as a *Prince of the Blood* ! ! !   He is protected by
the whole power of his brother, whose *vanity*, the leading
foible in his character, leads him to confer on the members
of his family, all the advantages and prerogatives of
Sovereign princes.   This conduct has rendered him the
object of incessant ridicule, and considerably diminished
his popularity.

' Another species of evil peculiar to a corrupt military
government, prevails in a very great degree, and has
become particularly offensive to the French, viz. the influence and insolence of generals.

' All the generals attached to Buonaparte, those who
supported him in his usurpation, and those who were with
him in Egypt, bear an exact resemblance to the minions
and favourites of the Roman Emperors.   These men have
the public treasure almost entirely at their disposal.
General Lasnes, one of the Consul's chief friends, spends
the enormous sum of *five hundred thousand livres* (upwards
of twenty thousand guineas ! ! !) a month, at Paris, where
he and his aids de camp occupy one of the most magnificent *hotels* in that capital.   Buonaparte, not being able to
supply his favourites with sufficient specie for defraying

---

[1] The *Porcupine*, No. 13, Nov. 13.
[2] *Ibid*. No. 28, Dec. 1.

their unbounded expences, grants them *congées d'exporta-tion*, i.e. an exclusive permission to export various articles the exportation of which is prohibited by law ; these *con-gées* are sold to mercantile men, who purchase them at a very high price.'

' To the facts, which we stated on Monday, respecting the prodigality of Buonaparte and his creatures, we may add the instance of General Ney. This Republican Bashaw has fixed his head-quarters at Neubourg, at the expence of which place, his table is furnished at the rate of *ninety pounds sterling a day !* The French have a proverb, the truth of which they and their neighbours now experience to their sorrow : " Il vaut mieux qu'une cité soit brûlée, q'un parvenu la gouverne "—A city had better be burnt to ashes, than submit to the rule of an upstart vagabond.' [1]

---

[1] The *Porcupine*, No. 30, Dec. 3, 1800.

CHAPTER XXI.

THE two plots against Napoleon's life which occurred in
this year must not be forgotten.   Let us have Combe's
version, which does not much exaggerate the facts of the
cases :—

> It seems the Jacobins against
> Our hero greatly were incensed :
> His levées, drawing-rooms, and so forth,
> They look'd upon as deeds of no worth ;
> The pageantry he held so dear,
> Did not Republican appear ;
> And, at such goings on distrest,
> Their indignation they exprest ;
> Our hero consequently saw
> The need of keeping them in awe ;
> So he contrived a plot, which seems
> The masterpiece of all his schemes ;
> And in this plot, too, he resolved
> His greatest foes should be involved.
> Fouché pretended, on th' occasion,
> (For Nap allow'd of no evasion)
> That some conspirators had got
> Daggers and pistols, and what not,
> To make the Conqueror their aim,
> When from the Opera he came.
> Nap to the Opera went indeed,
> One gave the signal, as agreed ;

Three men were instantly arrested
Three whom great Bonaparte detested.
They got it seems a dagger from one,
But carrying daggers now was common ;
He was from Nap at a great distance,
This proof, tho', was of no assistance ;
When the supposed assassination
Had undergone examination,
They seiz'd on others, as directed,
For having such a scheme projected ;
One prov'd at home that night he slept,
For being ill, his bed he kept ;
All this, however, had no weight,
For Nap's resentment was too great.
They suffered by the guillotine,
Which was his favourite machine ;
Save one, th' Italian too, I wot,
From whom the dagger had been got,
Nap banish'd him, and with him too,
Th' Italian patriotic crew ;
Four thousand, as historians say,
For no offence were swept away.

The first plot was that of October 10, 1800, and it has, certainly, somewhat of a police 'get up' about it. The First Consul knew all about it through an ex *chef de bataillon* named Harrel, who used to come every night to De Bourrienne, and tell him what the so-called conspirators had done. He supplied Harrel, at Napoleon's request, with money, &c. Napoleon was never in any danger, and four men perished by the guillotine.

Barre says : 'Still the persons designed, and arrested, on the very spot of the premeditated murder, were strictly searched about their proper persons, and neighbouring places, and not an arm, nor even a pin, was found. With what, then, could those pretended conspirators commit a murder, since, at the very moment, and on the very spot where it was to have been perpetrated, no kind of arms were found about them ?

'That such was the case, it was asserted, and never denied, in the course of the trial.

'The only witness was one Harel, an acknowledged spy of the police, holding the rank of Captain.

'And on the single evidence of a spy, devoted to, and paid by, the police, four men (Arena, Ceracchi, Demerville, and Topino-Lebrun,) were condemned to death. . . .

'Those unfortunate men having appealed from such iniquitous judgment, as grounded on many erroneous statements, and irregular proceedings, the court of appeals divided, when it was found that eight judges were for repealing, and eight for confirming, the judgment.

'The division being equal, five more judges were added to the sixteen, when the iniquitous judgment was confirmed.'

The other attempt upon Napoleon's life was genuine enough. On December 24, 1800, Haydn's Oratorio of the 'Creation' was to be performed at the Opera. He was sleepy, and disinclined to go, but was overpersuaded, and went. Luckily his coachman was drunk, and drove faster than usual. In the Rue St. Nicaise there was a loud explosion, two or three seconds after he had passed the place where it had occurred.

A barrel of gunpowder, surrounded by grapeshot, and pieces of iron, was fixed in a cart, and fired when Napoleon passed. He escaped, but twenty people were killed, and fifty-three wounded, including St. Regent who fired the train. The coachman was so drunk that he drove on, thinking it was only a salute that had been fired. There are several, and contradictory, versions of this event, but this seems to be the most authentic—

For this conspiracy ideal
Was soon succeeded by one real.
While the First Consul, with delight,
Was going to the play one night ;
His carriage pass'd a narrow way,
Where an infernal barrel lay—
This barrel of a sudden blew up,
And the combustibles all flew up.
With great dismay was Boney filled,
No wonder—some were hurt and kill'd ;
The windows of the carriage broke,
And most tremendous was the smoke :
The coachman luckily enough,
Had taken plenty of strong stuff ;
And, not regarding any evil,
Drove thro' the passage like a devil ;
His whip applied when there was need,
And saved his master by his speed.
Had coachee been of drink no lover,
With Nap it would have been all over.
The Jacobins (for, as related,
This party the brave Consul hated,)
Were mark'd for this assassination,
And many suffered transportation.
Indeed our hero firmly swore,
(As he had often done before,
For he would swear thro' thick and thin),
The British had a hand therein—
It seems the gentleman forgot
John Bull disdains a wicked plot.

Cobbett, of course, improves the occasion.[1] 'Miserable slaves ! For an instance of base flattery, surpassing anything we have hitherto seen, take the following from the *Chef du Cabinet*: " The explosion of the infernal machine

[1] The *Porcupine*, No. 60, Jan. 7, 1801.

broke *twenty-nine* pictures, out of *thirty*, which ornamented
an apartment in the street of St. Thomas. The single
picture which escaped, was that of the Chief Consul. One
would be ready to affirm (mark this) *that the same God,
who watches over the life of the first Consul, protected even his
likeness*"!!! What Emperor was it that talked of making
his horse a Consul? An English blood horse would be
disgraced by becoming the successor of Buonaparte.'

And again:[1] 'Buonaparte's embracing the Parisian
addressers, puts us in mind of the good old ceremony of
the *thief's kissing the hangman.*'

[1] The *Porcupine*, No. 61, Jan. 8, 1801.

CHAPTER XXII.

GENERAL FAST—ADULTERATION, AND COMPULSORY SALE OF STALE BREAD —WAR IN EGYPT—THE BOULOGNE FLOTILLA—NEGOTIATIONS FOR PEACE—RATIFICATION OF PRELIMINARIES—RECEPTION IN ENGLAND —GENERAL REJOICINGS.

IT is sad to take up the very first number of the 'London Gazette' for 1801, and find 'A Proclamation for a general Fast,' which was to be held on February 13, the reason wherefore is stated thus: 'WE, taking into Our most serious consideration the heavy Judgments with which Almighty God is pleased to visit the Iniquities of this land, by a grievous Scarcity and Dearth of divers Articles of Sustenance, and Necessaries of Life &c.'

The war bore grievously on the Commons, and, consequently, Napoleon was in like measure abhorred. Nothing short of the thought of approaching famine could have caused Parliament to pass, and the king give his royal assent to,[1] 'An Act to prevent until the Sixth Day of November, One Thousand Eight Hundred and One, and from thence to the End of Six Weeks from the Commencement of the then next Session of Parliament, the manufacturing of any fine Flour from Wheat, or other Grain, and the making of any Bread solely from the fine Flour of Wheat; and to repeal an Act, passed in the Thirty-Sixth Year of the Reign of His present Majesty, for permitting Bakers to make and sell certain Sorts of Bread, and to make more effectual Provision for the same.' This took effect on January 31, 1801.

[1] Dec. 31, 1800.

'An Act to prohibit, until the First Day of October, One thousand eight hundred and one, and from thence to the End of Six Weeks next after the then next Session of Parliament, any Person or Persons from selling any Bread which shall not have been baked Twenty-four Hours.' This Act was 41 Geo. III. cap. 17, and it recites the reason in the preamble: 'Whereas it is expedient to reduce as much as possible, at the present moment, the consumption of Wheat flour. And whereas it appears a considerable saving would arise if Bread was prohibited from being sold until it had been baked a certain time, &c.' The penalties of non-compliance ranging from 5s. to 40s.

Here is a receipt given for adulterated bread: 'Improvement of bread, with economy of flour, and saving of expense :—Take one pound of ground rice, put it in cold water sufficient to cover it, and something more, boil it, and it will absorb all the water, and weigh four pounds ; mix four pounds of flour with it, knead them well together, and lighten them with yeast, like common bread, and they will produce ten pounds ten ounces of excellent bread, which will not cost more than twopence halfpenny per pound, and will save one half in the consumption of flour. N.B. this bread will keep moist a week.'

When we remember that bad bread was on January 1, 1801, 1s. 9¼d. per quartern loaf, on March 5, 1s. 10½d., and although it dropped after harvest as low as 10¼d., yet closed December 31 at 1s. 0¼d., and that this bad bread had to be eaten stale, all through Boney, we cannot wonder that the people did not love him.   His direct presence was brought home to all and every one daily, by means of that most susceptible bodily organ, the stomach. It was hitting John Bull in a very vulnerable part.

The war in Egypt still kept on, and in February reinforcements of 15,330 men, under the command of Sir

Ralph Abercrombie, set sail in a fleet of 175 vessels or ships. In March they defeated the French under Menon, the rene-gade, but at the cost of the life of the brave Abercrombie.

On April 19, Rosetta surrendered to our forces, and on June 27 Cairo capitulated, on condition that General Belliard, with all his troops, arms, and baggage, should be taken back to France. On their march back to the coast, Menon, finding his cause hopeless, surrendered on the same terms, and thus ended the French occupation of Egypt.

With Napoleon's concordat with the Pope we have nothing to do, except that his satirists here did not forget to contrast his attendance at the solemn *Te Deum* at Notre Dame with his pseudo-Mahometanism in Egypt. What more affected us, was the arming along the Channel coast, and the Flotilla at Boulogne, which was to act as transport for the army for the invasion of England. The French themselves laughed at these little cockle-shells of boats, *teste* Madame Junot :—

' Boulogne was designated from the year 1801, as the chief station of the enterprise against England. The greatest activity suddenly prevailed in all ports of the Channel ; camps were formed on the coast, divisions of light vessels were organised, and multitudes were built. The Flotilla, as it was called, created apparently with the greatest exertion, and all the apparatus of preparation, spread, as was intended, alarm on the opposite shore. The Boulogne Flotilla was composed of extremely light boats, so small, that at Paris, where everything forms the subject of a jest, they were called walnut shells. Brunet, who at this time was a truly comic actor, performing in some piece which I do not remember, was eating walnuts, the shells of which, after a little preparation, he launched upon some water in a tub by his side. "What are you doing?" said his fellow actor. "Making des péniches," replied Brunet. This was the name by which the flat-bottomed boats of the flotilla were known at Paris. But poor Brunet was made to atone by twenty-four hours' imprisonment for his unseasonble joke on the Government; and the day after his release the same piece was performed. When Brunet should have made the interdicted reply, he was silent. The other actor repeated the inquiry as to what he was doing. Still Brunet made no answer, and the other with an air of impatience proceeded: "Perhaps you do not know what you are about?" "Oh yes!" said Brunet, "I know very well what I am about, but I know better than to tell." The laugh was general, and so were the applauses; and, in truth, nothing could be more droll than the manner in which this was uttered; Brunet's countenance in saying it was of itself sufficient to provoke universal hilarity.'

But, in very truth, John Bull was not much frightened: there was Nelson, and his fleet, and people had great faith in them. But Nelson could do little against this passive fleet. On August 3 he bombarded Boulogne, sunk five gun-boats, and damaged others; and on the 15th of the same month he tried to capture, or destroy, these gun-boats, but was unsuccessful in his attempt, as the French had chained them to the shore.

We now come to the principal event of the year, the Peace—over which there was much coquetting. As early as March, Lord Hawkesbury, the then Secretary of State for Foreign Affairs, addressed a letter to M. Otto, signifying King George's desire to enter into negotiations for the restoration of peace.

These negotiations for peace were naturally noticed, and one very good etching, by Roberts, 'Negotiation See Saw,' shows Napoleon and John Bull engaged in that pastime seated on a plank 'Peace or War.' Bonaparte says,

'There Johnny, now I'm down, and you are up—then I go up and you go down Johnny—so we go on.' John Bull does not enjoy the situation so much, but grumbles, 'I wish you would settle it one way or other, for if you keep bumping me up and down in this manner I shall be ruined in Diachilem Plaster.'

A somewhat elaborate etching, also by Roberts (no date, 1801), depicts 'John Bull's Prayer to Peace, or the flight of Discord.' He is on his knees praying the following to Peace: 'Sublime Descendant of Happiness, incline thine ear to the Petition of thy poor Patient, worn out oppressed I. Bull, who humbly prayeth thee that thou would'st in the first place exert thy influence, and be the means of restoring to me again those lost Liberties and Privileges I have been so basely rob'd of, and that you would'st be pleased also to put a speedy stop to cruel monopolizing, and e'er it be long, send me thy attendant Plenty, to comfort me and my long suffering numerous Family, and may that horrid Demon Discord never return again.' Peace, whom the eye of Providence watches over, replies: 'Thy Prayer shall be fulfill'd, Plenty awaits thee with all her blessings, her pace is slow but sure.' Bonaparte and Pitt, who is represented as covered with serpents, are retreating.

On October 1, preliminary articles of peace with France were signed at Lord Hawkesbury's office at Downing Street, by his Lordship, and M. Otto on the part of the French Government, and great were the rejoicings at the event, although not so great as they might have been. The 'Times' of October 3 says: 'The public were so impatient to express their feelings on the occasion of the News of the Preliminaries of Peace being signed, that almost all the public streets were illuminated last night. This was evidently not the wish of the Government, who have deferred a general illumination until the ratification of them comes back from France. Accordingly, none of the Public Offices were illuminated, nor either of the Theatres. The ratification of the Preliminaries is expected from Paris on Tuesday next.'

No wonder 'the public were so impatient to express their feelings,' their joy must have been so great. Long-suffering, they had borne the burden and heat of a long war, cheerfully too, and gladly must they have welcomed its conclusion.

In Paris the joy was the same. The 'Times,' October 10, says : 'The Intelligence . . . was announced to the inhabitants of Paris by discharges of Artillery, and was proclaimed by torch light throughout the streets. At night there was a general illumination. Never was joy more fervently expressed.'

One of the most practical tests of renewed confidence was the great variation of 3 per cent. Consols—in September $58\frac{1}{4}$; in October $69\frac{1}{2}$.

On October 10 came the preliminaries, ratified. Let us see the 'Times'' account :—'London October 12th. On Saturday morning, at ten o'clock, General Daurostan,[1] *Chef de Brigade* in the Artillery, and Aide de Camp to General Bonaparte, arrived at M. Otto's house in Hereford Street, with the ratification of the French Government of the Preliminaries of Peace signed on the 1st inst. between Lord Hawkesbury and M. Otto in Downing Street.

'The Preliminaries were ratified in Paris on the 5th ; but General Daurostan was not dispatched till Wednesday evening, in order to give time for a magnificent gold box to be made, in which the ratification was enclosed to Lord Hawkesbury. The General was also delayed by his carriage breaking down upon the road.

[1] Lauriston.

'After breakfasting at M. Otto's, the General, accompanied by the Minister, and Mr. St. John (Mrs. Otto's brother), proceeded to *Reddish's* Hotel, in St. James's Street, where he dressed, and afterwards went to Downing Street. On their way thither, the populace took the horses from the carriage, and drew it through the principal streets. As soon as the Ratifications had been exchanged, Lord Hawkesbury sent a letter to the Lord Mayor. . . . General Daurostan cannot fail to communicate to his Court the very flattering manner in which he had been received in London. His carriage having been drawn to St. James's Street, he alighted and came forward to the window, and bowed to the populace. On his way to Downing Street, they drew his carriage through the Park. Lord St. Vincent happening to be at the garden-gate of the Admiralty, the mob gave the gallant Admiral three hearty cheers, who, in return, recommended them to take care of the strangers, and not to overturn the carriage. . . . It is understood that there will be another illumination this evening. The Bank and Post Office have given notice of their intending to do so.'

Cobbett foamed at the mouth over this Peace, and his utterances are so caustic as to be well worth reproduction.[1] 'We request our readers to observe, that henceforth we shall be very particular in what we say about the most illustrious Sovereign Consul Buonaparte. Oh! how we shall extol him! We shall endeavour to give our readers the earliest information, when he rises, breakfasts, dines, sups, and spits. With all reverence, we shall treat of his lovely, chaste, and bonny Queen—thus by way of a touch :

'It is with superlative pleasure we inform our readers, that the last news from France represents the health of

---

[1] *Porcupine*, No. 291, Oct. 3, 1800.

the First Consul to be improving.   This glory of the
world, is returned to his country palace at Malmaison.

But it was after October 10, when the Ratification had
arrived, that Cobbett's wrath boiled over, and he appears at
his finest.   In the number for October 12, he gives vent to
his impassioned feelings in words like these : [1] 'On Saturday
last, such a scene was exhibited in this metropolis, as we
never expected to have lived to witness, and having
witnessed it, we care not how soon we resign our existence ! . . . a vile degraded rabble, miscalled Britons, took
the horses out of the carriage which contained the two
French Citizens, Otto and Lauriston—the latter of whom
they mistook for the brother of Buonaparte—and dragged
it from Oxford Street to Downing Street ; then back
through the Park, and, not content with taking the usual
carriage road, dragged it through the Mall, a place appropriated, exclusively, as a carriage road, to the use of the
ROYAL FAMILY !!!'

But Cobbett had good reason to be sore, for the mob had
smashed the windows of his dwelling-house in Pall Mall,
and at his office in Southampton Street, because he would
not illuminate ; so he takes his revenge in a peculiar manner.   ' He did not know that there existed in the country,
any force whatever, to compel his Majesty's subjects to
exhibit, at night, manifestations of joy at an event which,
in the morning, he had stated his reasons for believing to be
a subject of deep concern.   But he has unfortunately found
himself mistaken ; and he is, therefore, under the necessity
of apprizing his readers, that, until the principles of the
British Constitution, and the laws of the realm, which have
ever been objects of his fervent admiration, and most
zealous support, can rise superior to the destructive rage of
a senseless and infuriate rabble ; until he can derive that

[1] *Porcupine*, No. 298.

protection from the Police of the Country, which every
subject has a right to claim, but which he has, hitherto,
been unable to obtain ; until, in short, that "*tumult* of
exultation," and that "*delirium* of joy," which a Ministerial
writer so emphatically described, and so earnestly wished,
might *increase*, shall have subsided, the publication of The
Porcupine will cease, and the mob be left to exercise their
vengeance on an empty office.'

But he did not long leave the populace thirsting for his
utterances, for the paper was resumed on October 15.

> At length all parties pleased to yield,
> A treaty was in London seal'd ;
> And Nap with pleasure had to say
> That England own'd his Cons'lar sway.
> The Royalists were vex'd at this,
> They took the treaty much amiss ;
> It seem'd (as for a time it was)
> Destructive of the Bourbon cause.
> This Amiens treaty, as 'twas termed
> Was in October month confirm'd ;
> And London, tho' so ill repaid,
> Illuminations grand display'd.

CHAPTER XXIII.

AN unknown artist, probably Ansell, produced on October
26, 1801, a caricature of 'The Child and Champion of
Jacobinism new Christened (vide Pitt's Speech).' Bonaparte
is bending over a font, which is supported by Egyptian
sphinges, whilst a bishop calls out, 'Name this Child.' Addington and Pitt are the godfathers, and Lord Hawkesbury
is the godmother. Pitt replies, 'Deliverer of Europe and
Pacificator of the World.' Addington says, 'I hope he will
abolish the Slave Trade'; and the godmother mentions,
'You need not say anything about the march to Paris.'

Gillray (November 9, 1801) gives us a very elaborate
picture of 'Political Dreamings—Visions of Peace!—Perspective Horrors!' Windham, who was the leader of the war
party, is asleep, and his dreams are full of incident—too full,
indeed, to recapitulate here. But the principal scene in the
sleeping man's vision is Napoleon dragging to the guillotine by a halter, Britannia, whose trident is broken, as also
is her shield.

'The Balance of Power,' by Ansell (December 1, 1801),
shows a pair of scales, in which Bonaparte weighs down Pitt
and the Lord Chancellor. Pitt ruefully exclaims, 'So this is
the Balance of Power we have been making such a fuss about
—a pretty piece of business we have made of it. Curse
that sword of his, 'tis that has made us kick the Beam.'

Hostilities with France having ceased with the ratification of the preliminaries of peace, there was but little caricaturing of Napoleon, and none of an offensive character. Napoleon occupied his time in attending to home affairs, as also did the British Government. But the peace was not absolutely concluded, and much diplomatic wrangling took place, as usual, before the Peace of Amiens was really signed on March 27, 1802. Its principal articles must be briefly enumerated here, as they will be found of use in understanding forthcoming caricatures.

England restored to France, Spain, and Batavia, all the possessions which had been occupied or conquered during

the war, with the exception of Trinidad and Ceylon. Malta was to be restored to the Order of St. John of Jerusalem—the British troops to evacuate the island within three months, or sooner ; but Malta was to be independent, such independence being guaranteed by the Great Powers, and the ports to be open to the vessels of all nations, with the exception of those belonging to the Barbary Powers. These are the principal articles necessary for us to bear in mind.

Due credit was given to Bonaparte's astuteness, and our plenipotentiary, Lord Cornwallis, was considered no match for him.

The Caricature year of 1802 seems to open with one

by Ansell (January 9), 'A Game at Chess' between Bonaparte and Lord Cornwallis. Bonaparte says, 'Check to your King Remember this is not the first time, and I think a very few Manœuvres more will compleatly convince you that I am better acquainted with the Game I am playing, than you are aware of.' Cornwallis, tearing his hair, exclaims, 'Curse it, I shall lose this game. You are too much for me.'

This was followed by another from the same pencil (February 8), called 'Cross examination,' where Lord Cornwallis is button-holing Bonaparte, and saying, 'There is great delay in our negociation comeing to a conclusion, and I understand our People are very uneasy lest you should be Humbugging us—Your fleet having sail'd, has given cause for many conjectures, and to tell you the truth it puzzles me a little to know what your intention is.' Bonaparte's reply is plain and simple, 'I have to tell you, Sir, that I do not desire to give you the information you seem to wish for, and whether I sign or not, is of little consequence to the Republican government; our fleet I am in hopes will pick up something.'

In March 1802 Woodward produced a somewhat dreary picture called 'The National Institute's first Interview with their President.' Napoleon, seated under a canopy, says to Sheridan, Fox, Bedford, and Burdett, 'Gentlemen, you are welcome, and I invite you to the Honors of the sitting.' Sheridan, who is kneeling, holds a phial and box in his hands, and begs that Napoleon will 'Be pleased to accept some true poetic Tincture, and a small Box of Pizarro[1] Pills.' Fox, who has a money bag under his arm, says, 'I have brought a pound and a half of Patriotism for your eminence.' The Duke of Bedford opines that 'He'll not be displeased with a few Bedford

[1] An allusion to his play of that name.

biscuits ; ' and Burdett, with his hair, as usual, combed over his eyes, refers to his present, ' I have brought him a Phial of Genuine Bastile Balsam.'

But when once the peace was signed, much show was made of shaking hands and being friends. Englishmen went over to France in numbers ; Frenchmen reciprocated, but not to the same extent. This feeling is shown by the caricaturist, for on April 14, 1802, was published (artist unknown) a picture entitled ' A Peaceable Pipe, or a Con-sular Visit to John Bull.' Napoleon and John Bull are in amicable converse, smoking, and drinking beer. John Bull says, ' Here's to you, Master Boney Party ; come, take another whiff, my hearty !' To this hospitable invitation Napoleon replies, ' Je vous remercie, John Bull, I think I'll take another pull.' Mrs. Bull is hard at work mending John's breeches, which are wofully dilapidated : says she, soliloquising, ' Now we are at Peace, if my Husband does take a drop extraordinary I don't much mind, but when he was at war, he was always grumbling. Bless me, how tiresome these old breeches are to mend ; no wonder he wore them out, for he had always his hands in his pockets for something or other.'

As before said, with the peace came mutual intercourse between England and France, and there is a picture by Ansell (May 14, 1802), which represents ' A Trip to Paris, or John Bull and his Spouse, invited to the Honors of the Sitting !! ' Napoleon receives John Bull and Ireland, and when seated, Napoleon addresses them thus : ' Indeed, Mr. Bull, I am quite charmed with you—there is something so easy and polite in your manners.'

John Bull, however, is not to be taken in by such palp-able ' *blarney*,' and replies, ' Come—come Mounseer Bonny party, that's all gammon d'ye see. D—n me if I know more about politeness than a Cow does of a new shilling !!'

Ireland looks very angrily at her spouse, and remonstrates :
' For shame, Mr. Bull, what will the Jontleman think of
your Blarney about gammon and cows, and Bodder and
nonsense ; by St. Patrick, I must send you to Kilkenny to
larn good breeding.'

Some of these caricatures were rather dreary ; take, for
example, ' The Consular Warehouse or a Great Man nail'd
to the Counter ' (Cawse, May 20). Napoleon is keeping a
shop, selling, among other things, ' Preserved Promises,
Pickled Piety from Rome, Oil of Lodi, Marengo Olio, Bullet
Bolusses. advice gratis. N.B. One Pill is a dose. also Islands
for Home Consumption Martinique—St. Lucia.'   John Bull
has just bought two, paid for in good hard cash, and takes
his goods home with him.   Under one arm he carries the
' Island of Indemnity, ci-devant Ceylon '—under the other
is the ' Island of Security, ci-devant Trinidad.'   They hardly
seem to be John Bull's idea of a bargain, for he is saying,
' They be very light to be sure—but harkee, my worthy,—
you'll not forget to carry on a little trade with the Old
Shop ; if you don't, you know, a Rowland for an Oliver,
that's all.' Napoleon, however, reassures him with ' We'll
not talk of that at present, Mr. Bull ; all you have to do,
is to take care of your new Islands ; mind you don't tumble
down, and break them, before you get home—They are
very brittle, but a very good article for all that.'

As the year grew older, the *entente cordiale* grew colder.
Suspicions of Napoleon's intentions were aroused, and
Malta was not evacuated as per treaty.   One or two warning caricatures, stormy petrels, made their appearance, and
in the autumn of this year appeared ' The Corsican Conjurer raising the plagues of Europe.'   He is shewn with
huge cocked hat and an ample robe, which is held up by
the Devil, who encourages him, ' That's right my fine fellow
—If you don't kick up a pretty dust in the world, never

trust the Devil again—that's all.' Napoleon is waving a rod over a caldron, in which are serpents, and a devil, the steam from which is labelled, in different clouds, 'Anarchy, Pride, Murder, Confusion, Treason, War, Plunder, Revenge, Massacre, Avarice, Cruelty, Usurpation, Hatred, Horror, Envy, Blasphemy, Malice, Craft, Falsehood, and Terror.'

There is another one, 'Parcelling out John Bull,' which is a queer conceit. Napoleon has a huge pair of Compasses, with which he is measuring John Bull—congratulating himself that 'He really will make a pretty addition to my departments—he cuts out extremely well indeed.' There is the Wig Department, Department of the Head, Arm Department, Department of the Body, Fob Department, Breeches pocket Department, Right and Left Leg Divisions. But John Bull assures his friend, in no kindly spirit, 'Harkee Young one, you have forgotten the Fist Department, and if you don't take away your d—d Compasses, I'll give you a relish of it. Cut me out, indeed! why, I'll fight you with one hand tied behind me.' This caricature is neither signed nor dated, but it was undoubtedly issued in the autumn of 1802.

We have seen that it was fashionable for Englishmen to run over to France after the conclusion of peace, and Charles James Fox was no exception to the rule ; but he had to wait a little, until after the Westminster election, when, on July 15, he was returned head of the poll. He did not long delay the trip, and on July 29 he set out on his journey, accompanied by his wife, the Hon. St. Andrew St. John (afterwards Lord St. John) and a young Irishman named Trotter,[1] who wrote an exhaustive account of their journey. On the 4th of August, Napoleon had been elected

---

[1] *Memoirs of the Later Years of the Right Honourable Charles James Fox*, by John Bernard Trotter, Esq., late private secretary to Mr. Fox, London, 1811.

Consul for life, a step which might probably tend to con-
solidate peace, and which rendered his position equal to
any other European sovereign.   When Fox reached Paris,
it was rumoured that this was only preliminary to his taking
a higher rank, with the title of Emperor of the Gauls.   Just
then, Englishmen were in great favour at Paris, and Fox's
arrival created a great commotion.   All vied with each
other to pay him attention, and it was settled he should be

presented to the First Consul at his next *levée*, which took
place on September 3.

Caricaturists, like poets, must needs be allowed some
licence, and Gillray (November 15), in his picture of the
'Introduction of Citizen Volpone,[1] and his Suite, at Paris,'
draws slightly upon his imagination as to Napoleon's state
at this reception ; still the allegorical globes, and the introduction of Rûstan the Mameluke, add a fictitious dignity
to the picture.

The actual scene, as it was viewed by an eye-witness,[2]

------

[1] Fox.   [2] Trotter.

is thus described : 'We reached the interior apartment, where Buonaparte, First Consul, surrounded by his generals, ministers, senators, and officers, stood between the second and third Consuls, Le Brun and Cambacérès, in the centre of a semicircle, at the head of the room ! The numerous assemblage from the *Salle des Ambassadeurs*, formed into another semicircle, joined themselves to that, at the head of which stood the First Consul.'

Gillray's portrait of Charles James Fox is not very much exaggerated. Let us hope that of Mrs. Fox is. This lady, although she was married to Fox on September 28,

1795, was never introduced to his friends as his wife until this journey. She was always believed to be his mistress, Mrs. Armistead.[1] She made him a good and loving wife, and he was very fond of her.

Trotter describes the actual presentation thus : ' Buonaparte, of a small, and by no means commanding figure, dressed plainly, though richly, in the embroidered consular coat, without powder in his hair, looked like a private gentleman, indifferent as to dress, and devoid of all haughtiness in his air. . . . The moment the circle was formed, Buonaparte began with the Spanish

[1] Her real name, *vide his Marriage Register*, was Elizabeth B. Cane.

Ambassador, then went to the American, with whom he spoke some time, and so on, performing his part with ease, and very agreeably; until he came to the English Ambassador, who, after the presentation of some English Noblemen, announced to him Mr. Fox! He was a good deal flurried, and after indicating considerable emotion, very rapidly said, "Ah! Mr. Fox! I have heard with pleasure of your arrival—I have desired much to see you—I have long admired in you the orator, and friend of his country, who in constantly raising his voice for peace, consulted that country's best interests—those of Europe—and of the human race. The two great nations of Europe require peace;—they have nothing to fear; they ought to understand and value one another. In you, Mr. Fox, I see, with much satisfaction, that great statesman who recommended Peace, because there was no just object of war; who saw Europe desolated to no purpose, and who struggled for its relief."

'Mr. Fox said little, or rather, nothing, in reply,—to a complimentary address to himself, he always found invincible repugnance to answer; nor did he bestow one word of admiration or applause upon the extraordinary and elevated character who addressed him. A few questions and answers relative to Mr. Fox's tour terminated the interview.'

Other caricaturists took the matter up, for Fox's visit to Paris was naturally commented on; and there is an engraving by Ansell (November 8, 1802), 'English Patriots bowing at the Shrine of Despotism.' These 'Patriots' are Fox, Erskine, and Combe, the brewer, who was Lord Mayor. They are represented as bowing in the most lowly fashion—so low, indeed, that Fox has burst his trousers behind; and with one voice they assure Napoleon that they ' are, with the highest consideration, your Super Royal

Consulship's most Devoted, most Obsequious, and most honored Servants.' Bonaparte, seated in almost regal state, criticises them : 'Oh, from the World ! O'Connor's friends—Fox, ha ! how old are you ? A Brewer ; Lord Mayor, ha ! great pomp. Mr. Brief, ha ! a great Lawyer can talk well. There, you may go.'

Thus we see they did not quite get hold of the right version of this interview, as 'Taking leave' was satirised by a nameless artist (November 12, 1802), and represents Fox bowing very humbly to the First Consul, who is crowned with death's-head and cross-bones, daggers, pistols, and swords, and regards him in an extremely haughty manner.

IN June, Lord Whitworth was appointed ambassador
extraordinary, and minister plenipotentiary, to the French
Republic, and the state he then kept up was a striking
contrast to the plainness of Republican equipages. It was
different under the Empire ; but then the word Citizen had
not been dropped, and there was a certain affectation of
simplicity. The English attracted great attention by the
splendour of their equipages, and there is a caricature
(nameless, December 14, 1802) of 'Lord Whitworth's
Coachman at Paris.' His get-up is, certainly, 'exceeding
magnifical,' and is the wonder of the Parisians. It is
almost too much for his equanimity. for he is shown as
saying, ' How the Mounseers stare at me ! D—n me, if I
don't think they take me for the Ambassador.'

The effects of the peace were hardly realisable for a
time, and Woodward gives us an amusing caricature of the
state of the empire (December 20, 1802). It is called ' A
Peep at the Lion,' which is supposed to be on show. Outside the Exhibition Pitt is inviting Europe, generally, to
'Walk in Ladies and Gentlemen, and see the famous Lion.
Though I have some share in the concern, I have nothing
to do with showing him, I assure you—I am not his keeper ;
the Lion I used to show was very fierce, but this is quite quiet
and peaceable.' Inside, the Lion is shewn as lying down,

but with one eye open, Napoleon patting him on the head, saying, ' Poor fellow, poor fellow, what a beautiful Animal, —how sound he sleeps.' But the Chancellor, Lord Eldon, warns him, ' You had better not be too free with him Sir, In case of an accident. He is now asleep with one eye, and awake with the other.'

At the opening of the year 1803, although the storm clouds of war were ominously gathering, yet all seemed peace. The English enjoyed the rare treat of visiting France, and, generally, being of the better class, were well received. The year opens in a kindly spirit with ' The first

kiss these ten Years ! or the meeting of Britannia and Citizen François' (Gillray, January 1, 1803), which is a remarkably good caricature. Britannia, owing to the peace, has grown prosperous, and stout ; her trident and shield are put away in a corner, and the portraits of Napoleon and George the Third repose, in loving juxtaposition, on the wall, intertwined with palm-branches. Says Citizen François (his sword and cocked hat being laid aside), ' Madame, permettez me to pay my profound esteem to your engaging person ! and to seal on your divine Lips my everlasting attachment.' Madame Britannia replies, ' Monsieur, you are so truly a well bred Gentleman! and tho' you make me blush, yet you kiss so delicately, that I cannot refuse you ; tho' I was sure you would deceive me again !!!!'

A most amusing picture (Gillray, January 1, 1803) is that called ' German Nonchalance, or the vexation of Little Boney. vide the Diplomatique's late Journey through Paris.' It represents the Austrian ambassador being driven furiously through Paris, his luggage being directed ' à Londres.'

With the utmost *insouciance*, he is taking a pinch of snuff, calmly regarding Napoleon, who is standing on some

HOP	Step	Jump
FROM INDIGENCE IN CORSICA TO AFFLUENCE IN FRANCE.	FROM ASPIRING AMBITION TO THE SUMMIT OF POWER.	FROM CALAIS TO DOVER, WHERE LITTLE JOHN BULL DOES THE CORSICAN OVER.[1]

steps, and is in a fearful rage. With arms and legs outstretched, and his hat fallen off, he yells out, ' Ha, diable! va t'en, Impertinent! va t'en! is dere von Man oh Earth who not worship little Boney? Soldats! aux Armes! revenge! ah! Sacre Dieu, je suis tout tremblant.' The soldiers, however, although preparing to draw their swords, do not appear to be particularly anxious to avenge their insulted leader.

This incident arose from the Austrian minister neglecting

[1] January 1, 1803.   Artist unknown.

to pay his respects to the First Consul, whilst passing through Paris.

As an evidence of the uneasiness of public political feeling, take the following. In January 1803 was published a caricature by Raymond, called 'Leap Frog.' Napoleon has already jumped over the bowed backs of Holland and Spain. The poor Dutchman exclaims, 'He has left the Swiss and Italians a Mile behind—and as for me he has knocked my hat off and broken my pipe—pretty encouragement this to play at Leap-frog.' The don ruefully says that 'By St. Jago—my back is almost broken.' Napoleon is now jumping over Hanover, who plaintively asks, 'Why did I submit to this?' but the conqueror only says, 'Keep down your head Master Hanoverian, my next leap shall be over John Bull.' But that individual, who looks uncommonly belligerent, with clenched fists, exclaims, 'I'll be d—d if you do Master Corsican.'

The English Government, seeing how Napoleon was aggrandising himself, and seeing also that this country, alone, could save the liberty of Europe, did not hurry to conform with the treaty of Amiens, and surrender all the advantages gained by the late long struggle ; and although, with reluctance, the Cape, and other Batavian settlements, were given up, excuses were always to be found for not evacuating Malta.

On January 25, Lord Whitworth and Talleyrand had an interview, and the latter, after bitterly complaining of the licence of the British press, which he said ought to be curbed, or suppressed, asked plainly what were the intentions of the British Government with regard to Malta? It is to this interview, probably, that the following caricature owed its existence. How Cobbett lashed Addington, for his nepotism, in his 'Annual Register'!!

'The Evacuation of Malta' (Gillray, February 9, 1803)

is vividly, almost too graphically, depicted.   Ferocious little Bonaparte has hold of poor frightened Addington by his necktie, and, by flourishing his enormous sword, compels him to evacuate Malta, Egypt, Cape of Good Hope, St. Domingo, Guadaloup, and Martinique.   In vain Addington pleads, 'Pray do not insist upon Malta! I shall certainly be turned out! and I have a great many Cousins and Uncles and Aunts to provide for yet.' But his merciless enemy will hear of no compromise, and yells out 'All! All! you Jean F—t—e! and think yourself well off that I leave you Great Britain!!!'   A French officer mildly remonstrates, and suggests, 'My General, you had better not get him turned out, for we shall not be able to humbug them any more.'

Ansell executed an engraving (February 10, 1803) of the 'Rival Gardeners,' which represents Napoleon, and George III., tending their respective gardens, which are divided by the Channel.   Napoleon has a number of plants labelled 'Military poppies,' which flourish well; but he is greatly concerned about his principal flower, which has a very drooping head and flagging leaves.   He cannot understand it.   'Why, I don't know what is the reason; my Poppies flourish charmingly; but this *Corona Imperialis* is rather a delicate kind of a plant, and requires great judgment in rearing.'   His rival, however, points with pride to the sturdy British Oak, whose vigour is matchless, and is in full bloom, with a royal crown.   He replies, 'No, No, Brother Gardener, though only a ditch parts our grounds, yet this is the spot for true Gardening; here the *Corona Britanica* and yᵉ *Heart of Oak* will flourish to the end of the world.'

On March 8, the king sent a message to Parliament, respecting military preparations in the ports of France and Holland, and acquaints the House of Commons that 'he has judged it expedient to adopt additional measures of precaution for the security of his dominions;' and this gives us the key to the next caricature—

'Physical Aid, or, Britannia recover'd from a Trance, also the Patriotic Courage of Merry Andrew, and a peep thro' the Fog,' was published by Gillray, March 14, 1803, and is a very amusing picture. Bonaparte, and his flotilla, are crossing the Channel, and Sheridan, with fool's cap and bell, a tattered harlequin suit, a lathen sword, 'Dramatic Loyalty,' a shield with a Medusa's head, the snaky hair of which is labelled 'Envy, abuse, bouncing, puffing, detrac-

'A THEATRICAL HERO.'

tion, stolen jests, malevolence, and stale wit,' and a paper, in his sash, endorsed 'Ways and means to get a living,' calls out, 'Let 'em come! dam'me!!! Where are the French Buggabos? single-handed I'd beat forty of 'em!!! dam'me I'd pay 'em like Renter's shares, sconce off their half-crowns!!! mulct them out of their benefits, and come ye Drury Lane Slang over 'em.'

Britannia, suddenly aroused from her trance, screams out, 'Doctors and ministers of disgrace defend me,' and attempts to rise. Addington is attempting to recover her,

by holding a bottle of gunpowder to her nose, saying ' Do
not be alarm'd, my dear Lady! The Buggabos (the Honest
Gentlemen, I mean) are avowedly directed to Colonial service, they can have nothing to do Here, my lady—nothing
to do with US! do take a sniff or two to raise your Spirits,
and try to stand, if it is only upon one leg.' Lord Hawkesbury is presenting, in a feeble manner, to Britannia, her
spear—with broken point, and her shield, which is sadly
cracked, and bleats forth, ' Yes, my lady, you must try to
stand up, or we shall never be able to march to Paris.' Fox,
who is wilfully screening his face with his hat, exclaims,
' Dear me—what can be the reason of the old lady being
awaked in such a fright ? I declare I can't see anything of
the Buggabos!' On the ground lies the treaty of peace
torn.

On March 13, Napoleon behaved in a very rude, and
intemperate, manner to Lord Whitworth respecting the
non-evacuation of Malta—which scene is thus versified :—

> Our hero now, with great chagrin,
> Begg'd of Lord Whitworth to call in.
> Agreeably to his request,
> Th' Ambassador became his guest,
> And in the Cab'net of the Thuilleries,
> Napoleon play'd off all his fooleries.
> 'What is the cause,' he cried, ' of this?
> How comes it England acts amiss?
> I swear that every provocation,
> Daily augments my indignation ;
> Why are these libels to annoy me,
> Pensioned assassins to destroy me ?
> Why Malta's non-evacuation,
> And Alexandria, by your nation ?
> You'd fain keep Malta—I believe you,
> But part of France I'd rather give you.

Why all these provocations? why o' late,
The Amiens treaty dare to violate?'
Nap ask'd so many questions now,
That not an answer he'd allow.
Lord Whitworth moved his lips, but then
Our hero wagged his tongue again.
It seems Lord Whitworth wish'd to say,
France for infringements led the way ;
But when that she was pleased to stop,
And all her base aggressions drop,
The treaty England would fulfil,
For that, indeed, was England's will.
In spite of Nap's vociferation,
His Lordship made this observation :
' My sovereign's actions ne'er have been
Insidious, treacherous, or mean,
Because it is the king's desire
More to *preserve* than to *acquire*.'

CHAPTER XXV.

GENERAL UNEASINESS—CARICATURES THEREON—ADDINGTON'S NEPOTISM
—NAPOLEON'S DISCOURTESY TO LORD WHITWORTH—TRIAL OF JEAN
PELTIER.

'THE Political Cocks' (by Ansell, March 27, 1803) is very
graphic. Napoleon, a game cock armed with terrific spurs,
is calling across the Channel to Pitt, who, standing on the
British Crown, is crowing lustily. Napoleon says, 'Eh

THE POLITICAL COCKS.

Master Billy, if I could but take a flight over this brook, I
would soon stop your Crowing. I would knock you off
that Perch, I swear by Mahomet, the Pope, and all the Idols
I have ever worshipped.' Pitt, however, replies, 'Tuck-a-
roo—too—that you never can do!!!'

This was a fine time for the caricaturists, and their works
came thick and fast. Telling their own tale, they need no
explanation. 'An Attempt to swallow the World' (artist

unknown, April 6, 1803) shows Napoleon attempting this difficult feat—John Bull looking on, and remarking, ' I'll tell you what, Mr. Boneypartee, when you come to a little spot I have in my eye, it will stick in your throat and choak you.'

West (April 6, 1803) engraved ' John Bull teased by an Earwig.' Napoleon, drawn very small, is on John Bull's shoulder, pricking his cheek with his little sword. This annoys the old man, and, looking up angrily from his meal of bread (Ceylon), and cheese (Malta), he says, ' I tell you what, young one—if you won't let me eat my bread and cheese in peace and comfort, I'll blow you away, you may depend upon it.' To which the *Earwig* replies, ' I will have the Cheese, you Brute, you ; I have a great mind to annihilate you, you great overgrown Monster.'

' Easier to say than to do ' (I. Cruikshank, April 14, 1803) shows Bonaparte seated before a *New Map of the World*, attempting to erase the British Isles. A Dutchman, with a lighted candle, suggests, ' Got for d—n de ting —here take te candle, and burn tem out.' On the other side, a Spaniard says, ' Here, my friend, take the paste-brush, and stick a piece of your three-coloured flag over them.' Whilst a Jew, who has a label coming out of his pocket, ' Subscription to new loan,' says, ' I tink if I lend a little more monish at Turty per shent, it will soon annihilate dem.' Bonaparte reflects : ' I cannot scrape these little islands out of the map. As for your plan, Mynheer, we did try to burn them once, but they would not take fire ; and let me tell you, Don Diego, they are not so easily over-run with any flag as you may think ! I believe Moses's plan the best ; that, and a threat now and then may probably do the business.'

' An Attempt to undermine John Bull, or working through the Globe ' (Roberts, April 16, 1803), shows

Napoleon standing on ruins, surrounded by 'Territories pickaxed with impunity '—Switzerland, Italian Republic, Batavian Republic ; and he is now commencing operations with his pickaxe on John Bull, saying, ' O, the Pick axe is infinitely the best way—I shall soon be at the little fellow, that's his abode, I know it by the white cliffs.' John Bull is lying down, sword in hand, with his ear on the ground, and says, 'I hear you burrowing away, my fine fellow; but it won't do.—As soon as you pop your head above the surface, you shall be saluted with a few of John Bull's pop-guns.'

Another caricature (artist unknown, April 16, 1803), called ' A stoppage to a Stride over the Globe,' shows a colossal Napoleon bestriding the World, whilst a small John Bull, on England, is hacking at his foot, with a sword. Napoleon, in disgust, is calling out, ' Ah ! who is it dares to interrupt me in my progress ? ' ' Why, 'tis I, little Johnny Bull, protecting a little spot I clap my hand on, and d—n me if you come any farther—that's all.'

Ansell, too, the same date (April 16, 1803), drew ' The Governor of Europe, Stoped in his career, or Little B——n too much for great B——te.' Here a huge Bonaparte has attempted to put his foot on Britain, and John Bull has cut it off. Napoleon, dancing with pain and loss of blood, drops his sword, yells out, ' Ah, you tam John Bull ! ! You have spoil my *Dance* ! ! You have ruined all my Projets.' Little John Bull, pointing to his native land, says, ' I ax pardon, Master Boney, but as we says, *Paws off, Pompey,* we keep this little spot to ourselves, you must not dance here Master Boney.'

Rowlandson (May 1, 1803), brought out ' John Bull listening to the quarrels of State affairs.' Napoleon is talking to the Chancellor, and says, ' And so—if you do *so,* I do *so.*' The Chancellor, in an evident fright, exclaims tremulously, 'Oh! Oh!!' whilst old John Bull looks on, listening, all eyes and expectation, with his hair on end, 'I declare my very wig stands on end with curiosity. What can they be quareling about? O that I could but be let into the secret! If I ax our gentleman concerning it, it is ten to one if he tells me the right story.'

On May 2, 1803, Gillray produced a very effective caricature called 'Doctor Sangrado curing John Bull of Repletion, with the kind offices of young Clyster pipe [1] and little Boney. A hint from Gil Blas.' John Bull is seated, very weak indeed, held up by Lord Hawkesbury. Fox and

Sheridan are behind, bringing warm water, and everybody in the drawing is exhorting the patient to 'Courage.' Addington is performing the operation, and the blood streams forth copiously. Napoleon catches in his cocked hat, Ceylon, Malta, Cape of Good Hope, and West Indies; whilst young Clyster pipe holds out his hat, labelled 'Clerk of the Pells,' and catches a stream '3,000*l.* per annum.' This scandalous job, his father having given him this lucrative sinecure when he was very young, excited much adverse comment at the time.

'Britannia repremanding a Naughty Boy!' (artist unknown, May 3, 1803). Britannia, with a helmet on her

---

[1] A name bestowed on young Addington.

head, her shield by her side, a spear in one hand, and a
birch rod in the other, stands on the shore at Dover.   On
the top of the cliffs is a crown on a cushion.   Napoleon,
attired, as usual, in an enormous cocked hat, stands on the
shore at Calais, whimpering, 'I'm tired of this great hat, I
will have that crown.'   But says Britannia: 'Stay where
you are, you little troublesome Urchin.   If once you cross
the Dyke you'll get a good birchin!'

'Lunar Speculations' is the whimsical title of a picture
by Ansell, May 3, 1803.   Bonaparte is looking through a
large telescope, mounted on a tripod, at the moon ; and he
is saying : 'I wonder the Idea never struck me before !
The place would easily be taken, and has undoubtedly
great capabilities—Besides they would make me Emperor :—and then, the sound of the Title EMPEROR OF
THE FULL MOON—oh ! delightful !   I'll send for Garner [1]
and his balloons and set about the scheme immediately.'
John Bull, looking at him quizzically, and holding his very
fat sides, says : 'What! going to revolutionize the Moon,
Bonny ?   That's a good one, however—To be sure, you
talk'd of paying a visit to my little island, and one should
certainly be as easily accomplished as the other.'

The situation was getting more strained daily, and
Napoleon did not mend matters by his studied discourtesy
to Lord Whitworth.

> 'Indeed,' said Whitworth, 'you mistake,
> We wish a lasting peace to make.'
> 'Pay more respect to treaties, then,'
> Cried Nap, and raised his voice again ;
> 'What use are treaties ?—all my eye—
> If violated—fie—oh fie—
> What use are treaties ? woe to those
> Who don't respect them—they're my foes ;

---

[1] Garnerin, the aeronaut.

Yes, they're my foes—I tell you flat,
And I don't value them—not that.'
This said, his argument to back,
He with his fingers gave a crack,

. . . . .

The Company were all ashamed,
And his indelicacy blamed ;
His manners were so ungenteel,
That each now turn'd upon his heel.
England's Ambassador was bent
The Consul's conduct to resent.
He sent a note of all that pass'd
From the beginning to the last,
Then sought for passports, as advis'd ;
At this the Consul was surpris'd ;
But England now was irritated,
For in the *Moniteur* 'twas stated,
That she could never, single handed,
Contend with France—so he demanded
His passports—likewise he averr'd,
That war, he to suspense, preferr'd.
His lordship's wish they strove t' evade,
The passports daily were delay'd.
Lord Whitworth, soon as they were granted,
Set off for London, as he wanted.

By way of parenthesis, I may say that Napoleon made
loud complaint about the libels published about him in
England ; and, to show the impartiality of the Government,
and their desire to do justice, even at a time when war
between the two countries was almost morally certain, a
Frenchman, named Jean Peltier, was prosecuted for libelling
him, the indictment being 'That peace existed between
N. Bonaparte and our Lord the King ; but that M. Peltier,
intending to destroy the friendship so existing, and to despoil said Napoleon of his consular dignity, did devise, print,

and publish, in the French Language, to the tenor following, &c.'

It is never worth while to go into the words of the libel
(which appeared in a periodical called *L'Ambigu*), which
is purely political, and which would never be noticed
nowadays. I only introduce the episode to shew that the
English Government even went out of their way to conciliate Bonaparte, and that the libel, as usual, sprang
from French sources.

He was unanimously found guilty, and judgment was to
have been delivered next term, but, war being renewed, he
was never called upon to appear.

CHAPTER XXVI.

THE *ULTIMATUM*—LORD WHITWORTH LEAVES PARIS—DECLARATION OF WAR—CARICATURES PREVIOUS THERETO—SURRENDER OF HANOVER.

Now came the *ultimatums* on both sides. The presentation of an *ultimatum* is hardly a personal caricature of Napoleon, but it belongs to the history of the times. One picture was published May 3, 1803, by an unknown artist, and was called 'Waste Paper.' A French officer holds four *ultimatums* in his hand, and presents John Bull with No. 1. A servant, behind, carries a huge sack of *ultimatums*. The Frenchman thus speaks : 'Monsieur Jean Bull, I am come from De Grand Nation to present you vone *Ultimatum*. If you not like dat—I present you vone oder—I have got seventy tree Tousand *Ultimatum*, and you must agree to vone or de oder—or, begar, I sal kick you out of de Europe. My lacquey has got Dem in de Sac, and will leave dem for your consideration. Health and Fraternity, Citizen Bull !' John Bull uplifts his cudgel, and his bulldog growls. Says the old man, 'Hark ye, Mr. Frog ! I was just feeling in my pocket, for a little bit of waste paper, and you have just supplied me in time : so now get you gone, or I'll shew you the use of my Horns, by tossing you out of old ENGLAND.'

But this giving of *ultimatums* was not all on one side. I. Cruikshank (May 14, 1803) drew 'Ultimatum, or the Ambassador taking proper steps.' Our ambassador [1] is

[1] Lord Whitworth.

just stepping into his carriage, and, whilst doing so, presents Napoleon with an *ultimatum*, saying, with national courtesy, ' Be quick, or d— me I'm off.'   Napoleon is depicted as being deeply affected by this conduct.   He weeps copiously, and wrings his hands, whimpering, ' Pray stop, and I will agree to anything.'

There is a caricature by an artist unknown (May 18, 1803), called ' The Bone of Contention,' which is labelled MALTA.   Bonaparte, looking very fierce, menaces John Bull with his sword, exclaiming ' By the Bridge of Lodi ! by the plains of Marengo!! by everything that is great and terrible—I command you to surrender that bone !!!!' John Bull, however, has set his foot upon that bone, and is prepared to defend it with his oaken cudgel.   He laconically replies ' You be d—d.'

This subject was also treated by Ansell (June 14, 1803) in ' The Bone of Contention, or the English Bulldog and the Corsican Monkey.'   The monkey, in a fearful and wonderful cocked hat, calls out, ' Eh ! you Bull Dog, vat you carry off dat Bone for ? I vas come to take dat myself.   I vas good mind to lick you, but for dem Dam Tooths.'   Whilst John Bull, typified as a bulldog, has the bone, Malta, firmly between his teeth, and growls defiance.

Lord Whitworth left Paris on May 12, and arrived at Dover on the 17th,[1] where he met General Andreossi, the French minister, on the point of returning to France.   On the 18th, George III. sent his Declaration of War to both Houses of Parliament, and Nelson hoisted his flag on board the *Victory*, at Portsmouth, the same day.   Thus ended a peace which had existed only one year and sixteen days.

Of course, the caricatures were, necessarily, prepared a day or two before their publication, so the dates do not depend upon the events which took place.   Such an one is

[1] *St. James's Chronicle*, May 17/19, 1803.

'Armed Heroes,' Gillray, May 18, 1803, which is amusing. It is Addington who is bestriding the Roast Beef of Old England. Lord Hawkesbury sits behind him ; whilst the two other figures respectively represent Hely Addington and Bragge Bathurst, who were members of the Addington family, and had been provided with good places by their powerful relative.

Napoleon looks with hungry eyes on the beef, and exclaims :—

> Ah, ha ! sacrè dieu ! vat do I see yonder ?
> Dat look so invitingly Red and de Vite ?
> Oh by Gar ! I see 'tis de Roast Beef of Londres
> Vich I vill chop up, at von letel bite !

ARMED HEROES.

Addington is in a curious state of mind, between bluster and fear, calling out, ' Who's afraid ? damme ?—*O Lord, O Lord,—what a Fiery Fellow he is !*—Who's afraid ? damme ? —*O dear ! what will become of y[e] Roast Beef ?* Damme ! who's afraid ?—*O dear !—O dear !*'

The medicine bottles peeping out of his pockets are a delicate allusion to Addington's parentage, his father having been a physician.

The caricatures which follow are simply dated May ;

but, from their internal evidence, they precede the declaration of war. Bonaparte is represented as being excessively frightened at the prospect of a rupture with England, and, in May 1803, an etching (artist unknown) was produced, shewing 'A Little Man Alarmed at his own Shadow.' He is cowering, and trembling, and looking back at his lengthened shadow on a wall, saying 'Mercy on us—what tall figure is that. It surely can't be Johnny Bull? No, no, that cannot be, it is not lusty enough for him.'

A very graphic caricature is 'Maniac Ravings, or Little Boney in a strong Fit. Vide Lord W——'s [1] account of a visit to the Thuilleries.' Here he is depicted in a fearful state of frenzy; he has kicked over the consular chair, a globe (with all Europe expunged, except the British Isles), dashed his hat to the ground, upset a table, with all his writings on it, broken his sword and scabbard; and, whilst tearing his hair, stamps frantically on such papers as 'Wyndham's Speeches,' 'Cobbett's Weekly Journal,' 'Anti-Jacobin Review,' 'Wilson's Egypt,' &c. His 'Maniac Ravings' are veritably so. 'Oh Egypt, Egypt, Egypt! Oh, St. Domingo, Oh! Oh, the liberty of the English Press! English Bloodhounds! Wyndham! Grenville! Pitt! Oh I'm murdered! I'm assassinated!! London Newspapers! Oh! Oh! Oh! Revenge! Revenge! come Fire! Sword! Famine! Invasion! Invasion! Four Hundred and Eighty Frenchmen! British Slavery and everlasting Chains! everlasting Chains! O Diable! the Riches! Freedom! and Happiness of the British Nation! Ah! Diable, Diable, Diable! Malta! Malta! Malta! Oh, cursed Liberty of the British Press! Insolence of British Parliament! Treaty of Amiens! Damnation! British trade and commerce! Oh! Oh! Oh! English calumniating Newspapers! Oh, Sebastiani! Sebastiani! Oh, Georges! Arras! de Rolle! Dutheil!

[1] Whitworth.

O Assassins! Treason! Treason! Treason! Hated and Betray'd by the French! Despised by the English! and laughed at by the whole world!!! Oh, English Newspapers!!! English Newspapers!!!! English Newspapers!!!!!'

Woodward drew a picture (May 1803) of 'A great Man Intoxicated with Success,' and depicted Boney with a very 'how came you so?' expression of countenance, reeling along, and saying, 'Ah Johnny Bull, how are you my Boy—I am going to re-establish slavery—I am grown very Pious. I—I—I'll double my guards. I—I—I don't know what I'll do.' John Bull is utterly astonished at such conduct. 'Why, bless your heart, my fine fellow, you be Muzzy—I dare say you find it difficult to stand. Now, let me advise you—take a little Nap—if it's only for a quarter of an hour, you can't think how much it will refresh you.'

Another caricature, apparently by Woodward, was published in May 1803, 'Bonaparte and the Quaker.' Bonaparte's attitude is decidedly aggressive and bullying : 'So they are all Great Men in your Country, eh!—but I suppose they are like you—not very fond of fighting—is not that the case Master Quaker?' Brother Broadbrim replies, 'Little Man, it is not the case. I myself encourage not fighting. But if thou, or any of thy Comrades, darest to cross the great waters, my Countrymen shall make *Quakers* of you all.'

The national feeling was well expressed in a caricature (May 1803)—Bonaparte is represented as a mighty mushroom, looking, with no very benign expression of countenance, on John Bull, who, embracing the British Oak, exclaims, 'You may look as cross as you please, master Mushroom : but here stands the British Oak, and by St. George and the Dragon, not a leaf of it shall fall to the Ground.'

On May 28, George III., as Elector of Hanover, issued a proclamation, in which he said that, abiding by

the treaty of Luneville, he would, as Elector of Hanover,
take no part in the war. But, notwithstanding this, the
Electorate of Hanover surrendered, by capitulation, to
General Mortier on June 3. This prologue is necessary
for us to understand the following halfpenny broadside :—

A PEEP INTO HANOVER,

OR

*A faint Description of the Atrocities committed by the French in
that City.*

It will be remembered, that the Electorate surrendered without
Resistance. This we do not mention, as increasing our Com-
passion for the Inhabitants, which it certainly does not ; but as
increasing our abhorrence of the Invaders, who, without Provoca-
tion, or Pretext of Resistance, have perpetrated the Atrocities, of
which the following is a faint outline :

Ever since the Conquest, the whole Electorate has been a
scene of Pillage and Butchery, which is said to yield only to the
fate of Switzerland, in Spring 1798. The French Soldiers have
the most unbounded Indulgence of their ruling passions of Rapacity, Cruelty and Lust ;— *In the City of Hanover, and even in the
Public Street, Women of the Highest Rank have been violated by
the lowest of that brutal Soldiery, in presence of their Husbands and
Fathers, and subjected, at the same time, to such additional and
undescribable Outrages, as the brutal Fury of the Violators, enflamed
by Drunkenness, could contrive.* We have seen the names of some
of these unfortunate Ladies : but the Honour of their Families, and
the Peace of their own future Lives (if they can have peace) forbid
us to publish them. The Baron de K——, a well known partisan
of French Philosophy and Politics, went to the Commandant of
Hanover, and claimed his Protection, as an admirer of the French
Revolution ! but he found no more favour in the Sight of the
Aga of Sultan BONAPARTE's Janisaries, than the most loyal
Noblemen in Hanover. The French Officer told him, ' *All that*

Jacobinism is now out of Fashion—Go about your business!'' Nor have we heard that the Philosophers of Gottingen, the Enthusiasts of *Equality and Perfectability*, have been at all better treated.—

Such are the tender Mercies of the Wicked ! Such are the Gangs of ferocious Banditti, whom the MURDERER OF JAFFA let loose on the civilized World ! Such, and ten thousand times worse, is the Fate prepared *for England, if the valour of her people do not avert it ; for England will assuredly be more oppressed, in proportion as she is more dreaded, envied, and hated.* To shew any symptom of Neutrality in such a Cause, not to support it with all our might, IS THE FOULEST TREASON AGAINST THE PEOPLE OF ENGLAND ; and the poorest honest Labourer, who has a Mother, or a Sister, a Wife, or a Daughter, has, in truth, as much reason as the highest Duke in the Land to detest the Traitor. Englishmen think of this and profit by Example.

These were the kind of handbills (of which there are hundreds in variety) which were circulated, to arouse and stimulate martial fire and patriotic ardour in the Britannic mind. Their name is Legion, and I have had to read them all, in order to pick out the examples given in this book. They are curious, and help us, more than any other history, to gauge the temper of the times. It was a veritable scare. Hardly having felt any of the benefits of peace, the English were once more involved in war, with the almost certainty, this time, of having their, hitherto almost inviolate, islands invaded by the French. We can hardly wonder, therefore, at the hearty hatred our forefathers felt for the 'Corsican Ogre,' to whom all this turmoil was due ; and, to do them justice, they did hate him with a thoroughly genuine detestation—so much so, that they did not always scrupulously investigate the truth of some of the very questionable statements dished up for

them (and they were highly spiced). There can be no
manner of doubt but that these broadsides and handbills,
together with the caricatures, had the desired effect in
rousing the nation to a fervid patriotism, and, as they did
so, it is perhaps hardly right to question the legality of
their statements, but accept them according to the doctrine
that 'the end justifies the means.'

CHAPTER XXVII

PATRIOTIC HANDBILLS.

ON June 10, 1803, Gillray published an extra-sized picture of 'French Invasion—or Buonaparte Landing in Great Britain.' The French fleet is nearing land, and boats, full of armed men, are putting off. Bonaparte, and a large body of troops, including cavalry, have landed ; but, before they can scale the cliffs, and are yet on the shore, a few artillerymen, with two guns, have utterly routed them. It is *Sauve qui peut.* Napoleon, joining in the flight, throws away his sword ; the army is utterly demoralised, the ground being strewn with dead.

I. Cruikshank drew a not very interesting caricature, (June 10, 1803) of ' The Scarecrow's arrival, or Honest PAT giving them an Irish Welcome.' Napoleon, as a skeleton, is leading an army of skeletons, who are wading through the sea. He is just putting his foot on the shore, and, to encourage his troops, calls out, ' Now, my boys, halloo away — vil frighten Mr. Bull out of his wits, we vil make them quake like the Dutch, the Italian, the Swiss, and the rest of our Friends.' But a sturdy Irishman receives them with a shovel-full of mud in their faces. ' Och it is your own pratty figure it is, Master Bonny, d'ye think that Pat was to be blarney'd by such Scare Crows. No, no, Bother, the time is gone by : Pat's Eyes are wide open, and, look ye, if you don't imme-diately jump into the Sea to save your lives, I will shovel you all there to save mine.'

Here is a stirring appeal to the army :—

BRAVE SOLDIERS.

Defenders of your COUNTRY.

THE road to glory is open before you.—Pursue the great career
of your forefathers, and rival them in the field of honour. *A
proud and usurping* TYRANT (a name ever execrated by Englishmen) dares to *threaten our shores with* INVASION, *and to reduce
the free born Sons of Britain to* SLAVERY *and* SERVITUDE. For-
getting what English Soldiers are capable of, and ranking them
with the hirelings of the powers who have fallen his prey on the
Continent, he supposes his threat easily executed. *Give him a
lesson, my brave Countrymen, that he will not easily forget, and
that France may have by heart, for a Century to come !* Neither
the vaunting Hero (who deserted his own Comrades and Soldiers
in Egypt), nor the French Army, have ever been able to cope
with British valour when fairly opposed to it. Our Ancestors
declared that ONE ENGLISHMAN *was ever a match for* THREE
FRENCHMEN—and that man to man was too great odds in our
favour. We have but to feel their sentiments, to confirm them—
you will find that their declaration was founded on experience ;
and that even in our day, within these three years, an army of
your brave Comrades has convinced its admiring Country, that
the balance is still as great as ever, against the enemy. Our
EDWARD, *the illustrious Black Prince, laid waste the country of
France, to the Gates of Paris, and, on the Plains of Cressy, left* 11
Princes and 30,000 *men dead upon the Field of Battle—a greater
number than the whole English Army boasted at the beginning of
the action.* The same heroic Prince, having annihilated the Fleet
of France, *entirely routed her Army at Poictiers, took her King
prisoner, and brought him Captive to London, with thousands of
his Nobles and People, and all this against an Army* SIX TIMES AS
NUMEROUS AS THAT OF THE ENGLISH ! Did not our Harry the
Fifth invade France, and at Agincourt *oppose an Army of* 9,000
men, sickly, fatigued, and half starved, to that of the French,

amounting to 50,000 ; and did he not leave 10,000 of the enemy dead upon the field, and take 14,000 prisoners, with the loss of only 400 men ?

Have we not, within this century, to boast a MARLBOROUGH, who, (besides his other victories) at Blenheim slew 12,000 of the French, and made 14,000 Prisoners, *and in less than a month conquered* 300 *miles of Territory from the Enemy?* Did not the gallant WOLFE, in the year 1759, gain the Heights of Abra-ham with a handful of British Troops, and, afterwards, *defeat the whole French Army, and gain possession of all* Canada, *&c.?*

And are not the glories of our ABERCROMBY *and the Gallant* ARMY *of* EGYPT fresh in your minds ? *An Army of* 14,000 *Britons, who landed in the face of upwards of* 20,000 *troops of France,* and drove from a country, with whose strongholds they were acquainted, and whose resources they knew how to apply, a host of Frenchmen, enured to the Climate, and Veterans in arms ? *Did they not cut in pieces that vaunted Corps of Buonaparte's, whose successes against other Powers had obtained for it the appella-tion of* INVINCIBLE—And is not their Standard (all that is left of it) a trophy, at this moment, in our Capital ?

The Briton fights for his Liberty and Rights, the Frenchman fights for *Buonaparte,* who has robbed him of both ! Which, then, in the nature of events, will be most zealous, most active, and most terrible in the Field of Battle ? the independent sup-porter of his country's cause, or the Slave who trembles lest the arms of his comrades should be turned against himself ; who knows that his Leader, his General, his *Tyrant, did not hesitate, after having* MURDERED 4,000 *disarmed Turks, in cool blood, to* POISON 300 *of his own sick Soldiers, of men who had been fighting his battles of ambition, and been wounded in his defence*—English Soldiers will scarcely credit this, but it is on record, not to be doubted, never to be expunged. But more ; read and blush for the depravity even of an enemy. It is not that these bloody deeds have been perpetrated from necessity, from circumstances how-ever imperious at the moment ; they were the acts of cool and deliberate determination, and his purpose, no less sanguinary, is again declared in the event of success in his enterprise against

this Country.   Feeling that even the slavish followers of his fortune were not to be forced to embark in this ruinous and destructive expedition, he declares to them, in a public proclamation, or
decoy, that *when they have landed in this Country, in order to
make the booty the richer,* No Quarter *shall be given to the* Base
English *who fight for their perfidious Government—that they shall
be* Put to the Sword, *and their Property distributed among the
Soldiers of the Victorious Army ! ! !*   Say, is this the conduct of a
Hero? is this the man who is destined to break the spirit of
Englishmen? *shall we suffer an* Assassin *to enter our blessed
Country, and despoil our fields of their produce—to massacre our
brave Soldiers in cool blood, and hang up every man who has carried
arms ?*   Your cry is vengeance for the insult—and Vengeance is
in your own hands.   It must be signal and terrible !   Like the bolt
from Heaven, let it strike the devoted Army of Invaders !   *Every
Frenchman will find his Grave where he first steps on British
ground, and not a Soldier of Buonaparte's boasted Legions shall
escape the fate his ambitious Tyrant has prepared for him !*

BRITONS STRIKE HOME !

Or your Fame is for ever blasted,—Your Liberties for ever lost ! ! !

This is very bombastic and 'high-falutin,' but Englishmen were in a very grievous fright, nevertheless.

Still harping on the prospect of a French landing, we
have a caricature by T. West (June 13, 1803) of 'Britannia
correcting an Unruly Boy.'   Britannia has got Boney
across her knee, and, having taken down his breeches, is administering such a sound castigation with a birch rod, called
the *United Kingdom,* as to bring forth copious streams of
blood.   Needless to say, our hero is repentant, and prays
'Oh forgive me this time and I never will do so again.   Oh
dear! Oh dear! you'll entirely destroy the *Honors of the
Sitting.'*   But the stern matron still keeps on, with 'There
take that, and that, and that, and be more careful not to
provoke my anger more.'

We have an illustration of the homely proverb of 'Set a beggar on horseback &c.,' in 'The Corsican Beggar Riding to the Devil,' by Ansell (June 15, 1803). Here we have Hell treated in the mediæval manner, a huge, grotesque, dragon-like head, with outstretched jaws, vomiting flames. Napoleon, on a white charger, hugging himself with the idea that 'Sure they will make me Emperor,' is riding straight to it ; whilst two devils are in a high state of jubilation. ' One opines that ' He is sure to come ; we will finish your ambition,' the other politely calls out, ' Shew him in.' Ireland asks John Bull, ' Hey Johnny, who's that ?' and gets as a reply, ' Tis Boney going Post, brother Pat.' The Gallic Cock, crowing on its dunghill, screams, ' This is nothing new.'

Here is a passionate appeal, supposed to come from one of the softer sex :—

MEN OF ENGLAND.

It is said that some of you are so discontented, that you would join the Enemies against your Country—Is it possible that you are so misled as to believe that the Enemies to England would, whatever they pretend, be friends *to you*. Be assured, if you are so persuaded, that you are grossly imposed upon. What should make them your friends—What ties should bind them ? Think a little—and a very little proper reflection will be sufficient to make you see, that the Invaders of your Country, in their hearts, hate the inhabitants of it ; and will, in the end, themselves betray the Traitors to it.

The Invaders would nearly desolate your Country—and if Provisions are dear now, what would they be when numberless stacks of hay and corn were burnt—the cattle destroyed, and a horrid legion of desperate, faithless, lawless Invaders, to be maintained ? who would trample upon every tie, break all promises, make *tools* of you first, but soon sacrifice your wives, your daughters, your families, and yourselves, when you have served their purpose. If any few among you were guilty of plunder, you would, yourselves, soon be plundered and destroyed.

It has been the necessity of defending our country against its enemies that has made provisions dear ; but your wages have been increased in proportion—and though you may sometimes, in the course of events, suffer some hardships, as *everybody*, in their turn, must do, you may, unless it be your own faults, enjoy the greatest comforts—a peaceable home—a happy family—a quiet country, whose trade and consequence is envied by all the world—plentiful harvests—a government which respects you, and that your forefathers would have defended with the last drop of their blood—you have an excellent and lawful King, who will protect you ; and above all, you may have a blessing from God, who will reward you hereafter if you do your duty *here*. But from an Usurper, and Invader, you can have nothing to expect, but the being slaves to his lawless schemes for power. Let who will tell you the contrary, he comes only for plunder, and revenge, upon the only nation he fears. Will you be his instruments, his tools ? Can you, as Englishmen, lower yourselves in such a manner—to such a mean Usurper ? Heaven, from the beginning, intended you should have Kings and superiors—Equality was never intended—it never can be, on this earth—Heaven and reason forbid it—and Bonaparte, himself, has shewn you how little he intended to establish it. Your forefathers call to you from their graves—their warning voice tells you, that you would soon find the perfidy of his heart. The wretched condition you would bring yourselves and your families into, you would repent too late—deprived of every friend, but sure of ample punishment here, and hereafter.

People of England ! Sons of my beloved glorious Country ! You are now called upon by the women of your Country to protect them—Can you refuse to hear us ? Can you bear the thought of not only seeing *us* used with insult and barbarity,—of seeing your country bleed at every pore, but of being the occasion of these dreadful evils, in consequence of your mistaken opinions, and by suffering yourselves to be deceived, and cajoled, by foreign, ill designing wretches, who have only our, and your, ruin at heart.

Attend, Men of England,—you who may give conquest to your Country, safety to us, and everlasting glory to yourselves—Attend, Men of England, to the *solemn* truths told you by an honest

ENGLISHWOMAN.

It is a weak spot in these lucubrations that very few of them are dated, so that it is impossible to arrange them, like the illustrations, in chronological sequence. But this is of little matter ; the situation was the same, whatever might .be the month.

J. Smith (June 25, 1803) etched King George 'Playing at Bubbles.' The monarch is seated before a large tub of soap-suds, amusing himself by blowing bubbles, which are *Napoleon, flat-bottomed boats, invasion, and little ships*—and, judging by the king's placid countenance, caring very little for his creations.

A very excellent example of caricature is Gillray's 'King of Brobdingnag and Gulliver' (June 26, 1803). The burly king has the diminutive Bonaparte in the palm of his hand and is critically examining him through his glass. Says he, 'My little friend Grildrig you have made a most admirable panegyric upon yourself and country, but from what I can gather from your own relation, and the answers

I have with much pains wring'd and extorted from you, I
cannot but conclude you to be one of the most pernicious
little odious reptiles that nature ever suffered to crawl upon
the surface of the Earth.'

And, indeed, he well deserved this character, if he were
anything like the demon the English sought to make him
out. In one of the handbills, however, is a quotation from
' Denon's Travels in Egypt,' which is wrested to serve its
purpose in fomenting the Invasion furor.

To the infamous WRETCH, if there be such an one in England,
who dares to talk of, or even hopes to find *Mercy* in the Breast of
the *Corsican Bonaparte*, the *eternal sworn Foe of England*, the
Conqueror and Grand Subjugator of France.

If there be any Englishmen so base, or so foolish, as to wish
to trust to the *Mercy* of a French *Invading Army*, let him read
that which follows :—The accuracy and veracity of the account
cannot be doubted, it being an Extract from a Book, not only
written under the inspection of the French Government, but,
moreover, dedicated to the *Grand Consul.*

I shall make no comment on this most scandalous public
avowal, or rather, boast, of so inhuman and atrocious a proceeding, as the simple Fact sufficiently speaks for itself.

' We, who boasted that we were more just than the Mamelukes, committed daily, and *almost necessarily*, a number of iniquities : the difficulty of distinguishing our Enemies by their Form
and Colour, made us, every day, *kill innocent Peasants* ; the
Soldiers took Caravans of *poor Merchants* for enemies, and, before
justice could be done them, (*when there was time to do it*) two or
three of them were shot, a part of their cargo was *pillaged or destroyed*, and their camels exchanged for those of ours, which had
been wounded. The Fate of the People, *for whose happiness we
no doubt came to Egypt*, was no better. If, at our approach, terror
made them leave their houses, they found on their return, nothing
but *the Mud of which the Walls were composed* ; utensils, ploughs,
gates, roofs, everything served as fuel to boil our Soup ; their pots

were broken, their grain was eaten, their fowls and pigeons roasted, and nothing was left but the carcases of their dogs, *when they defended the Property of their Masters.* If we remained in their Villages, the wretches were *summoned to return*, under pain of being treated as *Rebels*, and, in consequence, *double Taxed ;* and when they yielded to these Menaces, came *to pay their Tax*, it sometimes happened, that, from their great number, they were taken for a body of Revolters, their sticks for arms, and they received *some discharges of Musketry before there was time for explaining the Mistake* ; the Dead were interred, and we remained friends, till a safe opportunity for revenge occurred. It is true, that when they staid at home, *paid the Tax, and supplied all the Wants of the Army*, they were saved the trouble of a Journey to a Residence in the Desert, *saw their Provisions consumed with regularity*, and *were allowed* a Part of them, preserved some of their gates, sold their eggs to the Soldiers, AND HAD BUT FEW OF THEIR WIVES AND DAUGHTERS VIOLATED ! '

Such was the Treatment which Egypt experienced ; a Country which the French were desirous to possess, and to conciliate ; very Different is their Design upon Great Britain, which it is their avowed Intention to Ravage, Plunder and Destroy.

CHAPTER XXVIII.

INEFFECTUAL attempts at mediation seem to have been made, but, situated as the two opposing Powers were, this could not be.

'Bruin become mediator' (artist unknown, June 1803) represents the Emperor of Russia as a bear, joining the hands of a Bull and a Monkey. The peacemaker thus addresses them, 'I wonder you civilized folks could not agree upon matters without reference to me, whom you have ridiculed as a Barbarian—but I suppose you think I must have more sense than yourselves, because I come further North.' The Monkey is giving his hand with 'I promise on the faith of a Frenchman (which is as any Birmingham Sixpence) to let you graze quietly in the Malta Paddock—and to love you with all my heart, as much as I do the Liberty of the French Nation.' The Bull says, 'Well Nappy, if you will leave off your Pranks and not think of skipping over to Egypt, and if you will promise not to hop the twig to Hanover, I will be reconciled.'

And again, a month later, is another caricature, called 'Olympic Games, or John Bull introducing his new Ambassador to the Grand Consul,' by I. Cruikshank (July 16, 1803), shewing us the little Corsican giving an ambassador a blow in the face with his clenched fist, saying, 'There

Sir, take that, and tell your master, I'll thrash every one who dares to speak to me : I'll thrash all the World. D— me I'll, I'll, I'll, be King of the Universe.' The astonished Ambassador exclaims, 'Why this is Club Law! this is the Argument of force indeed. The little Gentleman is De-rangé.' John Bull, however, is introducing a prize-fighter as his representative, telling Napoleon, 'There, my Boy, is an Ambassador who will treat with you in your own way— but I say, be as gentle with him as you can.' The pugilist looks on his adversary with contempt, 'What! is it that little whipper snapper I am to set to with? Why I think the *first round* will settle his hash.' The Austrian ambassador meanwhile remarks, 'The Monarch I represent, will return this insult with becoming Dignity.'

Martial enthusiasm was at its height, corps of volunteers were enrolled everywhere. The militia, 80,000 strong, had been called out on March 25 ; there was the regular army of 130,000, and, on June 28, the House of Commons agreed to the raising of 50,000 more, by means of conscription—of which England was to furnish 34,000, Ireland 10,000, and Scotland 6,000 ; whilst, on June 30, the Court of Common Council for the City of London resolved to raise, and equip, 800 men for the national service. This, be it remembered, only represented that portion of London within the city walls. Factions were for a time done away with, and men, of all shades of politics, stood shoulder by shoulder, as now, in the ranks of the different volunteer corps. Stirring broadsides were not needed, although they appeared, and the following may be taken as a good sample :—

ENGLISH MASTIFFS.

WE by this Address, publicly and solemnly, before God and our Country, pledge our Fortunes, Persons, and Lives, in the Defence of our Sovereign, and all the Blessings of our glorious Constitution.

There is not a Man that hears me, I am persuaded, who is not prompt and eager to redeem that pledge. There is not, there cannot be a Man here, who would leave undefended, our good, tried, and brave OLD KING in the Hour of Danger.

No, Sir ! we need now no Warning-voice ; no string of Eloquence ; no Thoughts that heat, and Words that burn, are necessary to raise a Host of hardy Men, when the King, the Parliament, and the Country are in Distress.[1] CALL OUT TO YORKSHIREMEN, ' COME FORTH TO BATTLE !' our Answer will be—One and All— ' WE ARE READY !—*There is the Enemy !*—Lead on !' Sir, that Enemy is not far off ; a very numerous, well appointed, ably commanded Army, to whom is promised the Plunder of England, are now hovering round, and Part of them in daily Sight of the Promised Land. They view it, like so many famished Wolves, Cruel as Death, and Hungry as the Grave, panting for an Opportunity, at any Risk, to come into our Sheep Fold ;—*but*, and if they should, is it not our Business, our first Duty, to have such a Guard of old, faithful ENGLISH MASTIFFS, of the old Breed, as shall make them quickly repent their temerity.

The Chief Consul of France tells us, that we are but a Nation of Shopkeepers : let us, Shopkeepers, then melt our Weights, and our Scales, and return him the Compliment in Bullets. Sir ; we may have a firm Reliance on the Exertions of as gallant a Fleet as ever sailed ; but the Fleet cannot perform Impossibilities ; it cannot be in two places at once ; it cannot conquer the Winds, and subdue the Storms. Though our old Tars can do much, they cannot do everything ; and it would be unsafe and dastardly to lie

---

[1] Is from Mr. Stanhope's speech at a meeting of Yorkshire noblemen and gentlemen, at the Castle, York, July 28, 1803, for the purpose of addressing the king on the situation of the country.

skulking behind them. With the Blessing of God, and a good Cause, we can do Wonders ; but if we depend upon our Naval Prowess only, we have much to fear. NO, SIR : England will never be perfectly safe, until she can defend herself as well by *Land*, as by *Sea* ; until she can defy the haughty Foe : if there was *even a Bridge* between Calais and Dover, and that Bridge in Possession of the Enemy, still can she say, in the Language of a good *English Boxing Match*, 'A FAIR FIELD AND NO FAVOUR.'

'Our good, tried, and brave OLD KING, in the Hour of Danger,' had made all snug, at least as far as human foresight could act. When the dreaded invasion came, he was to go either to Chelmsford or Dartford ; whilst the Queen, with the Royal Family and the treasure, were to go to Worcester, the city whose motto is 'Civitas in bello, et in pace, fidelis.' All the stores at Woolwich, including the artillery, were to be sent into the Midlands by means of the Grand Junction Canal ; in fact, every precaution was taken that forethought could devise : and there is but little doubt that, had Napoleon made good a landing, he would have had a warmer reception than he expected. Yet what disadvantages they laboured under compared to our days ! no Telegraphs, no Railways, no Steam. Of course it may be said that the enemy was in no better position ; but still a lucky wind might favour their crossing, and hinder our preventing it.

Loyal and patriotic poetry abounded ; here is a specimen :—

THE VOICE OF THE BRITISH ISLES.

TUNE—'*Hearts of Oak.*'

Away, my brave boys, haste away to the shore ;
Our foes, the base French, boast they're straight coming o'er,
To murder, and plunder, and ravish, and burn—
Let them come—we'll take care they shall never return ;

O 2

For around all our shores, hark ! the notes loudly ring,
   United, we're ready,
   Steady, boys, steady,
To fight for our Liberty, Laws, and our King.

They boast in the dark they will give us the slip :
The attempt may procure them a dangerous dip ;
Our bold Tars are watching in Ocean's green lap,
To give them a long *Jacobinical* nap.[1]
But should they steal over, with one voice we'll sing,
   United, we're ready, &c.

They knew, that united, we sons of the waves
Would ne'er bow to Frenchmen, nor grovel like Slaves ;
So ere they dare venture to touch on our strand,
They sent black Sedition to poison our land.
But around all our shores let the notes loudly ring,
   United, we're ready, &c.

They swore we were slaves, all lost and undone ;
That a Jacobine nostrum, as sure as a gun,
Would make us all equal, and happy, and free ;
'Twas only to dance round their Liberty's tree.
No, no ! round our shores let the notes loudly ring,
   United, we're ready, &c.

'Twas only to grant them the kiss call'd fraternal—
A kiss which all Europe has found most infernal ;
And then they maintained the effect could not miss—
We should all be as blest as the Dutch and the Swiss.
No, no ! round our shores let the notes loudly ring,
   United, we're ready, &c.

With lies, and with many a Gallican wile,
They spread their dread poison o'er Erin's green Isle ;
But now each *shillalah* is ready to thwack,
And baste the lean ribs of the Gallican Quack.
All around Erin's shores, hark ! the notes loudly ring,
   United, we're ready, &c.

---

[1] 'Death is an eternal sleep,' *vide* Robespierre's Decree.

Stout Sandy, our brother, with heart, and with hand,
And his well-try'd *Glaymore*, joins the patriot band.
Now Jack, Pat, and Sandy thus cordial agree,
We sons of the wave shall for ever be free.
While around all our shores, hark ! the notes loudly ring,
   United, we're ready, &c.

As they could not deceive, now they threaten to pour
Their hosts on our land, to lay waste and devour ;
To drench our fair fields, and our cities in gore,
Nor cease to destroy till Britannia's no more.
Let them come if they dare—hark ! the notes loudly ring,
   United, we're ready, &c.

My sweet rosy Nan is a true British wife,
And loves her dear Jack, as she loves her own life ;
Yet she girds on my sword, and smiles while I glow,
To meet the proud French, and to lay their heads low,
And chants 'tween each buss, while the notes loudly ring,
   My Jack, art thou ready ?
   Steady, boy, steady,
Go fight for thy Liberty, Laws, and thy King.

And Ned, my brave Lad, with a true British heart,
Has forsaken his plough, has forsaken his cart ;
E'en Dolly has quitted, to dig in a trench,
All, all, for the sake of a cut at the French ;
While he sings all day long, let the notes loudly ring,
   I'm ready, I'm ready !
   Steady, boy, steady,
To fight for my Liberty, Laws, and my King.

Away then, my boys ! haste away to the shore,
Our foes, the base French, boast they're straight coming o'er,
To murder, and plunder, and ravish, and burn—
They may come,—but, by Jove, they shall never return ;
For around all our shores, hark ! the notes loudly ring,
   United, we're ready,
   Steady, boys, steady,
To fight for our Liberty, Laws, and our King.

'The Final Pacification of Europe' (artist unknown, June 1803) shews that this desirable thing could only be accomplished by the death of Napoleon—so he is represented as being suspended from a gallows, whilst postboys, duly equipped with horns, and dressed in their different national garbs, are shouting, 'Good News for Russia, Prussia, Old England, Germany, and Switzerland.' Holland is excessively joyful: Mynheer calling out, 'Good news for Holland, ti-lol-de-riddle-lol.'

A very amusing caricature is 'Green Spectacles, or Consular Goggles' (artist unknown, June 1803), where Napoleon is represented as sitting on a rock called *Usurped Power*, and wearing an enormous pair of green goggles labelled 'Green eyed Jealousy,' through which he darts envious glances at Great Britain, West Indies, East Indies, Malta, and Egypt.

CHAPTER XXIX.

PATRIOTIC HANDBILLS, ETC.

WE meet with a slight notice of Toussaint l'Ouverture, and the war in St. Domingo, in a broadside dwelling on the consequences of a successful invasion : ' Here then there would be no *volunteering*, no *balloting*, unless, indeed, such Volunteers as were raised in France for the conquest of St. Domingo. And how were they raised ? Why, by every man having a bayonet put to his breast, being seized by force, and then *chained in couples like dogs*, and drove down in a string to the coast, for embarkation, like so many *Galley slaves*. This, though it may sound incredible to an Englishman's ear, is a fact known to all Europe.

' Such my brave Countrymen, would be your dreadful fate, could this blessed island be once subjugated to that haughty and merciless Tyrant, the Corsican Bonaparte. Where then, is the Man who would not die a thousand, and a thousand deaths sooner than submit to so cruel and unnatural a fate ? '

July was very prolific of these broadsheets, some of them taking the form of theatrical announcements, two of which are here given.

THEATRE ROYAL, ENGLAND.

IN REHEARSAL, AND MEANT TO BE SPEEDILY *ATTEMPTED*,

A FARCE

IN ONE ACT, CALLED THE

INVASION OF ENGLAND.

Principal Buffo .   . MR. BUONAPARTE,

Being his FIRST (and most likely his Last) Appearance on this Stage.

Anticipated Critique.

The structure of this Farce is very *loose*, and there is a moral, and radical, Defect in the Ground work. It boasts, however, considerable Novelty, for the Characters are ALL MAD. It is probable it will *not* be played in the COUNTRY, but will certainly never be *acted* in TOWN ; where ever it may be represented, we will do it the justice to say, it will be received with *Thunders* of . . . CANNON ! ! ! but we will venture to affirm will never equall the Success of

JOHN BULL.

It is however likely that the Piece may yet be put off on account of the Indisposition of the Principal Performer, Mr. BUONAPARTE. We don't exactly know what this Gentleman's Merits may be on the Tragic Boards of France, but he will never succeed here ; his Figure is very diminutive, he struts a great deal, seems to have no Conception of his *Character*, and treads the Stage very badly ; notwithstanding which defects, we think, if he comes here, he will get an ENGAGEMENT, though it is probable that he will, shortly after, be reduced to the situation of a SCENE SHIFTER.

As for the Farce, we recommend it to be withdrawn, as it is the opinion of all Political Critics, that if played, it will certainly be

DAMN'D.

' *Vivant Rex et Regina.*'

The other is :—

IN REHEARSAL,

THEATRE ROYAL OF THE UNITED KINGDOMS.

Some Dark, Foggy Night, about November next, will be ATTEMPTED, by a Strolling Company of French Vagrants, an Old Pantomomic Farce, called

HARLEQUIN'S INVASION

OR THE

DISAPPOINTED BANDITTI.

WITH NEW MACHINERY, MUSIC, DRESSES, AND DECORATIONS.

HARLEQUIN BUTCHER, BY MR. BUONAPARTE

FROM CORSICA.

(Who Murdered that Character in *Egypt, Italy, Switzerland, Holland,* &c.)

THE OTHER PARTS BY

MESSRS. SIEYES, LE BRUN, TALLEYRAND, MARET, ANGEREAU, MASSENA, AND THE REST OF THE GANG.

In the Course of the Piece will be introduced a Distant View of

Harlequin's Flat-Bottomed Boats

WARMLY ENGAGED BY THE

WOODEN WALLS OF OLD ENGLAND.

THE REPULSE.

OR, BRITONS TRIUMPHANT.

The Parts of John Bull, Paddy Whack, Sawney Mac Snaish, and Shone-ap-Morgan, by Messrs. NELSON, MOIRA, ST. VINCENT, GARDNER, HUTCHINSON, WARREN, PELLEW, S. SMITH, &c. &c. &c.

The Chorus of '*Hearts of Oak,*' by the JOLLY TARS and ARMY of OLD ENGLAND,

Assisted by a Numerous Company of Provincial Performers, Who have VOLUNTEERED their Services on this Occasion.

The Overture to consist of 'Britons Strike Home'—'Stand to your Guns'—'Rule Britannia' and

GOD SAVE THE KING.

The Dresses will be splendid ; the Band numerous and compleat. The whole to conclude with a GRAND ILLUMINATION, and a TRANSPARENCY displaying BRITANNIA receiving the Homage of GALLIC SLAVES.

*** No Room for Lobby Loungers.   *Vivant Rex et Regina.*

According to the caricaturist, Hanover had no special
attractions for Bonaparte. 'Boney in possession of the
Millstone' (Ansell, July 5, 1803) shews him as having a
fearfully large and weighty millstone hung round his neck,
called Hanover. He totters under the weight, and calls
out that 'It's cursed heavy! I wish it had been Malta!'
John Bull, dressed as a countryman, jeers him: 'What!
thee hast got it, hast thee? The Devil do thee good with
it—Old Measter Chatham used to say it was a Millstone
about my neck—so perhaps I may feel more lightsome
without it.'

'Flags of Truth and Lies' (artist unknown, July 10,
1803) is a representation of a typical Frenchman and
Englishman, as then imagined. The Frenchman holds a
tricoloured flag, and intimates that 'Mon grande Maître
bid-a you read dat, Monsieur!' and points to the following
text on the flag: 'Citizen first Consul Buonaparte presents
Compliments and Thanks to the Ladies and Gentlemen of
Great Britain, who have honored him with their visits at
Paris, and intends himself the pleasure of returning it in
person, as soon as his arrangements for that purpose can be
completed.' John Bull replies, 'And let your Grand Master
read that, Mounseer,' and points to his flag, the Union
Jack, on which is written 'John Bull does not rightly understand the Chief Consul's lingo—but supposes he means
something about Invasion; therefore the said John Bull
deems it necessary to observe that if his Consular Highness
dares to invade any Ladies or Gentlemen on his coast, he'll
be damn'd if he don't sink him.'

THE DEVIL AND THE CONSUL.

A New Song.

As the Devil thro' Paris one Day took a Walk,
BUONAPARTE he met,—and they both had some Talk ;
Great Hero, says *Satan*, pray how do you do?
I am well, cried the Consul, my Service to you.
   Derry down, down, down, derry down !

What News do you bring from your Empire below,
How is OLIVER CROMWELL ?   But very so, so !
I fancy he envies your *glories* so great ;
For he vows he ne'er reigned in such Splendor and State—
     Derry down, &c.

Tho' he often exerted himself in *my* Cause,
Still Britons from him, had some excellent Laws ;
How much below yours all his Merits must fall,
Who rules this *Republic* without Laws at all ! ! !
     Derry down, &c.

ALEXANDER, and CÆSAR, fine Heroes in Story,
Are jealous, I know, of your Deeds, and your Glory ;
Tho' they push'd thro' the Globe all their Conquests pell mell,
And rul'd *Monarchs* on Earth, now they're *Subjects* in Hell.
     Derry down, &c.

'Bout Religion at Rome you once made a great Pother,
Have pulled down one *Pope*, and then set up another !
In *Egypt* I've heard of your *wonderful* Works,
How Mahomet you worshipp'd, to flatter the Turks !
     Derry down, &c.

The Deeds you there acted with *Poison* and Ire,
On my Realms are recorded in Letters of Fire ;
Not an *Imp* in my Service, but boasts of your Fame,
And ' grins, horribly' grins—when he mentions your name.
     Derry down, &c.

You boast much, dear CONSUL, of Liberty's Tree,
You say that the *Dutch* and the *Swiss* are quite free !
If such Freedom as this to give Britain's your aim,
Try your skill, that I soon to yourself may lay claim !
                         Derry down, &c.

When the Time shall arrive that's determin'd by Fate—
That you quit for INVASION your Consular Seat ;
Fear not—if bold Britons should prove your o'erthrow,
You're sure of a *Seat* in my Kingdom below !
                         Derry down, &c.

DEATH OF THE CORSICAN FOX.

Gillray (July 20, 1803) produced the ' Death of the Corsican Fox—Scene, the last of the Royal Hunt,' in which
George III. holding his horse's bridle, with one hand holds
up the Corsican Fox, to throw to his hounds, St. Vincent,
Nelson, Sydney Smith, Gardner, Cornwallis, and others—
shouting merrily, meanwhile, 'Tally ho ! Tally ho! ho! ho!
ho ! '

CHAPTER XXX.

INVASION SQUIBS, CONTINUED—BONAPARTE'S TEN COMMANDMENTS, ETC.

THE NEW MOSES

OR

BONAPARTE'S TEN COMMANDMENTS.

Translated from a French Manuscript,

BY SOLIMAN THE TRAVELLER.

And when the great man came from Egypt, he used cunning, and force, to subject the people. The good, as well as the wicked, of the land trembled before him, because he had won the hearts of all the fighting men ; and, after he had succeeded in many of his schemes, his heart swelled with pride, and he sought how to ensnare the people more and more, to be the greatest man under the Sun.

The Multitude of the people were of four kinds ; some resembled blind men, that cannot see ; some were fearful, who trembled before him ; others courageous, and for the good of the people, but too weak in number ; and others yet, who were as wicked as the great man himself. And when he was at the head of the deluded nation, he gave strict laws, and the following commandments, which were read before a multitude of people, and in a full congregation of all his priests :

1. Ye Frenchmen, ye shall have no other commander above me, for I, Bonaparte, am the supreme head of the nation, and

will make all nations bow down to you, and obey me, as your Lord, and Commander.

2. Ye shall not have any graven images upon your coin, in marble, wood, or metal, which might represent any person above me ; nor shall ye acknowledge any person to excel me, whether he be among the living or the dead ; whether he be in the happy land of the enlightened French, or in the cursed island of the dull English ; for I, the Chief Consul of France, am a jealous hero, and visit disobedience of an individual upon a whole nation, and of a father upon the children, and upon the third and fourth generation of them that hate me ; and shew mercy unto those that love me, and humble themselves.

3. Ye shall not trifle with my name, nor take it in vain ; nor shall you suffer that any other nation treat it disrespectfully, for I will be the sole commander upon earth, and make you triumph over your enemies.

4. Remember, that ye keep the days of prayers, and pray for me as the head of the Nation and the future Conqueror of the base English. Ye shall pray fervently, with your faces cast upon the ground, and not look at the priest when he pronounces my name ; for I am a jealous hero, and delight in my priests, because they are humble, and I have regarded the lowliness of their hearts, and forgiven them all their past iniquities. And ye priests, remember the power of him, who made you his creatures, and do your duty.

5. Respect and honour all French heroes, that ye may find mercy in mine eyes for all your iniquities, and that ye may live in the land, in which I, the Lord, your Commander, live.

6. Ye shall not murder each other, save it be by my own commands, for purposes that may be known to me alone ; but of your enemies, and all those nations that will not acknowledge your, and my, greatness, ye may kill an infinite number ; for that is a pleasing sight in the eyes of your supreme commander.

7. Ye shall not commit adultery at home, whatever ye may do in the land of infidels, and the stiff-necked people ; for they are an abomination to the Lord, your Commander.

8. Ye shall not steal at home, but suppress your covetousness,

and insatiable desire of plunder, until ye may arrive in the land of our enemies. Ye shall neither steal from them with indiscretion, but seem to give with the left hand, when the right taketh.

9. Ye shall not bear false witness against your neighbour, if he should distinguish himself in the land of the enemies.

10. Ye shall not covet any thing of your neighbour, but everything of your enemies ; his jewels, his gold, his silver, his horse or ass, his maid, his daughter, his wife, or anything in which your hearts find delight ; and ye may take it, but still with cunning ; for the Lord, your Commander, loveth mildness, more than strength, to please the people when he plunders.—Use the sword in battle, cunning after it, look for plunder, but subject the people to me ;—herein lie all my commandments, and those who keep them shall be protected by my power and prosper in all my undertakings.

MASTER BONEY'S
HEARTY WELCOME TO ENGLAND.

Being the Song of Songs, and worth all the Songs in the World put together.

To be sung, or said, by every Jovial Fellow, who is a
True Lover of our good King and most happy
Constitution.

Should Boney come hither, our Britons declare,
They'd flog the dog well—you may surely guess where :
While others have vow'd, they would hang him as high,
As Haman the Jew—'twixt the earth and the sky.
      Boney down, down, down, Boney down.

Some say they will treat him no better than fleas,
And 'twixt thumb and finger they'll give him a squeeze ;
Whilst some by the ears, the vile Ruffian they'll lug,
And others will give him a good Cornish hug.
      Boney down, &c.

Nay, many would clap him in cage for a show,
At two pence a piece, Sirs—the price is too low :

Whilst others would drive him post haste to the Tower,
A *tit-bit* for tygers and wolves to devour.

Boney down, &c.

Stand by, says young Snip, don't you see my bold shears?
For the least I will have, is his nose or his ears ;
Says the Cook, I will baste him, and humble his pride,
Cries the Tanner, Pox take him, I'll tan his vile hide.

Boney down, &c.

Says the Butcher, I'll knock down the dog like an ox,
Cries the Constable bold—put the knave in the Stocks ;
Says the Chandler, when once to the Pill'ry he hies,
Rotten eggs will I furnish to bung up his eyes.

Boney down, &c.

Says the Doctor, I'm ready to give him a pill,
For the doctors, like Boney, they know how to kill ;
Says the Lawyer, I'll make the cur presently mute,
When once I shall bring him the cost of his suit.

Boney down, &c.

Cries the Huntsman, I long on his shoulders to ride,
I warrant a good pair of spurs I'll provide.
Says the Welchman, I'll toast him as I would toast cheese ;
Says Paddy, I'll whack him, as long as you *plase.*

Boney down, &c.

Cries a brave bonny Scot, Mon, gee mee his *lug*,
And I'll squeeze him as flat as a *bonnock* or bug ;
Says old Suds, I will shave him with razor so notch'd,
As shall leave his black muzzle most famously scotch'd.

Boney down, &c.

Says the Dust-man, I'll *dust* him—you know what I mean,
I'll give him a hide, all black, blue and green ;
Says the Mason, I'll case him in good bricks and mortar,
No, no, says Jack Ketch—don't you see this nice *halter ?*

Boney, down, &c.

Says the Baker, the Rogue in my oven I'll poke ;
Cries young Sweep—in the chimney I'll give him a smoke ;
The Cobler will give him a stitch in the heel,
And here's Moll, who would skin him as clean as an eel.
Boney down, &c.

But here's Tom the Miller, who swears he'll have Boney,
And grind him as close as—Old Hunks keeps his money,
Nay, stop, cries the Joiner, I'll saw off his head,
Cries the Surgeon, we'll have him as soon as he's dead.
Boney down, &c.

Then stretch the Dog out, and when flat on his back,
We'll cut out his heart to see if it's black ;
For sure such another, no mortal e'er saw,
Unless vomited forth, from old Belzebub's maw.
Boney down, &c.

But now for his flesh—we must lay bare his bones,
And then let him stand clear of Old *Davy Jones*,[1]
But Davy will have him, as sure as a gun,
So now Master Boney, here ends all your fun.
Boney down, &c.

The Soldiers will stick him—the Sailor he cries,
He'll never come hither, the Rascal's too wise ;
He knows that the Tars of Old England ne'er shrink,
But him, and his flat-bottom'd boats they will sink.
Boney down, &c.

'Twou'd weary your patience to hear folks repeat,
How Boney the *Pigmy* they're anxious to treat ;
So let him come hither, we'll soon make a ring,
Then fight till we die, for our Country and King.
Boney down, &c.

---

[1] Another name for old Nick.

Among the caricatures, West gives us (July 1803) 'A British Chymist Analizing a Corsican Earth Worm !!' Bonaparte is in a retort, being distilled, and George the Third is examining a cup of his extract, with a magnifying glass, saying, 'I think I can now pretty well ascertain the ingredients of which this insect is composed—viz.—Ambition and self sufficiency, two parts—Forgetfulness— one part—some light Invasion Froth, on the surface, and a prodigious quantity of fretful passion, and conceited Arrogance is the residue !! '

'Little Ships, or John Bull very Inquisitive' (artist unknown, July 1803), shews us Napoleon employed in cutting toy ships out of bits of wood ; he has already filled a large basket with them, and has two or three before him, on a table.   John Bull, with a terrific oaken cudgel, comes suddenly upon him, saying, 'I ax Pardon for coming in with my hat on, without knocking—but, hearing a nation thumping in your workshop—thought I may as well step up stairs, and see what the youngster is about.'   Napoleon replies, 'Don't be alarm'd Johnny—I am only making a few little Ships, for my own Private Amusement.'

The following broadside was printed with different headings, so as to sell in different counties—

TWENTY THOUSAND POUNDS
REWARD.

MIDDLESEX (to wit)

To all Constables, Head boroughs, Tithing Men, and other Officers
of the County of Middlesex, and to every of whom it may
concern,

WHEREAS a certain ill disposed Vagrant, and common disturber, commonly called, or known by the name of NAPOLEON BONAPARTE, *alias* Jaffa Bonaparte, *alias* Opium Bonaparte, *alias*

Whitworth Bonaparte, *alias* Acre Bonaparte, still continues to go about swindling and defrauding divers Countries, Cities, Towns, and Villages, under divers, various, and many false and wicked pretences, out of their Rights, Comforts, Conveniences, and Cash ; AND WHEREAS the said NAPOLEON BONAPARTE, *alias* Jaffa Bonaparte, *alias* Opium Bonaparte, *alias* Whitworth Bonaparte, *alias* Acre Bonaparte, hath been guilty of divers Outrages, Rapes, and Murders, at *Jaffa, Rosetta*, and elsewhere ; AND WHEREAS It is strongly suspected that the said NAPOLEON BONAPARTE, *alias* Jaffa Bonaparte, *alias* Opium Bonaparte, *alias* Whitworth Bonaparte, *alias* Acre Bonaparte, hath in contemplation at the Day of the Date of these presents, to land in some, (but in what, part is not yet known) of Great Britain or Ireland : WE DO hereby will and require, that in case the said NAPOLEON BONAPARTE, *alias* Jaffa Bonaparte, *alias* Opium Bonaparte, *alias* Whitworth Bonaparte, *alias* Acre Bonaparte, shall be found to *lurk*, and *wander* up and down your Bailiwick, that you bring before us the body of the said NAPOLEON BONAPARTE, *alias* Jaffa Bonaparte, *alias* Opium Bonaparte, *alias* Whitworth Bonaparte, *alias* Acre Bonaparte, on or before the Morrow [1] of All Souls, that he may be forthwith sent to our Jail for WILD BEASTS, situate, standing, and being, over Exeter 'Change in the Strand, without *Bail* or *Mainprize* ; and that he be there placed in a certain Iron Cage, with the Ouran Outang, or some other ferocious and voracious animal like himself, for the purpose of being tamed, or until a warrant shall issue to our beloved subject *Jack Ketch*, to deal with him according to Law and the *Virtue* of his Office ; and this in no-wise omit at your peril. Witness our hands

JOHN DOE and RICHARD ROE.

The said NAPOLEON BONAPARTE, *alias* Jaffa Bonaparte, *alias* Opium Bonaparte, *alias* Whitworth Bonaparte, *alias* Acre Bona parte, is a Corsican by birth, about five feet four inches in height of a swarthy black complexion, dark hair and eye brows, and resembles a great deal in person, a Bear-leader, or one of the

---

[1] November 3.

Savoyards who play on the reeds at Vauxhall : he is remarkable
for walking fast, and taking long strides, and has been thought to
squint, though it is, in fact, no more than a *cast* in the left eye,
with looking too much at one object—Old England—to which
over application, he also owes being afflicted with the Jaundice.

The above reward will be paid by the County immediately on
apprehension.

CHAPTER XXXI.

INVASION, *continued*—'BRITONS, STRIKE HOME'—BONAPARTE'S WILL.

AT this time much use was made of the phrase 'Britons, strike home!' which first appears in an adaptation of Beaumont and Fletcher's play of 'Bonduca,' or Boadicea—which was set to music by Henry Purcell in 1695. The few words are not in the original drama, but are interpolated with other songs, and form a solo and chorus.

But these simple words would hardly suit the times, so a brand new patriotic song was evolved, embodying the title

BRITONS, STRIKE HOME!

A New Song.

Should Frenchmen e'er pollute Britannia's strand,
Or press with hostile hoof this sacred land;
The daring deed should every Briton arm,
To save his native land from dire alarm;
Her free born Sons should instant take the field,
The Altar and the Throne at once to shield.

  Britons, strike home! avenge your Country's cause,
  Protect your *King*, your *Liberties*, and *Laws!*

Repel the Foe, that, desperate, dares invade
The land protected by great Sydney's shade;
And in the cause for which your Hampden bled,
Should ev'ry Briton's blood be freely shed;

A cause no less than Liberty and Life,
The poor Man's Home, his Children and his Wife.
> Britons, strike home ! &c.

The base Usurper comes—his troops advance,
And line, with threat'ning front, the shores of France ;
Already has the Despot given the word ;
Already has he drawn his blood stain'd sword ;
While *Jaffa's* plains attest th' Assassin's skill,
Poison and blood—the dagger and the pill.
> Britons, strike home ! &c.

No common war we wage, our *native land*
Is menac'd by a murderous, ruthless band ;
The Throne and Altar by their Chief o'erturn'd,
And at his feet one half the prostrate world !
' Plunder and Rape and Death ' 's the hostile cry,
' Fire to your towns—to Britons slavery ! '
> Britons, strike home ! &c.

Come, Bonaparte, come ! we are prepar'd ;
No British heart a foreign foe e'er fear'd.
What ! tho' an abject world in arms should rise,
In *England's* cause, a Briton death defies ;
If to herself she prove but firm and true,
Gaul, and her frantic Chief, she'll make to rue.
> Britons, strike home ! &c.

Plung'd in the deep, her navy we'll confound,
Or with French blood manure our British ground ;
Drive backward to the sea the Gallic slaves,
And whelm their host, like Pharaoh's, in the waves ;
Restore lost Peace and Plenty to our isle,
And make the land again with gladness smile.
> Britons, strike home ! &c.

There is an amusing picture by West (July 1803) called
Amusement after Dinner, or The Corsican Fairy display-

ing his Prowess.' George the Third and Queen Charlotte
are at dessert, which is, as was their whole *ménage*, frugal,
consisting only of a blancmange—the top ornament of
which is a fleet of ships, behind which is a pineapple (the
King fruit, as it was called on its introduction into England),
the summit of which bears a crown. The royal pair are
highly amused by the antics of the Corsican fairy (Napoleon)
who vapours about the table in huge cocked hat and enormous sword. Pointing to the blancmange, he says, 'If I
could but get over this dish of Blanche Mange, I would
soon invade the Pine Apple.'

In 'A Monstrous Stride,' by I. Cruikshank (July 25,
1803), Bonaparte is represented as flourishing his sword
and, having one foot on Turkey and Poland, is attempting
to put the other on Great Britain, but steps short, and
comes among the fleet guarding the English shores.
Underneath the picture is ' He will put his foot in it.'

There was a somewhat amusing political squib on
Napoleon, published some time in July of this year, entitled

BONAPARTE'S WILL.

In the name of my Trinity, the Goddess of Reason, Mahomet
the Prophet, and Pius the Pope ; We the most great, most mag-
nanimous, and most puissant BRUTUS ALY NAPOLEON BONA-
PARTE, son to a Spy, grandson to a Butcher, and great-grandson
to a Galley Slave, Emperor of the Gauls, First Consul of France,
President of Italy, Landamman of Switzerland, Director of Holland,
King of Etruria, Protector of Emperors, Dictator and Creator of
Kings, Electors, Princes, Cardinals, Senators, Generals, Bishops,
Prefects, Actors, Schoolmasters, &c., &c., &c., do declare, that
notwithstanding the adulation of our Slaves, and their assurances
of immortality, the pangs of our conscience, the decay of our
body, the fear of recoiling daggers, the dreadful anticipation of
infernal machines emitting fire and smoke, invented at Jaffa, and

the hissing breath of the poisonous serpents generated at El Arish, remind us that we soon must die, and that our power must die with us. We, therefore, according to the *Senatus Consultum* of our free Senate, do declare this to be our last Will and Testament, as follows :

Imprimis.

To our most beloved, and dearest *Ibrahim Rostan*, Mameluke, we give and bequeath after our decease, the crown of Henry IV., the sceptre of Saint Louis, and the throne of France and Navarre, the sovereignty and sovereign disposal of the lives and fortunes of thirty millions of Frenchmen, of six millions of Italians, of seven millions of Spaniards, of two millions of Helvetians, and of three millions of Batavians, (except as is hereafter excepted) and we enjoin and charge all the world to acknowledge, adore, and respect this Mameluke, *Ibrahim Rostan*, the African, as the natural and legal successor of us, *Brutus Aly Napoleon Bonaparte*, the Corsican.

We give and bequeath in reversion, to Citizen *Barras*, our dear Consort, much improved, and more enriched, but reserving to ourselves the disposal of her virtuous Maids of Honour, whom we give and bequeath to our *Legion of Honour*, as a reward due as well to the virtues of the one, as to the valour of the other.

We give and bequeath to our dearly beloved brother *Joseph*, the presidency of the Italian Republic, together with our dearly bought Minister *Talleyrand*, to be disposed of as his own property, in all future negociations.

To our dearly beloved brother *Lucien*, we give and bequeath our Batavian Republic, and our Minister *Chaptal*, who, hereafter, shall write his speeches, dictate his letters, and correct his spelling.

To our dearly beloved brother *Louis*, we bequeath our Helvetian Republic, and our Minister *Berthier*, accompanied with the sense of his Secretary *Achambau*, whose instructions, in some time, may enable him to become a good Corporal of Grenadiers.

To our dearly beloved brother *Jerome*, we bequeath, *in petto*, the sovereignty of the seas, with our minister of Marine, and all the admirals of our navy, doubting, however, if their united efforts will make him a good midshipman.

To our dearly beloved *Mother*, we give and bequeath his Holiness, the *Pope*, and our uncle, Cardinal *Frere*[1]; with a Pope, and a Cardinal, in her possession, her stay in purgatory must be short, and in Heaven long.

To our dearly beloved sisters, Mistresses *Bacchiocchi*, *Murat*, *Santa Cruce*, and *Le Clerc*, we give and bequeath our family honours, chastity, modesty, and moderation.

To our dear son in law, *Eugenius Beauharnais*, we give and bequeath *Parma* and *Plaisance*,[2] with our dear countryman *Sebastiani*, who will instruct him to drive like a coachman, and ride like a postillion.

To our much beloved daughter in law, Madame *Fanny Beauharnais*, as a reward for her loyalty, we bequeath a representation, in wax, of the scaffold of her father, and the throne of her mother, both designed by the revolutionary modellers, *Barras* & Co.

To our dear uncle, Cardinal Frere,[1] we give and bequeath the triple crown of St. Peter, *in petto*, and to all our nameless known and unknown relatives, we give and bequeath the kingdom of *Etruria*, to be disposed of to the highest bidder, and its value laid out in mourning rings, to be equally distributed amongst them, and certain Continental Princes hereinafter mentioned.

We give and bequeath to our dear friend the King of *Spain*, an Etrurian mourning ring, and four family pictures, representing the Bourbons dethroned, the Bourbons degraded, the Bourbons repenting, and the Bourbons forgiven.

We give and bequeath to the King of *Naples*, three marble statues, after a model by his Queen, representing Faith, Loyalty, and Constancy; and to the Kings of *Sardinia*, we bequeath our promises of honour, to be equally divided between them.

We give and bequeath to his Holiness the *Pope*, the doctrines of the Goddess of Reason, the Alcoran of Mahomet, and the atheism of our Institute; all true relics; besides, to himself, his successors, and College of Cardinals, we bequeath concordant

[1] Fesch.   [2] Placentia.

mourning rings, from the manufactory of our Counsellor of State *Portalis.*[1]

We give and bequeath to his Imperial Majesty the Emperor of *Germany*, two drawings, representing Hope amongst the ruins of *Turkey*, and Desire contemplating *Bavaria*, designed by Citizen *Dupe*, and sold by Citizen *Plot*.

We give and bequeath to his Imperial Majesty the Emperor of *Russia*, three pictures, representing Louis XVI. upon the Throne, Louis XVI. in the Temple, and Louis XVI. upon the Scaffold ; by Citizens *Loyalty*, *Monarchy*, and *Warning*.

We give and bequeath to our dearest friend the King of *Prussia*, the landscape of Hanover, with the Imperial Crown in perspective, by Citizens *Royalty*, *Jacobin*, and *Rebel*.

We give and bequeath to our natural Ally the Emperor of the *Turkish Empire*, the description of our Conquests of *Egypt*, our flight from *Egypt*, and our future return to *Egypt*, by Citizens *Treachery*, *Cowardice*, and *Design*.

We give and bequeath to his Majesty the King of the United Kingdoms of *Great Britain*, and *Ireland*, the United Navy of Holland and France, commanded by Citizen *Envy*, mann'd by Citizen *Coalition*, and lost by Citizen *Invasion*.

We give and bequeath to his Majesty the King of *Sweden*, the French original representation of the assassination of *Gustavus III.* to remind him of vengeance, honour and duty.

We give to our dear friend the King of *Denmark*, an original painting, of the insults, torments, and death, of his Queen *Caroline Matilda* ; designed and executed by two celebrated French artists, Citizens *Intrigue* and *Crime*.

We give and bequeath to the Regent of *Portugal*, a Code of our Revolutionary Laws of Nations, and a chapter of the Rebel Etiquette of Grenadier Ambassadors, explained and illustrated by Citizens *Sans Culottes*, *Rudeness*, and *Impudence*.

We give and bequeath to our friend the Elector of *Bavaria* the Bible of the *Theophilanthropes*, and the Concordat of *Portalis*, as an assistance to his patriotic illuminated ministers, in their political reformations, and religious innovations.

[1] Who had the chief share in promoting the Concordat with the Pope.

We give and bequeath to our chosen Grand Master of *Malta*, the Musical Opera of the Capture of *Malta*, performed in 1798 with a Concerto by Citizen *Treason*, and in 1800 with a Bravura, by Citizen *Valour*, with the farcical afterpiece of the *Recapture*, performed at *Amiens*, by Citizens *Fraud* and *Treaty*.

To all other *Continental Sovereigns*, who have accepted more or less of our bountiful indemnities, we give and bequeath our mourning rings of honour ; and to all other ambassadors, ministers, agents, and deputies, who have negociated, intrigued, bribed, or begged indemnities, we give and bequeath, with our consciences of honour, the revolutionary principles of *Necker*, the ex-minister, the probity, and disinterestedness of *Talleyrand*, our minister, and the honour and virtue of *Fouché* our senator, to be equally divided amongst them, share and share alike.

We give and bequeath to all *Sovereigns* upon earth, who have acknowledged our Corsican Kingdom of *Etruria*, and to their ministers and counsellors, *Iron* mourning rings, from the axe of the Guillotine, of the *Luneville* manufactory, bearing the following inscription, '*Monarchy degraded, and Monarchy dishonoured, Feb.* 1801.'[1]

We give and bequeath to the *Citizens of the Republics* in *Italy*, *Switzerland*, and *Holland*, our Corsican Mourning rings, with an inscription, '*Liberty lost*, 1801, *and unrevenged*, 1803.'

N.B.—We give and bequeath to the *Citizens* of the *United States* of *America*, the funeral speeches on the tombs of the Liberty of *France*, *Germany*, *Switzerland*, *Italy*, and *Holland*, translated and published by Citizen *Plot*, in *Louisiana*.

To all our *Senators, Legislators, Tribunes, Counsellors, Ministers, Generals, Cardinals, Bishops, Prefects*, &c., &c., &c., and to all other of our *Slaves* of every denomination and description, whether *Rebel, Royalist*, or *Regicide Jacobins* ; either *Traitors, Apostates, Murderers*, or *Plunderers*, we give and bequeath the Cannon of *St. Napoleon*, the dagger of *St. Brutus*, the poison of *St. Aly*, the Guillotine of *St. Robespierre*, and the halter of *St. Judas* ; all true relics, to be equally divided amongst them.

We give and bequeath to the Manes of all the Citizens

---

[1] The Treaty of Luneville was signed Feb. 9, 1801.

butchered by us at Toulon, murdered by us at Paris, and poisoned by us in Egypt ; our confession to our Cardinal Bishop at Paris, and our absolution from his Holiness the *Pope*.

We command, and desire most earnestly, not to be buried in any Church or Church-yard, in any mosque or pantheon, but in the common sewer of *Montmartre*, where the corses of our worthy predecessors, *Marat* and *Robespierre*, were deposited ; but for the quiet of our soul, we do order, and put into requisition, *La Revalliere*, high priest to the *Goddess* of *Reason*, *Mercier*, the atheist of the Institute, *Amarat*, the mufti of *Constantinople*, and *Pius* the *Pope* of *Rome*, to say prayers over our tomb, and to read '*Domine salvum fac Consulem*,' *sic transit Gloria mundi !*

Lastly, to *Louis* the XVIII. commonly called the Pretender, and to all Princes of the *House* of *Bourbon*, their heirs, executors, administrators, and assigns, we give and bequeath our everlasting hate ; and it is our further will and pleasure, that, if any potentate or power, shall harbour the said *Louis* XVIII. or any of the said princes, such harbouring shall be a good cause of war ; and the potentate and power guilty of such humanity, and hospitality, shall be punished by a Coalition of Powers as a violater of the law of nations, and contrary to the rights of man.

In Witness whereof, we have hereunto set our hand and seal the 25th day of Prairial, (14 June, 1803) in the eleventh year of the French Republic, one and indivisible.

BRUTUS ALY NAPOLEON BONAPARTE.

As a specimen of the bombast of the time, we may take the subjoined illustration of what our Tars would do with Napoleon.

INVASION.

CHAPTER XXXII.

INVASION   SQUIBS,   *continued*—'BRITONS   TO   ARMS'—BRAGGADOCIO--
NAPOLEON'S EPITAPH.

A MOST ghastly picture, which should not be called a
caricature, yet is meant so to be, is by Gillray (July 26,
1803), and is called 'Buonaparte forty-eight Hours after
Landing!' A crowd of rural volunteers are assembled,

and one of them hoists the head of Napoleon upon a pitch-
fork, calling out ' Ha, my little Boney ! what do'st think of
Johnny Bull, now? Plunder Old England! hay? make
French slaves of us all! hay? ravish all our Wives and

Daughters! hay? O Lord, help that silly Head! To think that Johnny Bull would ever suffer those lanthorn Jaws to become King of Old England Roast Beef and Plum pudding.' Whilst on the top of the engraving is inscribed, 'This is to give information for the benefit of all Jacobin Adventurers, that Policies are now open'd at Lloyd's—where the depositer of One Guinea is entitled to a Hundred if the Corsican Cut throat is alive 48 Hours after Landing on the British Coast.'

Ansell also takes up this gruesome subject (August 6, 1803) in 'After the Invasion. The Levée en Masse, or Britons Strike Home.' The French have landed, but have been thoroughly defeated; the British soldiers driving them bodily over the cliffs, into the sea. The women are plundering the dead, but complain bitterly of the poverty of their spoil. 'Why, this is poor finding, I have emptied the pockets of a score and only found garlic, one head of an onion, and a parcel of pill boxes.' A rural volunteer, who has Bonaparte's head on a pitchfork, addresses two comrades thus: 'Here he is exalted, my Lads, 24 Hours after Landing.' Says one of the countrymen, 'Why, Harkee, d'ye zee, I never liked soldiering afore, but, somehow or other, when I thought of our Sal, the bearns, the poor Cows, and the Geese, why I could have killed the whole Army, my own self.' The other remarks, 'Dang my Buttons if that beant the head of that Rogue Boney—I told our Squire this morning, What do you think, says I, the lads of our Village can't cut up a Regiment of them French Mounseers? and, as soon as the Lasses had given us a Kiss for good luck, I could have sworn we should do it, and so we have.'

Of loyal and patriotic songs, there are enough and to spare, but one was very popular, and therefore should be reproduced :—

BRITONS TO ARMS !!!

Written by WM. THOS. FITZGERALD, Esqr.,
And Recited by him at the ANNUAL MEETING of the
LITERARY FUND, at GREENWICH.
14 July, 1803.

Britons to Arms !—of apathy beware,
And let your Country be your dearest care ;
Protect your Altars ! guard your Monarch's throne,
The Cause of GEORGE and FREEDOM, make your own !
What ! shall that England want her Sons' support,
Whose Heroes fought at Cressy—Agincourt ?
And when great MARLBOROUGH led the English Van,
In France, o'er Frenchmen triumphed to a man !
By ALFRED's great, and ever honoured, Name !
By EDWARD's prowess, and by HENRY's fame !
By all the generous Blood for Freedom shed,
And by the Ashes of the Patriot Dead !
By the bright Glory Britons lately won,
On Egypt's Plains, beneath the burning Sun !
Britons to Arms ! defend your Country's Cause,
Fight for your King ! your Liberties ; and Laws !
Be France defied, her slavish yoke abhor'd,
And place your safety only on your Sword.
The Gallic Despot, sworn your mortal Foe,
Now aims his last,—but his most deadly blow ;
With England's Plunder tempts his hungry Slaves,
And dares to brave you, on your Native Waves !
If Briton's right be worth a Briton's care,
To shield them from the Son of Rapine—swear !
Then to Invasion be defiance giv'n—
Your Cause is just—approv'd by Earth and Heaven.
Should adverse winds our gallant Fleet restrain,
To sweep his 'bawbling [1] vessels' from the main ;

---

[1] 'A bawbling vessell was he Captain of,
    For shallow draught and bulk unprizable.'— *Twelfth Night*, act 5, sc. i
Trifling, insignificant, contemptible.

And Fate permit him on our Shores t'advance—
The Tyrant never shall return to France ;
Fortune, herself, shall be no more his friend,
And *here* the Hist'ry of his Crimes shall end—
His slaughter'd Legions shall manure our shore,
And England never know Invasion more.

This was the stilted sort of stuff given to our forefathers, to inflame their patriotic zeal, and this example is of good quality compared to most. Here is another one, which I give, as having the music, published July 30, 1803 :—

BRITONS TO ARMS !

Cheerly my hearts of cour-age true, The hour's at hand to try your worth ; a glo-rious pe-ril waits for you, And val-our pants to lead you forth. The Gal-lic fleet ap-proaches nigh, boys, Now some must conquer, some must die, boys; But that ap-pals not you nor me, For our watchword, it shall be : Brit-ons strike home, re-venge your coun-try's wrongs, Brit-ons strike home, re-venge your country's wrongs.

Undaunted Britons now shall prove
  The Frenchman's folly to invade
Our dearest rights, our country's love,
  Our laws, our freedom, and our trade ;
On our white cliffs our colours fly, boys ;
Which we'll defend, or bravely die, boys ;
For we are Britons bold and free,
And our watchword it shall be
            Britons strike home, &c.

3.

The Tyrant Consul, then too late,
  Dismayed shall mourn th' avenging blow
Yet vanquish'd, meet the milder fate
  Which mercy grants a fallen foe :
Thus shall the British banners fly, boys,
On Albion's cliffs still rais'd on high, boys,
And while the gallant flag we see,
We'll swear our watchword still shall be
            Britons strike home, &c.

About the last caricature in this month was by I.
Cruikshank, who depicted Napoleon (July 28, 1803) as
' Preparing to invade.' He is pouring himself out a bumper,
and soliloquising, ' I must take a little Dutch Courage,
for I am sure I shall never attempt it in my sober senses !
Besides, when John Bull catches me, I can plead it was
only a Drunken Frolick ! Diable ! if I not go, den all my
Soldiers call me one Braggadocio, and one Coward, and if
I do, begor, dey vil shew me in the Tower, as one very
Great Wild Beast.'

I. Cruikshank (July 28, 1803) tells us ' How to stop
an invader.' Napoleon, and his army, are represented as
having landed, and he is asking ' Which is the way to

London?' A countryman replies, giving emphasis to his words by driving his pitchfork deeply into the Consul's breast, 'Why, thro' my Body—but I'se be thro' yourn virst.' His wife, as a type of what was expected of the women of England, is emptying the offensive contents of a domestic utensil over him. Bulldogs are let loose, and are rapidly making an end of their enemies, in which laudable enterprise they are materially assisted by prize-fighters and carters.

The month of August was very fruitful in caricature, for in that month, and in September, the Invasion scare was at its height.

There was an immense amount of Gasconading and Braggadocio going about, as senseless as it was improbable. Take this for example: 'The Consequence of Invasion, or the Hero's Reward. None but the brave deserve the fair. The Yeomanry Cavalry's first Essay' (Ansell, August 1, 1803). A stout yeoman is swaggering about, with his sword drawn, and carrying a pole, on the top of which is Bonaparte's head, and, lower down, he grasps some fifteen or twenty bleeding heads of decapitated Frenchmen. He is saying, 'There, you Rogues, there! there's the *Boney parts* of them. Twenty more; Killed them!! Twenty more; Killed them too!! I have destroyed half the army with this same Toledo.' Women from all parts are coming to hug and caress him, saying, 'Bless the Warrior that saved our Virgin Charms.' 'Ah! bless him, he has saved us from Death and Vileation.' 'Take care, I'll smother him with kisses.' One lady says to a man, not a Volunteer: 'There you Poltroon look how that Noble Hero's caressed!' whilst the poor wretch thus addressed exclaims, 'Ods Niggins, I wish I had been a Soldier too, then the Girls would have run after me, but I never could bear the smell of Gunpowder.'

'John Bull offering Little Boney fair play' is the title
of one of Gillray's pictures (August 2, 1803), and depicts
the fortified coasts on both sides of the Channel, with John
Bull, as a Jack Tar, stripped to the waist for action.   He
wades half across to hurl defiance at his foe.   'You're a
coming ?   You be d—d !   If you mean to invade us, why
make such a rout ?   I say little Boney, why don't you come
out ? yes, d—n ye, why don't ye come out ?'   Meanwhile Boney, secure in his fortress, and with his flotilla safe
on shore, looks over the parapet, and says, ' I'm a coming !
I'm a coming ! ! !'

His epitaph was even obligingly written for him during
his lifetime, and here it is :—

EPITAPH

Underneath a GIBBET, *over a* DUNGHILL *near* HASTINGS,
close by the SEA BEACH.

Underneath this Dunghill
Is all that remains of a mighty Conqueror,
NAPOLEON BUONAPARTE.
Who, with inflexible Cruelty of Heart,

And unexampled depravity of Mind,
Was permitted to scourge the Earth, for a Time,
With all the Horrors of War :
Too ignorant, and incapable, to do good to Mankind,
The whole Force of his Mind was employed
In oppressing the Weak, and plundering the Industrious:
He was equally detested by all ;
His enemies he butchered in cold Blood ;
And fearing to leave incomplete the Catalogue of his Crimes,
His friends he rewarded with a poison'd Chalice.
He was an Epitome
Of all that was vicious in the worst of Tyrants ;
He possess'd their Cruelty, without their Talents ;
Their Madness, without their Genius ;
The Baseness of one, and the Imbecility of another.
Providence, at last,
Wearied out with his Crimes,
Returned him to the Dunghill from which he sprung ;
After having held him forth
On the neighbouring Gibbet,
As a Scare-crow to the Invaders of the British Coast.
This Beach,
The only Spot in our Isle polluted by his footsteps ;
This Dunghill
All that remains to him of his boasted Conquest.
Briton !
Ere you pass by
Kneel and thank thy God,
For all the Blessings of thy glorious Constitution ;
Then return unto the peaceful Bosom of thy Family, and continue
In the Practice of those Virtues,
By which thy Ancestors
Merited the Favor of the Almighty.

I. Cruikshank, in 'Johnny Bull giving Boney a Pull'
(August 7, 1803), brought out a caricature in which is
graphically depicted the total annihilation of the French

flotilla, and John Bull is dragging Napoleon, by a cord round his neck, to a gallows, surrounded by people waving their hats in token of joy. Napoleon, not unnaturally, hangs back, remarking,'Ah! Misericordi! Ah! Misericordi! Jean Bool, Jean Bool, hanging not good for Frenchmen.' But John pulls along manfully, exclaiming, 'I shant *measure the Cord*, you F——. I am sure it is long enough for a dozen such Fellows as you.'

A picture by West (August 8, 1803), 'Resolutions in case of an Invasion,' is divided into six compartments. A tailor, with his shears, says, 'I'll trim his skirts for him.' A barber, 'I'll lather his wiskers.' An apothecary, with a pestle and mortar, 'I'll pound him.' A cobbler, 'I'll strap his Jacket.' A publican, 'I'll cool his Courage in a pot of Brown Stout.' An epicure, 'I'll eat him.'

The punishment, for any attempt at invasion, was prophesied as being his certain downfall, and a nameless artist (August 12, 1803) produced an engraving of 'A rash attempt, and woful downfall'—Bonaparte snatching at the British Crown.

> But as he climb'd to grasp the Crown,
> She knock'd him with the Scepter down,
> He tumbled in the Gulph profound,
> There doom'd to whirl an endless Round.

Britannia is represented as standing on a cliff, with a crown upraised in her left hand, and a sceptre in her right. Napoleon is shewn as tumbling into the infernal regions, to the great joy of attendant demons.

'Observations upon Stilts' is by an unknown artist (August 12, 1803), and represents Bonaparte upon a huge pair of stilts. He is looking over to England, through a telescope, and is saying, 'How very diminutive everything appears from this astonishing elevation. Who is that little man, I wonder, on the Island, the other side the ditch ? he seems to be watching my motions.'   John Bull, the person referred to, is also using his telescope, exclaiming, ' Why surely that can't be Bonny, perch'd up in that manner. Rabbit him ! if he puts one of his Poles across here, I'll soon lighten his timbers.'

CHAPTER XXXIII.

'HARLEQUIN Invasion' is by West (August 12, 1803).
Napoleon is a Harlequin, and points with his wooden sword
'Invincible' to Great Britain, which is surrounded by goodly
ships of war.   Pantaloon, as the Pope, typifying Italy, lies
dead, and Holland, dressed as a Pierrot, does not relish the
command of his master, who tells him, 'As Pantaloon is no
more, I insist on your joining me to invade that little island.'
Poor Holland replies, 'D—m me—if I do, Master—for I
don't like the look of their little ships—can't you let me be
at quiet—whisking me here, and there, and everywhere.'

1.

Ladies and Gentlemen, to day
    With scenes adapted to th' occasion
A Grand new Pantomime we play,
    Entitled—Harlequin's Invasion.

2.

No comic Pantomime before
    Could ever boast such tricks surprising ;
The Hero capers Europe o'er,
    But hush ! behold the Curtain rising.

3.

And first that little Isle survey,
    Where sleeps a Peasant boy, so hearty ;
That little Isle is Corsica,
    That peasant boy is Bonaparte.

4.

Now lightnings flash and thunders roar,
    Dæmons of witchcraft hover o'er him ;
And rising thro' the stage trap door,
    An evil genius stands before him.

5.

His arms in solemn state are cross'd,
    His voice appalls th' amaz'd beholders ;
His head in circling clouds is lost,
    And crimson pinions shade his shoulders.

6.

Mortal, awake ! the phantom cries,
    And burst the bonds of fear asunder !
My name is *Anarchy* ; arise !
    Thy future fortunes teem with wonder.

7.

To spread my reign the earth around,
    Here take this sword, whose magic pow'r,
Shall sense, and right, and wrong confound,
    And work new wonders ev'ry hour.

8.

Throw off that peasant garb, begin
    T' assume the party colour'd rover,
And, as a sprightly Harlequin,
    Trip, lightly trip, all Europe over.

9.

He spoke, and instant to the view
    Begins the curious transformation ;
His mask assumes a sable hue,
    His dress a pantomimic fashion.

10.

Now round the Stage, in gaudy pride
    Capers the renovated varlet,
Shakes the lath weapon at his side,
    And shines in blue, and white, and scarlet.

11.

High on a rock, his cunning eye
    Surveys half Europe at a glance ;
Fat Holland, fertile Italy,
    Old Spain, and gay, regenerate France.

12.

He strikes, with wooden sword, the earth,
    Which heaves with motion necromantic ;
The nations own a second birth,
    And trace his steps with gestures antic.

13.

The *Pope* prepares for war, but soon
    All pow'rful Harlequin disarms him,
And changing into *Pantaloon*,
    Each motion frets, each noise alarms him.

14.

With trembling haste he seeks to join
    His daughter *Gallia*, lovely rover !
But she, transform'd to *Columbine*,
    Her father scorns, and seeks her lover.

15.

The *Dutchman* next his magic feels,
    Chang'd to the *Clown*, he hobbles after ;
Blund'ring pursues the light of heels,
    Convulsing friends and foes with laughter.

16.

But all their various deeds of sin,
    What mortal man has ever reckon'd?
The mischief plann'd by Harlequin,
    Fair Columbine is sure to second.

17.

They quickly kill poor *Pantaloon*,
    And now our drama's plot grows riper,
When e'er they frisk it to *some tune*,
    The Clown is forc'd to *pay the piper*.

18.

Each foreign land he dances through,
    In some new garb behold the Hero,
Pagan and Christian, Turk and Jew,
    Cromwell, Caligula and Nero.

19.

A Butcher, Harlequin appears,
    The rapid scene to Egypt flying,
O'er captive Turks his steel up rears,
    The stage is strew'd with dead and dying.

20.

Next by the crafty genius taught,
    Sportive he tries Sangrado's trick,
Presents a bowl, with poison fraught,
    And kills his own unconscious sick.

21.

Hey pass ! he's back to Europe flown,
  His hostile foll'wers disappointed :
Kicks five old women from the throne,
  And dubs himself the Lord's Anointed.

22.

In close embrace with Columbine,
  Pass, gaily pass, the flying hours ;
While prostrate at their blood stained Shrine,
  Low bow the European powers.

23.

Touch'd by his sword, the morals fly,
  The virtues, into vices dwindling,
Courage is turn'd to cruelty,
  And public faith, to private swindling.

24.

With Atheist Bishops, Jockey Peers,
  His hurly burly Court is graced ;
Contractors, Brewers, Charioteers,
  Mad Lords, and *Duchesses disgraced.*

25.

And now th' Invasion scene comes on ;
  The patch'd and pyeball'd renegado,
Hurls at Britannia's lofty throne
  Full many an Insolent bravado.

26.

The trembling Clown dissuades in vain
  And finds too late, there's no retreating,
Whatever Harlequin may gain,
  The Clown is sure to have a beating.

27.

They tempt the main, the canvas raise,
  A storm destroys his valiant legions ;
And lo ! our closing scene displays
  A grand view of th' infernal regions.

28.

Thus have we, gentlefolks, to day,
  With pains proportion'd to th' occasion,
Our piece perform'd : then further say,
  How like you Harlequin's Invasion ?

BOB ROUSEM'S

EPISTLE TO

BONYPART.

This comes hoping you are well, as I am at this present ; but I say, Bony, what a damn'd Lubber you must be to think of getting *soundings* among us English. I tell ye as how your Anchor will never hold ; it isn't made of good Stuff, so luff up, Bony, or you'll be *fast aground* before you know where you are. We don't mind your Palaver and Nonsense ; for tho' 'tis all Wind, it would hardly fill the Stun' sails of an English Man of War. You'll never catch a Breeze to bring ye here as long as you live, depend upon it. I'll give ye a Bit of Advice now ; do *try* and Lie as near the *Truth* as possible, and don't give us any more of your *Clinchers*. I say, do you remember how Nelson came *round* ye at the Nile ? I tell ye what, if you don't take Care what you are about, you'll soon be afloat in a way you won't like, in a High Sea, upon a Grating, my Boy, without a bit of soft Tommy to put into your lanthorn jaws. I tell you now, how we shall fill up the Log-Book if you come ; I'll give ye the Journal, my Boy, with an Allowance for *Lee way* and *Variation* that you don't expect. Now then, at Five A.M. Bonypart's Cock-Boats sent out to amuse

our ENGLISH MEN-OF-WAR with *fighting*, (that we like).   Six A.M.
Bonypart lands, (that is, if he can); then we begin to blow the
Grampus ; Seven A.M. Bonypart in a Pucker ; Eight A.M. Bonypart
running away ; Nine A.M. Bonypart on board ; Ten a.m. Bonypart
sinking ; Eleven a m. Bonypart in *Davy's locker;* Meridian,
Bonypart in the North Corner of ——, where it burns and freezes
at the same time ; but you know, any port in a storm, Bony, so
there I'll leave ye.   Now you know what you have to expect ; so
you see you can't say I didn't tell ye.   Come, I'll give ye a Toast:
Here's Hard Breezes and Foul Weather to ye, my Boy, in your
Passage ; here's *May you be Sea Sick;* we'll soon make ye *Sick of
the Sea* ; Here's, May you never have a Friend here, or a Bottle
to give him.   And to conclude : Here's the French Flag where
it ought to be, under the ENGLISH.

his
Bob + Rousem.
mark

P.S.   You see as I coudn't write, our Captain's Clerk put the
Lingo into black and white for me, and says *he'll charge it to you.*

Woodward (August 13, 1803) illustrated a very amusing
little ballad.   The picture is simple.   Napoleon, as usual,
with an enormous cocked hat and sword.   John Bull, of
ample rotundity, with his oaken cudgel.   It is called ' John
Bull and Bonaparte !! to the tune of the Blue Bells of
Scotland.

When, and O when, does this little Boney come ?
Perhaps he'll come in August, perhaps he'll stay at home ;
But it's O in my heart, how I'll hide him should he come.

Where, and O where, does this little Boney dwell ?
His birth-place is in Corsica—but France he likes so well,
That it's O the poor French, how they crouch beneath his spell.

What cloathes, and what cloathes, does this little Boney wear ?
He wears a large cock'd hat, for to make the people stare ;
But it's O my oak stick ! I'd advise him to take care !

What shall be done, should this little Boney die ?
Nine cats shall squall his dirge, in sweet melodious cry ;
And it's O in my heart, if a tear shall dim my eye !

Yet still he boldly brags, with consequence full cramm'd,
On England's happy island his legions he will land ;
But it's O in my heart, if he does, may I be d—d.'

In June of this year, Bonaparte, and Josephine, took a
tour into Belgium, and the Côtes du Nord. What it was
like, cannot better be told than in the words of De Bourrienne. 'Bonaparte left Paris on June 3 : and, although
it was not for upwards of a year afterwards, that his brow
was encircled with the imperial diadem, everything con-
nected with the journey, had an imperial air. It was
formerly the custom, when the kings of France entered the
ancient capital of Picardy, for the town of Amiens to offer
them, in homage, some beautiful swans. Care was taken
to revive this custom, which pleased Bonaparte greatly, because it was treating him like a king. The swans were
accepted, and sent to Paris, to be placed in the basin of the
Tuileries, in order to show the Parisians, the royal homage
which the First Consul received, when absent from the
Capital.' So it was all through his progress. The caricature
here described is, of course, exaggerated, but it shows the
feeling which animated the popular breast on this particular journey.

'Boney at Brussels' is by I. Cruikshank (August 14,
1803), and here he is represented seated on a throne, with
a Mameluke, armed with sword and pistol, on each side of
him. He is provided with a huge fork in each hand, with
which he is greedily feeding himself from dishes provided
in the most humble and abject manner by all kinds of
great dignitaries.

He has his mouth full of an 'Address to the Deified

Consul.' The next morsel, which is on one of the forks, is
'To the Grand Consular Deity,' and the other fork is dug well
into 'We burn with desire to lick the Dust of your Deified
feet.' A prelate begs him to 'Accept the Keys of Heaven
and Hell;' and other dishes are labelled 'Act of Submission,' 'Your most abject Slave, Terror of France,' and 'The
Idol of our Hearts, Livers, Lights, Guts, and Garbage,
Souls and all.'

'John Bull out of all Patience!!' is by Roberts (August
16, 1803), and represents him in a Cavalry uniform, and a
most towering rage, astride of the British Lion, which is
swimming across to France. He is shouting out, ' I'll be
after you, my lads—do you think I'll stay at home waiting
for you? If you mean to come, d—n it, why don't you
come? do you think I put on my regimentals for nothing?'
Boney and his army are running away, the former calling
out 'Dat is right my brave Friends, take to your heels, for
here is dat dam Jean Bool coming over on his Lion.'

The subjoined illustration also does duty for 'The Sor-
rows of Boney, or Meditations in the Island of Elba, April
15, 1814,' but, having priority, it appears here as:—

'CROCODILE'S TEARS

OR

BONAPARTE'S LAMENTATION

A NEW SONG.

Tune 'Bow, wow, wow.'

By gar, this Johnny Bull— be a very cunning elf, Sir,
He by de Arts and Commerce thrive, and so he gain de pelf, Sir;
But he no let us rob de land—or else, with naval thunder,
He'll send dat lion bold, Jack Tar, and make us all strike under.
Lack, Lack a day, fal lal, &c.

By gar, de British Bulvarks be—a very grand annoyance,
I'm told, against all EUROPE join'd, they've often dar'd defiance!
Then what can France and Holland do? By gar, dat day me rue,
    Sir,
When I de peaceful Treaty broke—to England prov'd untrue, Sir.
          Lack, lack a day, fal lal, &c.

And then, when in von passion thrown, by gar, I took occasion,
To shew de *Gasconade de France!* and threat them with Invasion !

John Bull, he made at me de scoff, and call'd me Gasconader,
By gar, me find he ne'er will flinch—from any French Invader !
          Lack, lack a day, fal lal, &c.

And now, what vex me worse than all, John Bull prepare for war,
    Sir,
For, fraught with vengeance, he send out that valiant dog, Jack
    Tar, Sir,
By gar, he sweep de Channel clean, and den he mar our sport, Sir,
He either take de ships of France, or block them in de port, Sir,
          Lack, lack a day, fal lal, &c.

This spoil'd my scheme for sending troops from Gallia's shore to
    Dover,
So then, by gar, me send them off, and then they took Hanover ;
But, for to ratify the terms, th' ELECTOR did not choose, Sir,
Because, I'm told, the British King, to sign them did refuse, Sir.
               Lack, lack a day, fal lal, &c.

O ! next I make more gasconade, and then most loudly boast, Sir,
That I would send flat-bottom'd boats, and soon invade de coast,
    Sir,
' *That all the men in arms I found, by gar, I'd take their lives, Sir,*
And put to sword the Britons all, their children, and their wives,
    Sir ! ! !'
               Lack, lack a day, fal lal, &c.

I found my boasting threats are vain, for now, all ranks, by gar,
    Sir,
From fifteen, up to fifty-five, are all prepar'd for war, Sir,
They swear, 'no Gallic yoke they'll bear, or Corsican's proud
    sting, Sir,
But, bravely for their Freedom fight, their Country, and their
    King ! Sir.'
               Lack lack a day, fal lal, &c.

And then they talk of warlike deeds—of *Edward the Black*
    Prince, Sir,
And how their *Harries* fought of old—true courage to evince, Sir,
In modern times, a *Nelson* brave ! and *Abercrombie's* fame, Sir,
O'er Gallia's fleets and armies too, have spread eternal shame, Sir.
               Lack, lack a day, fal lal, &c.

By gar, me always thought, till now, I was a mighty *Hero* !
But then, I'm told, the people say, me cruel was as Nero,
Because *three thousand Turks* I slew, they say I was to blame, Sir,
As also when at Jaffa I—did poison sick and lame, Sir.
               Lack, lack a day, fal lal, &c.

By gar, I find my ardor fail, and all my courage cool, Sir,
De *World* confess I am de *knave*—de *English* call me *fool*, Sir ;
Hard fate ! alas, that I am both ! my heart, of grief, is full, Sir,
By gar, me wish I was at *peace !* with honest *Johnny Bull !'* Sir.

      Lack, lack a day, fal lal, &c.

CHAPTER XXXIV.

INVASION SQUIBS, *continued*—THE BOTTLE CONJUROR—PIDCOCK'S
MENAGERIE.

IN order to understand the next caricature, it is necessary to go back to January 16, 1749, when a famous hoax
was played on the public. The 'Gentleman's Magazine' for
that month says, 'A person advertised that he would, this
evening, at the *Theatre* in the *Hay-market*, play on a common walking cane the music of every instrument now used,
to surprising perfection ; that he would, on the stage, get
into a tavern quart bottle, without equivocation ; and while
there, sing several songs, and suffer any spectator to handle
the bottle ; that, if any spectator should come mask'd, he
would, if requested, declare who they were ; that, in a private room, he would produce the representation of any
person dead, with which the party requesting it could converse some minutes as if alive, &c.'

The bait took, and the theatre was crowded : patience
was exhausted, and some one in the pit calling out that
' For double prices, the conjurer will go into a pint bottle,'
an uproar began, which ended in the wreckage of the house,
which was made into a bonfire outside, and the carrying
off of the treasury.

With this introduction we can the better understand
' Britannia blowing up the Corsican Bottle-Conjurer,' by
I. Cruikshank (August 17, 1803), which represents Napo-
leon being violently ejected into the air, in an extremely

disorganised condition, from the mouth of a bottle which is labelled 'British Spirits composed of True Liberty Courage, Loyalty and Religion,' and in which is seated Britannia, helmed, and armed with spear and shield.

THE CORSICAN MOTH !

Woodward designed 'The Corsican Moth' (August 22, 1803), which, flying towards the candle, exclaims: 'It is a very fierce flame; I am afraid I shall singe my wings!' George III. consoles himself with: 'Thou little contemptible insect, I shall see thee consumed by-and-by.'

This very vivid caricature explains itself. The French
Court are consuming all the good things to be got by the
invasion of England in anticipation, when the fearful
'Mene, Mene, Tekel Upharsin,' the mystic handwriting on
the wall, appears. Napoleon is in consternation, but his
wife and the assembled guests do not seem to notice it.
Josephine is here, as generally, depicted as being very fat.
She was not so at this time, nor for some time after.
Madame Junot says: 'I observed that Josephine had
grown very stout since the time of my departure from
Spain. This change was at once for the better and the
worse. It imparted a more youthful appearance to her

THE HANDWRITING ON THE WALL.

face ; but her elegant and slender figure, which had been
one of her principal attractions, had entirely disappeared.
She was now decidedly *embonpoint*, and her figure had
assumed that matronly air which we find in the statues of
Agrippina, Cornelia, &c.' The three ladies behind her
chair are supposed to represent Pauline, who was afterwards the Princess Borghese, the Princess Louise, and the
Princess Joseph Bonaparte.

'A Knock Down blow in the Ocean, or Bonaparte
taking French leave,' is by some unknown artist (August
24, 1803). John Bull, stripped to the waist in true pugi-
listic style, has encountered Bonaparte in the Channel, and,

with one well-directed blow, has sunk him, leaving only
his hat and boots to tell the tale. With great satisfaction
the old man says : 'There, my lad, I think that blow will
settle the business. D—n me, he is gone in such a
hurry he has left his hat and spurs behind him.' The
English give ringing cheers : 'John Bull for ever! Huzza!
Huzza! Bravo! Bravo!' But the French look very rueful,
and, wringing their hands and weeping, exclaim : 'Ah!
misericorde, pauvre Bonaparte. O dat Terrible Jean
Bool.'

AN INVASION SKETCH.

If there be one Person so lost to all Love for his Country,
and the British Constitution, as to suppose that his Person or his
Property, his Rights and his Freedom, would be respected under
a Foreign Yoke, let him contemplate the following Picture—not
Overcharged, but drawn from Scenes afforded by every Country :
Italy, Holland, Switzerland, Germany, Spain, Hanover, which has
been exposed to the Miseries of a French Invasion.

LONDON, 10 *Thermidor— Year*——.

General BONAPARTE made his public entrance into the capital,
over London Bridge, upon a charger from his BRITANNIC MAJESTY'S
Stables at Hanover, preceded by a detachment of Mamelukes.
He stopped upon the bridge for a few seconds, to survey the
number of ships in the river ; and, beckoning to one of his Aid-
de-camps, ordered the French flags to be hoisted above the
English—the English sailors on board, who attempted to resist
the execution of this order, were bayonetted, and thrown over-
board.

When he came to the Bank, he smiled with complaisance
upon a detachment of French grenadiers, who had been sent to
load all the bullion in waggons, which had previously been put in
requisition by the Prefect of London, Citizen MENGAUD, for the
purpose of being conveyed to France. The Directors of the

Bank were placed under a strong guard of French soldiers, in the Bank parlour.

From the Bank, the FIRST CONSUL proceeded, in grand procession, along Cheapside, St. Paul's, Ludgate Hill, Fleet Street, and the Strand, to St. James's Palace. He there held a grand Circle, which was attended by all his officers, whose congratulations he received upon his entrance into the Capital of these once proud islanders. BONAPARTE, previous to his arrival, appointed two Prefects, one for London, and one for Westminster. Citizen MENGAUD, late Commissary at Calais, is the Prefect of London, and Citizen RAPP, of Westminster. He also nominated Citizen Fouché to the office of Minister of Police. The Mansion-house has been selected for the residence of the Prefect of London, and Northumberland House for the residence of the Prefect of Westminster. As it has been deemed necessary to have the Minister of Police always near the person of the FIRST CONSUL, Marlborough House has been given to Citizen Fouché. Lodgings have been prepared elsewhere, for the late owners of that splendid Palace.

London was ordered to be illuminated, and detachments of French Dragoons paraded the principal streets, and squares, all night.

11 *Thermidor.*

BONAPARTE, at five o'clock in the morning, reviewed the French Troops on the Esplanade at the Horse Guards. A Council was afterwards held, at which the following Proclamations were drawn up, and ordered to be posted in every part of the City :

BY ORDER OF THE FIRST CONSUL.

PROCLAMATION.

St. James's Palace.

Inhabitants of London, be tranquil. The Hero, the Pacificator, is come among you. His moderation, and his mercy, are too well known to you. He delights in restoring peace and liberty to all mankind. Banish all alarms. Pursue your usual occupations. Put on the habit of joy and gladness.

The FIRST CONSUL orders,

That all the Inhabitants of London and Westminster remain in their own houses for three days.

That no molestation shall be offered to the measures which the French Soldiers will be required to execute.

All persons disobeying these Orders, will be immediately carried before the Minister of Police.

(signed)   BONAPARTE.
The Minister of Police   FOUCHÉ.

PROCLAMATION

To the French Soldiers.

Soldiers! BONAPARTE has led you to the Shores, and the Capital of this proud island. He promised to reward his brave companions in arms. He promised to give up the Capital of the British Empire to pillage. Brave Comrades take your reward. London, the second Carthage, is given up to pillage for three days.

(signed)   BONAPARTE.
The Minister of War, par interim   ANGEREAU.

The acclamations of the French soldiery—*Vive Bonaparte—le Heros—le Pacificateur—le Magnanime*—resound through every street.

12th, 13th, 14th, Thermidor.

LONDON PILLAGED! The doors of private houses forced. Bands of drunken soldiers dragging wives, and daughters, from the arms of husbands, and fathers. Many husbands, who had the *temerity* to resist, butchered in the presence of their Children— Flames seen in a hundred different places, bursting from houses which had been set fire to, by the *vivacity* of the troops. Churches broken open, and the Church plate plundered—The pews and altars converted into stabling—Four Bishops murdered, who had taken refuge in Westminster Abbey—The screams of women, and of children, mix with the cries of the soldiers—*Vive la Republique! Vive Bonaparte!*

St. Martin's Church converted into a *depôt* for the property acquired by the pillage of the soldiery.

15 *Thermidor.*

A proclamation published by the First Consul, promising *protection* to the inhabitants.

The houses of the principal Nobility and Gentry, appropriated to the use of the French Generals. Every house is required to furnish so many rations of bread and meat for the troops.

At a Council of State, presided over by Bonaparte, the two Houses of Parliament are solemnly abolished, and ordered to be replaced by a Senate, and a Council of State. General Massena appointed Provisional President of the former, and General Dessolles of the latter. The Courts of Law are directed to discontinue their sittings, and are replaced by Military tribunals.

16 *Thermidor.*

A contribution of twenty millions ordered to be levied upon London. A deputation was sent to Bonaparte to represent the impossibility of complying with the demand, the Bank and the Capital having been pillaged. After waiting in the ante-chamber of the Consul for four hours, the deputation are informed by a Mameluke guard, that Bonaparte will not see them. Two hundred of the principal citizens ordered to be imprisoned till the contribution is paid.

17 *Thermidor.*

A plot discovered by Fouché against the First Consul, and three hundred, supposed to be implicated in it, sent to the Tower.

Insurrections in different parts of the Capital, on account of the excesses of the soldiers, and the contribution of twenty millions. Cannon planted at all the principal avenues, and a heavy fire of grape-shot kept up against the insurgents.

Lords Nelson, St. Vincent, and Duncan, Messrs. Addington, Pitt, Sheridan, Grey, twenty Peers and Commons, among the latter is Sir Sidney Smith, tried by the Military tribunals, for having been concerned in the *insurrection* against France, and sentenced to be shot. Sentence was immediately carried into execution in Hyde Park.

17 *Thermidor.*

The Dock-yards ordered to send all the timber, hemp, anchors, masts, &c., to France. The relations of the British sailors at sea, sent to prison till the ships are brought into port, and placed at the disposal of the French. Detachments dispatched to the different Counties to disarm the people.

The Island ordered to be divided into departments, and military divisions—the name of London to be changed for *Bona-part-opolis*—and the appellation of the country to be altered from Great Britain, to that of *La France insulaire*—Edinburgh to take the name of *Lucien ville*—Dublin, that of *Massen-opolis.*

BRITONS! can this be endured?—Shall we suffer ourselves thus to be parcelled off?—I hear you one and all say, No! No! No!—To your Tents, O Israel!—for BRITONS NEVER WILL BE SLAVES.

PIDCOCK'S GRAND MENAGERIE,

With an exact representation of

BUONAPARTE,

THE LITTLE CORSICAN MONKEY,

As he may probably appear at the above Receptacle of Foreign Curiosities, on, or before, Christmas 1803.

Ladies and Gemmen!

This surprising Animal was taken by Admiral JOHN BULL, of the TRUE BRITON, one of his Majesty's principal Line of Battle Ships. He possesses the Cunning of the Fox, the Rapacity of the Wolf, the bloodthirsty *Nater* of the Hyena, the tender Feelings of the Crocodile, and the Obstinacy of an Ass. He has rambled over several parts of the world, where he played a number of wicked and ridiculous Tricks, particularly in Egypt; there he had

like to have been *nabbed* by Sir Sidney Smith, but contrived to
steal away to France, where, after a Time, exerting all the bad
Qualities he possesses, he so far got the better of his own species
as to reign King Paramount over Thirty Millions of poor deceived
Monkeys. 'Come, come, Jacko; don't look Melancholy, you
shall have your Gruel with a Crust in it presently.' Ladies and
Gemmen, if I was to quit him an Instant, he would play a thousand
figaries; break all your Crockery, drink up your Wine, play the

Devil and Doctor Faustus with your Wives and *Darters*,; eat
your Provisions, steal your Goods and Chattels, and commit more
Mischief here, than he did in Egypt. He's of unbounded Ambition, and, by some fortunate Strokes of good Luck, more than by
his Abilities, proved very successful in his Deceptions; but this
Luck was not to last for ever. Puft up, as full as a blown bladder,
with conceit, he thought he *coud* conquer the four Quarters of the
Globe: when, sailing with a party of large Baboons, who were

called his body Guard, he stole, one dark Night, out of Boulogne Harbour, to make an attack, and seize the Island of Great Britain; where he assured his Companions of immense Wealth by their Plunders. But Admiral BULL coming up with him by break of day, when he was half Seas over, gave them a Broad Side, and *woud* have sunk them outright; but seeing the Crew were nothing but a Collection of miserable, deluded, poor, Brutes, he turned them adrift, and only seized their Leader to shew him as a *Curiosity.*[1]

A suggestion was made that two could play at the game of Invasion, and ' John Bull landed in France ' is a caricature by West (August 29, 1803). He is in cavalry uniform, and, mounted on his lion, is pursuing the French troops, who, bestriding frogs, are in full flight. The terrible old man roars out, ' D—m me, but I'll put your Cavalry to the hop—-I only wish I could find out your Commander.' But Boney is looking out of a cottage chimney, remarking, ' Mercy on me, what a terrible fellow. I think I am tolerably safe here ! '

West (August, 1803) describes the ' Three plagues of Europe.' Bonaparte figures as ' The Turberlent Mr. Fightall ' ; Pitt as ' The Honourable Mr. Taxall ' ; and the Devil as ' The Worshipful Mr. Takeall.'

---

[1] Pidcock's Menagerie was one of the best and largest that used to exhibit in Bartholomew and other fairs : the animals being hired from Cross's famous collection in Exeter 'Change. At this time (1803) Pidcock was probably dead, as he exhibited in 1769. The show was afterwards known as Polito's.

CHAPTER XXXV.

SONG.

THE INVASION.

Come listen every Lord and Lady,
   'Squire, Gentleman, and Statesman,
I've got a *little Song* to sing,
   About a *very great Man !*
And, if the Name of BONAPARTE
   Should mingle in my Story,
'Tis with all due submission
   T' his Honour's Worship's Glory.
          Bow, wow, wow, &c.

The kindness of this philanthropic
   Gentleman extending,
From Shore to Shore, Colossus like,
   Their grievances amending,
To Britain would reach, if he could,
   From fancied Ills to save ye ;
But tho' he likes us vastly well,
   He *does not like our Navy !*
          Bow, wow, wow, &c.

With Egypt, once, he fell in Love,
   Because it was the high Road,

To India, for himself and friends
   To travel by a nigh Road ;
And after making mighty Fuss,
   And fighting Day and Night there,
'Twas vastly ungenteel of us,
   Who would not let him stay there.
         Bow, wow, wow, &c.

A Nobleman was sent to him,
   For Negotiation able,
And BONAPARTE kindly set
   Him down at his own Table,
And in a Story, two Hours long,
   The Gentleman was heard in,
Whilst our Ambassador declar'd
   He could not get a word in.
         Bow, wow, wow, &c.

With Belles and Beaux the drawing-room
   One morning it was quite full,
And BONA, like *a Bantam cock*,
   Came crowing rather spiteful ;
He then began to huff and bluff,
   To show that War his Trade is ;
He scolded all the Englishmen,
   And frighten'd all the Ladies ! ! !
         Bow, wow, wow, &c.

From Malta, next, he took his Text,
   My Lord look'd rather blue on 't ;
For every Trick the Consul had,
   My Lord had one worth *two* on 't ;
Why, Gen'ral, says he, 'Sdeath and Fire,
   Unless you cease these Capers,
They'll publish every word you say
   In all the English Papers.
         Bow, wow, wow, &c.

My Lord, says he, you needs must see,
   I pity British Blindness,
And wish to open all your Eyes,
   Out of pure Love and Kindness,
To make a generous People free,
   My Legions shall pell mell come,
What think you then?—Why, Sir, I think
   They'd be more free **than** *welcome.*
            Bow, wow, wow, &c.

When I come o'er, I'll make all Britons
   Live in perfect bliss, Sir,
I'm sure they will receive me just
   As kindly as the Swiss, Sir.
The Odds an hundred are to one
   I fail, tho' Fortune's Minion.
Says our Ambassador to him,
   I'm quite of your opinion.
            Bow, wow, wow, &c.

My Lord, says he, I'll take the Field.
   You'd better take the Ocean.
My plans are deep.— *Why, yes, they'll reach*
   The Bottom, I've a Notion.
What would the English think to see
   Me 'twixt Boulogne and Dover?
Why, General, they'd surely think
   Your Worship half seas over!
            Bow, wow, wow, &c.

Your Government I'll tame, says he,
   Since War you are so fond on ;
I've got my will in Paris here,
   And wish the same in London ;
I'll rule your great *John Bull!* says he,
   I have him in the Ring, Sir.—

Says John, I'll not be rul'd by you,
  Nor any such a *Thing*, Sir.
      Bow, wow, wow, &c.

Then bring my Flag, invincible,
  A Scot took it long ago, Sir.
For now I think, your ships I'll sink,
  And never strike a Blow, Sir,
A clever Man has found a plan,
  A plan he's surely right in,
For if you beat the British Fleet,
  It must not be at Fighting.
      Bow, wow, wow, &c.

Quite frantic now, he vows Revenge,
  The Moment that he's landed,
And proudly boasts, we cannot hope
  To fight him single handed.
What, single handed, we can do,
  His troops shall know full well soon ;
For him, he learn'd it long ago,
  From *single handed* Nelson.
      Bow, wow, wow, &c.

Now, since their Minds are quite made up,
  Let me on this Occasion,
Make one request to Neptune : Should
  They dream of an Invasion ;
To bring them safely out of Port,
  On gentle Billows guide them,
To where a set of British Boys
  May anchor close beside them.
      Bow, wow, wow, &c.

Reference is made to Napoleon's attempts to stir up
sedition in Ireland in 'An attempt on the Potatoe bag,'
by some artist unknown (August 1803). It shows an

Irishman trudging along towards Dublin, having on his
back a huge sack of potatos, which Napoleon is slitting,
allowing the potatos to escape. Says Bonaparte : ' I say,
Paddy, Give up the bag quietly, and you shall have this
Purse of Gold.' But Paddy replies : ' I see what you are
at, you sly Teaf of the World ; you may cut out a few of
the Potatoes that are rotten at the core—but, by St.
Patrick, you'll never get the whole bag—so you may
pocket your Cash, and march home and be D—d.'

Dean Swift's ' Gulliver ' is very frequently used as a
motif for caricature, and Charles etched (August 1803)
' Gulliver and his Guide, or a Check String to the Corsican.'
King George, as King of Brobdingnag, is seated in a
gallery, looking through the invariable glass at Gulliver
(Napoleon), who is climbing a flight of steps to get at him ;
but he has a rope round his neck, which is held by a sailor
armed with a stout oak cudgel. Says the King: ' Ay,
what ! what ! Does the little Gulliver want my C $_{***}$ n !
Let him come, and he will soon find how 'tis protected.
Hearts of oak are our ships, Jolly tars are our men, &c.
&c.' Napoleon, throttled by the rope, exclaims : ' If these
fellows did not keep such a tight hand over me, I would
soon try how that Ornament would fit my head.' Whilst
the sailor, who has him in hand and checks his advance,
calls out : ' Avast there, my little fellow ; for, D—n my
Timbers, if I don't take you Aback before you reach the
end of your Intended travels. So pull away, pull away, I
say, for the tight little bit of land in the Ocean.'

There is a charming libel on Napoleon in a periodical
publication, called ' Ring the Alarum Bell,' No. 3, August 27,
1803 (I believe it only reached four numbers), the heading
of which is, ' Atrocities of Brutus Napoleone Ali Buonaparté, who now pretends to be at war for restoring the
Knights of Malta, and who told the Egyptians ' (July 1798),

'that he was a true Mussulman, and had been to Malta, on purpose to drive from thence those Christian Infidels, the Knights!!!'

After a most scurrilous and incorrect version of his life, this precious paper gives us a thrilling account of '*The Corsican's Drowning his own wounded Soldiers, and his Thievery.*

' During the early engagements at Mantua with General Wurmsur, the hospital for the French who were wounded was at Como. Some officers, who are ready to swear to the truth of their assertion, passing through this town in the month of April 1800, were informed by the inhabitants that one morning they beheld, with unspeakable horror, the dead bodies of a number of French soldiers floating upon the surface of the lake, whom this infamous assassin, Buonaparté, had ordered to be cast into it on the preceding night. Every one of these unfortunate wretches were soldiers who had suffered amputation of some member or other! This monster caused, at the same time, not only the dead, but even the sick, in the hospitals to be thrown pell-mell into a ditch at Salo, on the Lake of Guarda. It is a fact, well-known in Upper Italy, that the Curate of Salo died with grief at the sight of this horrible transaction.

' The pecuniary robberies of the Corsican are innumerable. At Leghorn he caused a servant of the Grand Duke to bring him all the plate belonging to that Prince, and kept himself an inventory, in order to examine whether any article was missing. At Pisa a British nobleman (the Marquis of D——) was robbed of his carriage, and other effects, by a party of French Hussars. Buonaparte appropriated the carriage to himself, and afterwards made use of it at Milan. France was then in a state of profound peace with the Grand Duke. At Milan, Buonaparte imprisoned

the Nobles, and, in order to procure their release, their con-
sorts brought their diamonds to the wife of the Usurper.'

The following might well go as companion to 'Pidcock's
Menagerie' :—

Most Wonderful

WONDER OF WONDERS.

Just arrived, at Mr. BULL'S MENAGERIE, in British Lane, the
most renowned and sagacious MAN TIGER, or Ourang Outang
called

NAPOLEON BUONAPARTE ;

HE has been exhibited through the greatest Part of Europe, particularly in Holland, Switzerland, and Italy, and lately in Egypt—
He has a wonderful faculty of Speech, and undertakes to reason
with the most learned Doctors in Law, Divinity, and Physic—He
proves, incontrovertibly, that the strongest POISONS are the most
Sovereign Remedies for Wounds of all kinds ; and by a Dose or
two, made up in his own Way, he cures his Patients of all their Ills
by the Gross—He PICKS the POCKETS of the Company, and by a
Rope,[1] suspended near a Lantern, shews them, as clear as Day, that
they are all richer than before—If any Man in the Room has
empty Pockets, or an empty Stomach, by taking a Dose or two of
his POWDER of HEMP, he finds them on a sudden full of Guineas,
and has no longer a Craving for Food ; If he is rich, he gets rid
of his tædium vitæ ; and, if he is over-gorged, finds a perfect Cure
for his Indigestion.—He proves, by unanswerable Arguments, that
Soupe Maigre, and *Frogs*, are a much more wholesome food than
Beef and *Pudding*—and that it would be better for OLD ENGLAND,
if her Inhabitants were all *Monkeys* and *Tigers* as, in times of
Scarcity, one half of the Nation might devour the other half.—He
strips the Company of their Cloaths, and when they are stark
naked, presents a PAPER on the POINT of a BAYONET, by reading
which they are all presently convinced that it is very pleasant to

---

[1] Hanging them.   A revival of the old Revolutionary cry of 'À la
Lanterne !'

be in a state of Nature.—By a kind of hocus-pocus Trick, he breathes on a Crown, and it changes suddenly into a Guillotine.—He deceives the eye most dexterously; one Moment he is in the Garb of the MUFTI: the next of a JEW, and the next Moment you see him the POPE.—He imitates all Sounds; bleats like a *Lamb*; roars like a *Tiger*; cries like a Crocodile; and brays most inimitably like an Ass.

He used also to perform some wonderful Tricks with *Gunpowder*; but he was very sick in passing the Channel, and has shewn great aversion to them ever since.

Admittance, One Shilling and Sixpence.

N.B. If any Gentleman of the *Corps Diplomatique* should wish to see his OURANG OUTANG, Mr. Bull begs a Line or two first; as on such Occasions, he finds it necessary to bleed him, or give him a Dose or two of cooling Physic, being apt to fly at them, if they appear without such preparation.

'John Bull and the Alarmist' is as well drawn as any of Gillray's caricatures (September 1, 1803). Sheridan, in the character of a bill-sticker, having under his arm a sheaf of 'Loyal Bills, Sherry Andrew's Address, Playbills,' &c., and, with a *bonnet rouge* peeping out of his pocket, is telling John Bull the two last lines of the first verse of the subjoined song.

The old boy stands resolutely before the throne, which he is ready to defend with his huge oak cudgel carved with a bulldog's head, and, whilst nourishing himself on a tankard of ale, tells his informant his opinion of his intelligence in the words of the second verse :—

John Bull as he sat in his old Easy Chair,
An Alarmist came to him, and said in his Ear,
' A Corsican Thief has just slipt from his quarters,
And is coming to Ravish your Wives and your Daughters !'

' Let him come, and be D—d !' thus roar'd out John Bull,
' With my Crab-stick assured I will fracture his Scull,
Or I'll squeeze yᵉ vile reptile twixt my Finger and Thumb,
Make him stink like a Bug, if he dares to presume.'

' They say a full Thousand of Flat bottomed Boats,
Each a Hundred and Fifty have, Warriors of Note ;
All fully determin'd to feast on your Lands,
So I fear you will find full enough on your hands.'

John smiling arose, upright as a post,
' I've a Million of Friends bravely guarding my Coast,
And my old Ally, Neptune, will give them a dowsing,
And prevent the mean rascals to come here a lousing.'

I know not from what source the statistics relative to the strength of the French flotilla, contained in the sub-joined broadsheet, are taken. It purports to be an ex-tract from a French letter :—

CITIZENS OF ENGLAND

BONAPARTE

INVASION :

Read the following detailed Account of his Preparations, and ask yourselves whether those who tell you so, are your Friends or your Enemies.

'The Alertness of our People, employed in the several Yards along the Coasts, never had a parallel. I reckon 11,000 Ship-Carpenters, and their necessary Assistants, Labourers, &c., employed here, and at *Calais, Dunkirk,* and *Ostend,* besides those at Work on the Boats preparing at *Ghent, Bruges,* and *Antwerp.*

'At *Boulogne,* we have 36 Gun Boats ready, each carrying three heavy Pieces of Ordnance, Two fore, and One aft ; besides 152 of what are called *Flat Bottomed* Boats ; but they are now generally *rounded below,* and *keeled.* In three Weeks Time, we expect to have as many more in a State of perfect Readiness.

'At *Calais,* several of the *Floating Batteries,* that opposed LORD NELSON, when he attacked Boulogne, are now fitting up, and about seventy boats that will carry 150 Men each.

'At *Dunkirk,* and the adjacent Canals, there are 47 *Gun boats ready,* with remarkable heavy Ordnance ; and not less than 220 Boats for carrying men. They count upon being able to send 400 of these vessels (great and small) to Sea, in less than Three Weeks.

'At *Ostend,* the *Gun Boats, Floating Batteries,* and *Vessels for carrying Soldiers,* that are now, and will be, completed during the present month, amount to 487. They work here during the Whole of the Moonlight nights.

'I cannot, at present, exactly ascertain what Number of Men

are employed, at *Bruges* and *Ghent*; but they are extremely numerous. Such is the case at Antwerp.'

But not one of these vessels dared shew her nose out of harbour, for every French port in the Channel was blockaded by English men-of-war, of which there were some five hundred, of different sizes, afloat. Sometimes this blockading business got tiresome, and it was relieved by an occasional landing, on which occasions mischief to the French, in some shape or other, was always included in the programme ; or a vessel would be cut out, or a few shells would be thrown into a town such as Dieppe or Havre — anything to vary the monotony. At home they were bragging and blustering of what they would do ; afloat they were *doing*, and we cannot tell from what fate their action saved us.

Woodward drew an amusing sketch of 'John Bull shewing the Corsican monkey' (September 3, 1803), who is represented as seated on a Russian bear, which is muzzled and led by John Bull, who thus expatiates on his charge to the delighted audience : 'My friends and neighbours, this is no monkey of the common order ; he is a very cholerick little gentleman, I assure you.   I had a vast deal of trouble to bring him to any kind of obedience—he is very fond of playing with globes and sceptres — so you may perceive, I let him have one of each made of Gingerbread—in order to amuse him in a strange country.'

A not very witty picture, 'Buonaparte on his Ass,' by an unknown artist (September 14, 1803), represents Bonaparte on a donkey, which has got itself in a terrible mess through trampling on Italy, Switzerland, Holland, and Hanover, and is endeavouring to reach Malta, which, however, is protected by the British Lion.   Napoleon opines that, 'This d—d ass gets so entangled and unruly, I'm afraid I shall never be able to reach Malta.'

O'er countrys I'll trample, where threats may prevail,
But must let those alone where they will not avail,
For on looking around me to find where to prance,
To touch Malta, might be destruction to France.

Woodward drew (September 16, 1803) ' The Corsican
Macheath,' with Napoleon singing :—

Which way shall I turn me ?
How can I decide
The Prospects before me ?
I long for to stride.
But 'tis this way—or that way,
Or which way I will,
John Bull at his Post,
Is prepared with a Pill.

CHAPTER XXXVI.

INVASION SQUIBS, *continued*—TALLEYRAND'S DISINCLINATION TO INVADE ENGLAND.

'A FULL and particular Account of the Trial of Napoleon Buonaparte before John Bull,' drawn by Woodward, etched by Cruikshank (September 14, 1803), is a broadside not remarkable for artistic merit ; it does not even give a fair idea of Napoleon's features. The letterpress is as follows :—

The Court being opened, and John Bull on the bench, Napoleon Buonaparte was put to the Bar, charged with various high crimes, thieving, and misdemeanours. Counsellor Tell Truth opened the case on the part of the prosecution, as follows :

Counsellor. May it please your worship Mr. John Bull, and Gentlemen of the Jury, From the Indictment now before you, you will perceive the prisoner stands charged as follows : that he, Napoleon Buonaparte, on the 28th of December, 1793, caused at Toulon, when the siege was over, fifteen hundred men, women, and children, to be fired upon with grape shot ; that by these means he became a favourite of Robespierre, and, in concert with that destroyer, did on the 13th Vendemaire, October 4, 1795, sweep the streets of Paris near the Pont Neuf with artillery, and covered the steps of St. Roch with heaps of slaughtered bodies ; the persons massacred on the whole amounted to about eight thousand. At Pavia, the magistrates having interfered to save the people from the bayonet, were bound together, and shot by his order ; he also burnt the town of Benasco, and massacred the inhabitants. At Alexandria he gave up the city to his soldiers for four hours ; the old people, women, and children, flew to the mosques, but the mosques were no protection from brutal fury, though Buonaparte professed himself a Turk ;—at Jaffa, horrid to relate ! three thousand eight hundred prisoners were marched to a rising ground, and there destroyed by means of musquetry, grape shot, and the bayonet ; in short, his various massacres, robberies, and pillage, are too numerous to bring forward. I shall only observe, that this gentle, this merciful man, at the above place, Jaffa, finding his hospitals crowded with sick of his own army, caused the whole to be poisoned ; thus, in a few hours, five hundred and eighty soldiers died miserably by order of their General—; so says Sir Robert Wilson.

John Bull. Mercy on me, Mr. Tell Truth, let me hear no more, it will lift my wig off with horror ! ! !

Counsellor T. T. I shall briefly observe, that this man, after overrunning all Italy, France, Holland, Switzerland, stealing our beloved George's horses at Hanover, and various other sacrifices to his unbounded ambition, had the audacity to declare he would invade the happy shores of Great Britain, and disturb the fireside of honest John Bull and his children ; but he was stopped in his career by a single English seaman, who will lay the particulars before the Court. Crier, call in Tom Mizen.

Crier. Tom Mizen, come into Court.

John Bull. Now, Mister Mizen, what have you to say ?

Tom Mizen. You must know, Mr. Bull, having, as it were, lashed myself to a love of my King and Country, and hearing the land lubber at the bar was about to bring over his Cock boats ; I thought myself, in duty bounden, to see what sort of game he was after ; so, rigging out my little skiff the Buxom Kitty, I clapped a few pounders aboard, with an allowance of grog, and set sail ; when I got near Bull-hog-ney—I think they call it so in their palaver—but I never can think of their outlandish palaver, not I—howsomdever I soon spied a little gun boat or two, and on board one of them I saw a little pale-faced olive-coloured man in a large cocked hat, taking measure of the sides : may I never set sail again, said I, if that is not little Boney—so I made no more ado, but got ready my cordage and grappling irons, and after one broadside, towed the little gentleman into Brighton.

John Bull. Bravo, Mister Mizen—now let us hear what Mynheer Dutchman has to say.

Dutchman. Indeed, Mynheer Bool, I have nothing to say in his favour—he has robbed me of my liberty, my money, and everything that is dear to me.

Italian. I am precisely in the same position.

Swiss. And I.

The Pope. I once had a voice in the senate, but he has totally abridged my power.

Hanoverian, &c. We are one and all tired of his tyrannical usurpation.

John Bull. Then it appears to me no one will speak in his favour.

From the Court. Not one.

John Bull. Well then—what has the prisoner to say in his own defence?

Buonaparte. I am a man of few words, and leave my defence entirely to my counsel.

The Devil, as Counsellor for the Prisoner. Mr. Bull, and Gentlemen of the Jury, I blush for the first time in my life; it is well known I am the father of lies and mischief, and have had the prisoner at the bar a considerable time in training, but he really goes so much beyond my abilities, that I entirely give up to the discretion of the Jury.

John Bull. I shall very briefly, gentlemen, sum up the evidence; you have heard a long and serious detail of the prisoner's cruelties in different parts of the world. The conduct of our worthy countryman, Tom Mizen, you must all admire; you perceive there is not one person to speak in his favour; and even his old counsel the Devil will have nothing to do with him—I therefore leave him to your verdict.

The Jury, without leaving the Court, pronounced the prisoner *Guilty.* John Bull then passed sentence, as follows:

NAPOLEON BUONAPARTE—after a fair trial, you have been found guilty of various high crimes and misdemeanours, in different parts of this world. I am a man that delights not in blood;

I therefore sentence you to be turned over to the care of my trusty and beloved friend Mr. Pidcock, proprietor of the Wild beasts over Exeter 'Change in the Strand ; there to be publicly shewn to my fellow citizens, inclosed in an iron cage for three months ; after the expiration of which time, I sentence you to be trans- ported to your native town of Ajaccio in Corsica for three months, and, for the remainder of your life, to be hung up by your legs in the mines of Mexico.

Mr. Pidcock attended with a cage, and disposed of the prisoner according to his sentence ; he appeared extremely hardened during the whole of the trial. The Court was un- commonly crowded.

' Buonaparte's Soliloquy at Calais, written and designed by G. M. Woodward,' was published September 21, 1803. It is as follows :—

> To go or not to go? that is the question ;—
> Whether 'tis better for my views to suffer
> The ease and quiet of yon hated rival,
> Or to take arms against the haughty people,
> And by invading, end them? T' invade,—to fight,—
> No more ! and by a fight, to say we end
> The envy and the thousand jealous pangs
> We now must bear with ; 'tis a consummation
> Devoutly to be wish'd.   T' invade—to fight—
> To fight ?—perchance be beat : aye, there's the rub ;
> For in our passage hence what ills may come,
> When we have parted from our native ports,
> Must give us pause ;– there's the respect
> That makes th' alternative so hard a choice.
> For who would bear their just and equal laws,
> Their sacred faith, and general happiness,
> That shew in contrast black our tyrant sway,
> Our frequent breach of treaty, and the harms
> Devouring armies on the people bring,
> When he himself could the dark shame remove

By mere invasion?   Who would tamely view
That happy nation's great and thriving power,
But that the dread of falling on their coast,
(That firm and loyal country, from whose shores
No enemy returns,) puzzles the will,
And makes us rather bear the ills we have,

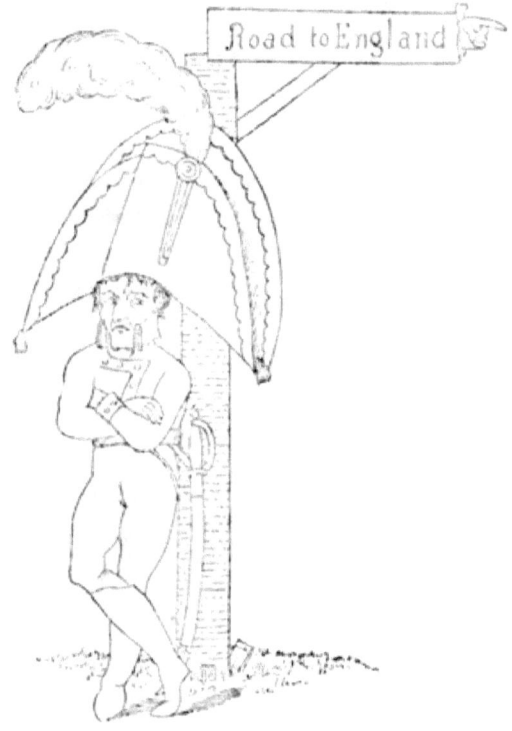

Than fly to others that we know not of?
Thus conscience does make cowards of us all ;
And thus the native hue of resolution
Is sicklied o'er with the pale cast of thought ;
And enterprises of great pith and moment,
With this regard, their currents turn awry,
And lose the name of action.

'The Fable of the Bundle of Faggots exemplified, or Bonaparte **baffled**,' by an unknown artist (September 20, 1803), shows Napoleon unable to break the bundle of *Britons.* His foot rests on a heap of broken faggots, all conquered nations, but this is too hard a job for him, as he confesses : 'Au diable ! all I can do, they'll neither bend or break.'

An unknown artist (September 1803) gave us, 'A Peep at the Corsican Fairy.' Here little Boney is chained to a table and padlocked by *The British Navy.* An Italian, Swiss, Dutchman, and Spaniard are looking curiously at him, thus making their remarks : 'Monsieur John Bull, I think I have seen this little Gentleman before—he was with us in Italy.' 'We shall never forget him in Switzerland.' 'My frow once persuaded me to show our house, and he took possession of the whole premises.' 'By St. Diego, he is a curious little fellow.' John Bull is showing him, and has a sweetmeat labelled 'Malta' in his hand : 'Oh yes, sir, he is a great Traveller—but don't come too near him ; he is very cholerick ; he put himself into a great passion with me about the sugar plumb I hold in my hand—indeed, if it was not for my little chain and padlock, I could not keep him in any sort of order.'

It is well known that Talleyrand was averse to the intended invasion of England, and some time in September 1803, Gillray produced 'The Corsican Carcase Butcher's Reckoning Day, New Style, *No Quarter* Day !' a portion of which is here given. Talleyrand (his ecclesiastical status expressed by the cross on his partially military cocked hat) restrains Napoleon from invading England, although the Conqueror has on his seven-league boots. In the distance are the white cliffs of Albion, surrounded by ships of war, and a huge bull bellows defiance. At the open door the Russian bear looks in, enraging Napoleon almost to frenzy.

On the ground is a coop full of foxes labelled 'From Rome, not worth killing.' 'The Germanic Body' lies in a sadly mutilated condition, having lost its head, feet, and hands ; one of the latter—the right hand—lies close by, labelled 'Hanover.'   A poor, lean, gaunt dog, 'Prussia,' is in a

kennel 'put up to fatten.' The food provided for it is blood, or 'Consular Whipt Syllabub.'   In a trough lie the bodies of six Mamelukes, 'Jaffa Cross breeds,' whose blood drains into a receptacle 'Glory.'   On the walls are hung a sheep, 'True Spanish Fleec'd'; a dead Monkey,

'Native Breed'; an ass 'from Switzerland,' and a pig 'from Holland.'

BONEY AND TALLEY.

THE CORSICAN CARCASE BUTCHER'S RECKONING DAY.

NEW STYLE. *No Quarter Day!*

1.

Says Boney the Butcher to Talley his man,
One settling day as they reckon'd,
    'Times are hard—'twere a sin,
    Not to keep our hand in '—
Talley guessed at his thoughts in a second.

2.

Then he reach'd the account book—turn'd over awhile ;
'I have it—see here are the Dutch, Sir.'
    Boney cries 'It appears
    That they're much in arrears.'
Quoth Talley ' *They don't owe us much, Sir !* '

3.

'Here's Parma, Placentia ; there's Naples and Rome.'
Talley smil'd ' They are nothing but bone, Sir ! '
    ' For the present pass Prussia ;
    What think you of Russia ? '
' *'Twere as good that we let her alone, Sir !* '

4.

' My ambition unsated, my fury unquenched,
Let Europe now shake to her bases :
    For my banner unfurl'd,
    I defy all the world,
And *spit in th' ambassadors' faces.* '

5.

Seeing raw-head and bloody bones wondrous irate,
Talley turn'd o'er the leaf with his finger ;
    ' Here's Hanover—if—'
    'If what ?' in a tiff
Cries Boney, 'Tell Mortier to bring her.

6.

' Let her bleed till her life strings are ready to burst,
To drain her let Massena shew you ;
    The job being done,
    And all her fat run,
We'll give up her trunk to—*you know who.*

7.

'This will do for a breakfast—read on.'   Talley read,
Each page they conn'd over and over,
    ' I can find nothing here ;
    We must stop, Sir, I fear.'
Boney scowl'd, *and then pointed to Dover.*

8.

' Shall I want employ—whilst a breed there exists
So sleek, and so tempting to slaughter ?
    Reach my cleaver and steel,
    I'll not sit at a meal—
Till '—Talley cries 'Think of the *Water.*'

9.

' A soul such as mine, by the Koran I swear,
Such childish impediment scorns, Sir ;
    I will bait this great Bull,
    And his crest I will pull.'
Cries Talley ' *Remember his horns, Sir.*'

10.

'Psha ! my mouth 'gins to water, and yearns for the feast,
Such dainty, such delicate picking ;
　　By his horns I will seize him,
　　Goad, worry, and teaze him : '
Quoth Talley—'*He's given to kicking.*'

11.

'Let him kick, let him toss, and for mercy implore,
Be mine the proud task to refuse it ;
　　The fates shall obey,
　　I will have my way ; '
Talley mutters, '*I hope you won't lose it.*'

12.

'Sound the cleaver and marrow bones,' Boney exclaims,
'Strait this herd in my power shall be, Sir ; '
　　'Should you once reach the shore,'
　　(Talley said somewhat lower,)
'You'll soon be at top of the tree, Sir.'

13.

'Don't jest with thy master, thou recreant knave !
Am I, Sir, or am I, Sir, no king ?
　　By the Prophet I swear '—
　　'Cry you mercy—forbear ! '
Quoth Talley, '*I thought you were joking.*'

14.

'Am I such a lover of jibes or of jests,
Do I ever smile ? ' Boney cried, 'Sir ; '
　　'No, that I may say
　　But to blast or betray ; '
(But this, Talley uttered aside, Sir.)

15.

He calls on Great Mahomet, swears by his beard,
The Lama he begs to be civil ;
  Now tells all his complaints
  To the Calendar Saints,
And now sends them all to the Devil.

16.

Thus prepared, he clasp'd firm the dread steel in his hand,
And wielded his cleaver on high, Sir ;—
  'Oh thou Bull, thou *Grand Bête* !
  Oh thou barb of my Fate !
This day thou most surely shalt die, Sir ! '

17.

Tho' artful and cunning some madmen appear,
The simplest expedient will turn 'em ;
  Talley saw what he meant ;
  On the schemes he was bent,
And fully resolv'd to adjourn 'em.

18.

Now Boney grown wilder, his eyes seem'd to start,
And loudly began he to bellow ;
  When Talley seized hold
  Of this hero so bold,
And pinion'd *the poor little fellow.*

19.

'Oh, brave, great, and noble, magnanimous man ! ! ! ! ! !
To save thee thy servant is bound, Sir ;
  The Sea it is deep,
  And the shores they are steep,
Most certainly you will be drown'd, Sir.

20.

'Think how precious your life is to France and to me,
Obey then your fate, and don't mock it ;
    Think what we shou'd do,
    Mighty Sir, without you,
With our *liberties all in your pocket.*

21.

'Nay—*sweet, gentle* Sir' (Boney kick'd with all might),
'Oh !—this chivalry's quite out of fashion !'
    Talley had his own way,
    Not a word did Bo say,
For speak he could not for his passion.

22.

'Dread Sir, your great project is worthy yourself,
Your knife shall soon hit the bull's throat, Sir,
    I'd only premise,
    Were I fit to advise,
'*Twould be better to order a boat*, Sir.'

23.

'A boat, aye, a boat ! why there's reason in that,'
Boney cries with a scowl of delight, Sir ;
    For the truth must be told,
    He knew Talley of old,
And felt in a devilish fright, Sir.

24.

Boney thought that the boat was a much safer plan,
He voted the counsel discreet, Sir ;
    Quoth Talley ''Tis done,
    And the day is your own,
Just—take—care—to avoid the Fleet, Sir.'

25.

Talley cautiously then let the little man down,
When the little man softened his features ;
    Yet though little in size, Sir,
    His soul is as high, Sir,
As the cross at the top of Saint Peter's.

26.

Little Boney shook hands then with Talley the good ;
(*And thought how he best might dispatch him*)
    Whilst Talley as meek,
    Kiss'd the Mussulman's cheek,
(*And swore in his heart to o'er match him.*)

27.

They drank to their hopes—hob a nobb'd to their scheme,
Which promis'd such royal diversion ;
    Thus cordial they sat,
    And, in *harmless chit chat,*
Sketch'd the *plan of this water excursion.*

28.

When the boat will be ready we none of us know,
Talley swears 'twill be here in a trice, Sir ;
    But it must be confess'd,
    Boney's not in such haste,
Since he thought of the business twice, Sir.

29.

Then a health to the Butcher ! and life long enough,
That he once of the Bull may a view get,
    For, whenever we meet,
    If he *skulk from the* FLEET,
We will find him head quarters in NEWGATE.

CHAPTER XXXVII.

INVASION SQUIBS—VOLUNTEERS.

'THE Corsican Locust' (West, September 1803) shows him hovering over a picnic party, saying : 'Bless me, how comfortably these People live.' The party consists of an Englishman, Irishman, and a Scotchman. The first has roast beef, plum-pudding, and a foaming tankard, before him, and, regarding the insect, says : 'As sure as I'm alive, that Corsican locust smells the Roast Beef and Plumb pudding.' Paddy has only 'praties,' but looks up at it, and asks : 'Perhaps, my Jewel, 'tis a potatoe or two you want, but the divil a halfpeth do you get from me.' The Scotchman, with his basin and spoon in his hands, thinks : 'Perhaps the Cheeld would like a little o' my Scotch Broth—but Sandy is too cunning for that.'

'The Grand Triumphal Entry of the Chief Consul into London' is by an unknown artist (October 1, 1803). He is escorted by volunteer cavalry, and is seated, bareheaded and handcuffed, with his face towards the tail of a white horse,[1] his legs being tied under its belly. The horse is led by two volunteers, one of whom carries a flagstaff with the tricolour under the Union Jack, and on the summit is perched Boney's huge hat, labelled 'For Saint Pauls.' One of the mob is calling out : 'We may thank our Volunteers for this glorious sight.'

---

[1] Indicative of Hanover.

Of ' The Corsican Pest, or Belzebub going to supper,' by Gillray (October 6, 1803), only a portion is given in the

THE CORSICAN PEST, OR BELZEBUB GOING TO SUPPER.

illustration, but nothing of moment is omitted. The following are the lines under this broadsheet :—

> Buonaparte they say, aye good lack a day !
>> With French Legions will hither come swimming,
> And like hungry Sharks, some night in the dark,
>> Mean to frighten our Children and Women.
>>>> Tol de rol.

> When these Gallic Foisters gape wide for our Oisters,
>> Old Neptune will rise up with glee,
> Souse and Pickle them quick, to be sent to old Nick,
>> As a treat from the God of the Sea.
>>>> Tol de rol.

Belzebub will rejoice at a Supper so nice,
  And make all his Devils feast hearty ;
But the *little tit bit*, on a fork, he would spit,
  The Consular Chief, Buonaparté !
                    Tol de rol.

Then each Devil suppose, closely stopping his nose,
  And shrinking away from the smell,
' By Styx,' they would roar, ' such a damn'd Stink before
  Never entered the kingdom of Hell.'
                    Tol de rol.

Full rotten the heart of the said Buonaparte,
  Corrupted his Marrow and Bones,
French evil o'erflows, from his Head to his Toes,
  And disorder'd his Brains in his Sconce !
                    Tol de rol.

His pestiferous breath, has put Millions to Death,
  More baneful than Mad dog's Saliva,
More poisonous he, all kingdoms agree,
  Than the dire Bohan-Upas of Java—
                    Tol de rol.

By the favour of Heaven, to our Monarch is given
  The power to avert such dire evil,
His subjects are ready, all Loyal and Steady,
  To hurl this damn'd Pest to the Devil.
                    Tol de rol.

An unknown artist (October 11, 1803) gives us ' The
Ballance of Power or the Issue of the Contest.' The hand
of Providence is holding the balance, and John Bull, whose
good qualities are named ' Valour, Justice, Honor, In-
tegrity, Commerce, Firmness, Trade, Heroism, Virtue,' is
rapidly ascending ; and, according to his own account,
' There's a sweet little Cherub that sits up aloft, will take

care of the fate of John Bull. But poor Boney, with a
heavy burden on his back of 'Shame, Disgrace, Obloquy,
Cruelty, Murder, Plunder, Rapine, Villainy, and Hypocrisy,'
is sinking into the earth, which emits flames to consume
him.

'Thoughts on Invasion, both sides the water,' by
Charles (October 11, 1803), shows us the English coast
defended by volunteers. John Bull, laughing, is seated in
a chair, under which is a cornucopia, running over with
corn, wine, beef, and all kinds of provisions. The old boy
is chuckling: 'I can't help laughing at the thought of Invasion, but there is no knowing what a mad man may
attempt, so I'll take care to have my coast well lined, and
I think 80,000 such men as me, able to eat all the Boney
rascals in France, and if they mean Invasion, I have sent
a Specimen of Bombs into Calais!' The ships are shown
in the act of bombarding that place, while Boney sits very
miserable, with a tricolour foolscap on his head, moaning:
'I wish I had never promis'd to Invade this terrible John
Bull, but how shall I avoid it, with Credit to myself and
honour to the French Nation? and this bombarding Calais
gives me the Bl—— Blu—— Blue Devils.' A blue devil
behind him is saying: 'You must go now, Boney, as sure
as I shall have you in the end.'

'The little Princess and Gulliver' is by Ansell (October
21, 1803), and, of course, the Gulliver is Napoleon, whom a
Brobdingnagian princess (Charlotte of Wales) has plunged
into a basin of water, and, with her fist, keeps beating him
as he rises to the top, saying: 'There you impertinent,
boasting, swaggering pigmy—take that. You attempt to
take my Grandpapa's Crown indeed, and plunder all his
subjects; I'll let you know that the Spirit and Indig-
nation of every Girl in the Kingdom is roused at your
Insolence.'

' The Centinel at his Post, or Boney's peep into Walmer Castle!!' (Ansell, October 22, 1803) shows Boney, with a boat-load of troops, arrived on the English Coast, but they are at once disconcerted by the appearance of the sentinel, Pitt, who challenges, 'Who goes there?' With abject fear depicted on the countenance of Bonaparte and his followers, the former exclaims: 'Ah! Begar—dat man alive still. Turn about, Citoyens—for there will be no good to be done—I know his tricks of old!!'

There are two caricatures on the same subject, one attributed to Gillray, but signed C.L.S. (October 25, 1803), the other by I. Cruikshank, to which the same date is attributed. One is evidently copied from the other, for the *motif* is the same in both. I prefer the former, and therefore describe it. It is called 'French Volunteers marching to the Conquest of Great Britain, dedicated (by an Eye Witness) to the Volunteers of Great Britain.' A mounted officer leads a gang of chained, handcuffed, and pinioned, scarecrow-looking conscripts, some of them so weak that they have to be carried in paniers on donkey-back, or drawn on a trolley; whilst a poor, dilapidated, ragged wretch, also chained by the neck, and with his hands tied behind him, brings up the rear of the procession.

' John Bull guarding the Toy Shop' (J. B., October 29, 1803) shows a shop-window containing such toys as the India House, St. James's, the Bank, Custom House, Tower, and the Treasury. Little Boney, with his handkerchief to his eyes, is weeping, and crying: ' Pray, Mr. Bull, let me have some of the Toys, if 'tis only that little one in the Corner' (the Bank). But John Bull, who is in full regimentals, and armed with his gun, replies, in his rough, insular way: ' I tell you, you shan't touch one of them—so blubber away and be d—d.'

The volunteer force was a great factor in face of the

Invasion, and it was computed to number 350,000 men.[1]
We know, in our own times, that, at a mere whisper of invasion, men enrolled themselves as volunteers by thousands,
and we have never heard that whisper repeated. The
enthusiasm of the citizen army was very great, and twice
in October 1803 (on the 26th 14,500 men, and on the 28th
about 17,000), the King reviewed these volunteers in Hyde
Park. It will be curious briefly to note some particulars
respecting the pay and clothing of volunteers. They are
taken from the circular papers of regulations which were
sent from Lord Hobart's office to the Lords Lieutenant of
the different counties.

8. When not called out on actual service, constant pay to be
allowed for 1 Sergeant and 1 Drummer per Company, at the same
rates as in the disembodied Militia ; the pay of the Drummer to
be distributed at the discretion of the Commandant ; pay (as disembodied Militia) for the rest of the Sergeants and Drummers,
and for the Corporals and private men, to be allowed for two days
in the week, from the 25th of February to the 24th of October,
and for one day in the week from the 25th day of October to the
24th of February, both inclusive, being 85 days pay per annum, but
for effectives only, present under arms, on each respective day.
Pay may, however, be charged for persons absent by sickness, for
a period not exceeding three months, on the Commanding Officer's
Certificate to that effect. Sergeants 1/6, Corporals 1/2, Drummers and Privates 1/.

9. If a Corps, or any part thereof, shall be called upon, in case
of any riot or disturbance, the charge of constant pay to be made
for such services must be at the rates before specified, and must
be supported by a Certificate from his Majesty's Lieutenant, or
the Sheriff of the County ; but, if called out in case of actual
Invasion, the Corps is to be paid and disciplined in all respects as

---

[1] The Marquis of Hartington in a speech in the House of Commons, March
17, 1884, said 'there were now 209,365 volunteers enrolled, of whom 202,478
were efficient.'—*Morning Post*, March 18, 1884.

the Regular Infantry, the Artillery Companies excepted, which are then to be paid as the Royal Artillery.

10. The whole to be clothed in Red, with the exception of the Corps of Artillery, which may have Blue clothing, and Rifle Corps, which may have Green, with black belts.

Allowance for Clothing.

£3 3 9 for each Sergeant,
  2 12 0 for each Corporal,
  2 3 6 for each Drummer,
  1 10 0 for each Private Man,

and to be repeated at the end of three years ; the Sergeant Major, and 1 Sergeant, and 1 Drummer per Company, to have clothing annually.

11. An annual allowance to be made for each Company in lieu of every contingent expense heretofore defrayed by Government, viz. £25 for companies of 50 Private men, with an additional allowance of £5 for every 10 Private Men beyond that number.

There is an amusing caricature (October 18, 1803) illustrating Talleyrand's disinclination to the projected invasion of England.

In his 'Voyage to Brobdingnag,' Lemuel Gulliver, speaking of his enemy the King's Dwarf, says : ' He had before served me a scurvy trick, which set the queen a-laughing, although at the same time she was heartily vexed, and would have immediately cashiered him, if I had not been so generous as to intercede. Her majesty had taken a marrow-bone upon her plate, and, after knocking out the marrow, placed the bone again in the dish erect, as it stood before ; the dwarf, watching his opportunity when Glumdalclitch was gone to the sideboard, mounted the stool that she stood on to take care of me at meals, took me up in both hands, and squeezing my legs

together, wedged them into the marrow bone above my
waist, where I stuck for some time, and made a very ridiculous figure.   I believe it was near a minute before any
one knew what was become of me ; for I thought it below
me to cry out.   But, as princes seldom get their meat hot,

THE KING'S DWARF PLAYS GULLIVER A TRICK.

my legs were not scalded, only my stockings and breeches
in a sad condition.   The dwarf, at my entreaty, had no
other punishment than a sound whipping.'

    There was also a squib about the same master and
man :—

BUONAPARTE

AND

TALLEYRAND.

It is well known that Monsieur TALLEYRAND always objected
to the Invasion of England, as a mad Attempt, that must end in
the destruction of the Invaders. Having been favoured with a
Note of a Conversation between him and the Chief Consul on this
Subject, I have attempted, for the Entertainment of my Countrymen, to put it into Rhyme.

A. S.

BUONAPARTE.

TALLEYRAND, what's the state of my great preparation,
To crush, at one stroke, this vile, insolent nation,
That baffles my projects, my vengeance derides,
Blasts all my proud hopes, checks my arrogant strides.
Boasts a *Press unrestrained*, points its censure at ME,
And while Frenchmen are Slaves, still presumes to be free?

TALLEYRAND.

In a Month, Sire, or less, your magnanimous host,
Their standards shall fix on the rude British Coast.

BUONAPARTE.

'Tis well—let the troops be kept hungry and bare,
To make them more keen—for that Island's good fare.
Give them *drafts upon London*, instead of their pay,
And rouse them to *ravish, burn, plunder,* and *slay.*
Prepare, too,—*some draughts,* for the sick and the lame ;
You know what I mean.

TALLEYRAND.

As in Syria ?

BUONAPARTE.

The same !

That *England I hate*, and its armies subdued,
The *slaughter of Jaffa* shall there be renew'd.
Not a wretch that presumes to oppose, but shall feel
The flames of my fury, the force of my steel.
Their daughters, and wives, to my troops I consign ;
So shall **vengeance**, sweet vengeance, deep-glutted, be mine,
Their children —

TALLEYRAND.

What ! massacre them, my dread Lord ?

BUONAPARTE.

Why not ? with *me* PITY *was never the word !*
That island once conquer'd, the world is my own,
And its ruins shall furnish the base of my throne.

TALLEYRAND.

What a project ! how vast !—yet allow me one word ;
Sir, the English are brave, and can wield well the sword.
In defence of their freedom, their *King*, and their soil,
Not a man but would dare the most perilous toil.
Should our troops but appear, they will rush to the field,
And will die on the spot to a man e'er they yield.
In defence of their honour, their women will fight,
And their navy, triumphant, still sails in our sight.

BUONAPARTE.

Hush, hush, say no more lest some listeners should hear,
And our troops should be taught these fierce Britons to fear.
They are brave ; and my soldiers have felt it—what then ?
Our numbers are more—to their five, we are ten.
Say their sailors are skilful, oak hearted, and true,
One army may fail, yet another may do.
And though thousands should fatten the sharks in the sea,
There are thousands remaining, *to perish for me.*
In a night, or a fog, we will silent steal over,
And surprise unexpected, the Castle of Dover.

Then to gull the poor dupes of that navy bound land,
You have lies ready coin'd—*'tis your trade*, at command.
We will tell them, and swear it, our sole end and aim,
Is to make them all equally rich—all the same.
I see by your smile you interpret my meaning,
That where my troops reap, they leave nothing for gleaning.
They soar at a palace, they swoop to a cot,
And plunder—not leaving one bone for the pot.
Now, Sir, to your duty, your business prepare,
Leave the rest to *my* Genius, *my* fortune, *my* care.

        [*Exit Buonaparte, Talleyrand looking after him.*

TALLEYRAND.

Your fortune, I fear, Sir, will play you a trick :—
Notwithstanding his **vaunts**, he is touch'd to the quick.
What folly ! what madness, this project inspires,
To conquer a nation, whom liberty fires.
Even now from their shores, loudly echoed, I hear
The song of defiance **appalling** mine ear.
Their spirit **once rous'd**, what destruction awakes !
What vengeance, the wretched invaders o'ertakes.
Prophetic, I plead, but my warning is vain,
Ambition still urges, and maddens his brain :
Fired with hopes of rich **booty**, his soldiers all **burn**,
THEY MAY GO, SOME MAY LAND, BUT NOT ONE WILL RETURN.

J. B. (November 5, 1803) produced 'Boney in time for
Lord Mayors Feast.' At this banquet a sailor produces
Napoleon chained, and with a collar round his neck. He
thus introduces him : 'Here he is, please your Honors.
We caught him alive, on the Suffolk Coast. He was a
little queerish at first, but a few Stripes at the Gangway
soon brought him about. I told him he was just in time
for the Lord Mayor's Show. What does your honor think
of him for the Man in Armour ?' The Lord Mayor, glass
in hand, says : 'Ay, you see how we live at this end of the

town, but you get no Roast beef here, Master Boney—Let
him have plenty of Soup Maigre—and in the evening take
him up to the Ball Room for the amusement of the Ladies
—Come, heres the glorious Ninth of November.'

'Destruction of the French Gun Boats—or Little Boney
and his friend Talley in high Glee' is presumably by
Gillray, though not signed by him (November 22, 1803).
It represents the total destruction of the French flotilla by
the English fleet—which Napoleon, mounted on Talleyrand's shoulder, is watching with great glee through a
rolled-up paper (Talleyrand's plan for invading Great
Britain), which is being used in lieu of a telescope. He
shouts out, in great delight, 'Oh my dear Talley, what a
glorious sight! We've worked up Johnny Bull into a fine
passion! My good fortune never leaves me! I shall now
get rid of a Hundred Thousand French Cut Throats whom
I was so afraid of! Oh, my dear Talley, this beats the
Egyptian Poisoning hollow! Bravo Johnny! pepper 'em
Johnny!'

Ansell is answerable for 'Boney's Journey to London,
or the reason why he is so long in coming, i.e. because he
travels like a Snail with his house at his back' (November
23, 1803). He is portrayed as being in a wooden house,
drawn by his soldiers, who are being unmercifully whipped
with a knout-like weapon. Napoleon, calling out to the
officer who is administering the punishment, 'You Vaga-
bones, make haste, Vite, Vite, or I shall not get to London
by Christmass. Give them more of the Fraternal Whip,
the dam Rascals do not know the value of Liberty.'

END OF THE FIRST VOLUME.

Spottiswoode & Co., Printers, New-street Square, London.

www.ingramcontent.com/pod-product-compliance
Lightning Source LLC
Chambersburg PA
CBHW060557030726

47498CB00005B/1423